FRANZI

THE HERO

Part I: 1939

PAUL DICKINSON

APS Books,
4 Oakleigh Road,
Stourbridge,
West Midlands,
DY8 2JX

APS Books is a subsidiary of the

APS Publications imprint

www.andrewsparke.com

Copyright ©2020 Paul Dickinson

All rights reserved.

Paul Dickinson has asserted his right to be identified as the author of this work in accordance with the Copyright Designs and Patents Act 1988

Drawings courtesy of Bill Houston

First published worldwide by APS Books in 2020

No part of this publication may be reproduced, stored in or introduced into a retrieval system, or transmitted, in any form, or by any means (electronic, mechanical, photocopying, recording or otherwise) without the written permission of the publisher except that brief selections may be quoted or copied without permission, provided that full credit is given.

A catalogue record for this book is available from the British Library

ISBN 978-1-78996-214-7

Dedication

To My Wonderful Wife Sally-Ann, who put up with my 'Franzi' moments!

And to the crews of HMS Courageous and HMS Royal Oak, 1939

And especially for Franzi the Orangutan 1925-1959

Chapter 1

Regents Park – Wednesday 26th July 1939

Franzi sat as high as he could on his "tree" and watched the proceedings. Of course, it wasn't a real tree, there wasn't room for that, but you had to make do.

It hadn't been a good summer. The weather wasn't quite right and there seemed to be something wrong with the people.

For one thing, there was that horrible ululating siren that seemed to panic everyone and send them running. He wasn't quite sure where to, but they came back when the sirens sounded again, this time with a steady tone. Sometimes after the first siren men in uniform ran about with football rattles. That seemed to panic people even more. They fumbled at the boxes they were all carrying and pulled out strange masks that they fitted over their heads.

No-one seemed to pay attention to Franzi, well not after he'd ignored all attempts to get him inside.

No, it was very odd and the number of children he saw declined over the months until one day there were no children or adults only staff.

He'd slept well and expected to go out as usual. He was hungry and he liked eating out rather than staying in.

This morning though he couldn't go outside as the door was shut and locked.

What on earth was going on? He had a major scratch and waited for Bert. He'd tell him what was up.

**

The wheel squeak on Bert's small cart alerted Franzi that he was on his way. He stopped outside the door and banged on it with his broom.

Franzi ambled across to the door and banged back.

A hatch opened.

"Now then Franzi, special day today mate. Off on a trip you are" said Bert.

Franzi whistled in reply.

"I'm not coming with you, but I'll send along some notes to tell 'em how to take care of you and give you the treats you like"

Franzi wasn't convinced and blew a raspberry.

"It'll be alright lad – you see. Now here's some grub" said Bert pushing a large tray through another hatch at the bottom of the door.

Franzi reached out a hand to Bert and "rumbled".

"You know I shouldn't. They don't like it but since it's the last time I'll see you for a while" said Bert. He stood back from the door and lit up a cigarette. "There ya go", he passed it through the hatch.

Franzi took it, sat down, and had a long drag. It was alright but not as good as those clove cigarettes he'd smoked out in Java before coming to London. Just one of the "bad habits" that he'd picked up as a youngster living with District Officer Whyte in Borneo, strong tea and whisky being the other main ones.

"Well then, I'll be back in a little while and we'll sort you out to travel. You've not been on a train before, have ya?"

Franzi stared back and said nothing.

"It's a fine way to travel. Not a long journey, normally. Not sure now with a War coming. I'll put plenty of your treats in with you" and with that Bert closed the hatch and wandered off with his squeaking trolley.

Franzi finished the cigarette and crushed it out before eating the dog end.

He sighed. This wasn't fun at all. He wanted to be outside seeing what was going on. May as well eat then.

**

Sometime later as Franzi was getting bored in his room he heard voices outside and something large being wheeled up.

Bert was speaking "Well he's not going to like that. It needs larger holes."

"Bigger holes mean he can get his arms through," said another voice, John Baker, the "Gaffer".

"Well," said Bert "He won't do any harm. You know how calm he is."

"Normally," said John "But you're not going to be with him, I am. And he gets mischievous around me"

"That's cos you won't give him a fag" replied Bert.

"You know they're bad for him," said John

"Well that's why he tries to mug you to get at your packet" laughed Bert.

"I suppose I'll let him have one if it keeps him calm on the journey. We should have had more notice of this though. The other animals went off in the vans but they've decided they can't wait until they're back for another trip"

"He'll be fine. He loves travelling. He only slept in his crate on the ship over from Borneo if you remember."

"Yes, he spent a lot of time sitting up the radio mast" chuckled John.

"Come on then," said Bert, and the door opened revealing the two keepers, big trolley, and the crate on top.

"Now then Franzi look at this," said Bert, showing him the open crate. "You fancy getting inside?"

Franzi ambled across to the crate and eyed it suspiciously. It looked much smaller than when he'd travelled in it from Borneo a couple of years back. Of course he'd grown and was now a handsome looking chap with red hair, moustache, and beard. His wide cheeks flanges marked him out as a mature male.

He'd even started to find Daisy "interesting in some ways.

Bert had put some fruit inside as well as greens and there was a pile of straw. He'd also put in an old tyre and a couple of branches to keep Franzi amused.

Sighing Franzi walked over to Bert and hugged him, until Bert shouted "Not so bloody tight, Franzi!".

Franzi let him go and went into the crate, picking up a piece of fruit before turning around to the door and sitting down with a thump.

Bert and the Gaffer closed the door and bolted it shut, adding a padlock to keep the bolt secure.

Franzi was sure he could get out of the crate anytime he wanted. They'd forgotten how powerful he was now. Not that he wanted to at the minute. This was an adventure! Much better than being shut in his room or even the enclosure.

The two men took up the trolley handle and pulled him along. His 80 kg not causing them too much of a problem as they made their way towards the Main Entrance where a truck was waiting.

The driver and his mate helped Bert and the Gaffer to push the trolley up onto the flatbed and made it fast with ropes.

"Just have to wait for the boss to come and see us off," said the Gaffer.

"You got everything I put together for Franzi," asked Bert?

"All safe and sound. I'll make sure he's settled in right before I come back. There's talk of a female keeper up there."

"Oh he'll like that. He's started to get an eye for the ladies" laughed Bert.

"Franzi already to go John?" asked a distinguished, bespectacled and suited gentleman.

"Yes Doctor," said the Gaffer.

"Right then." Dr Geoffrey Vevers, the zoo's curator, turned to smile and nod at Franzi "Off you go then".

Franzi blew a loud raspberry.

"Well I say Franzi" exclaimed Dr Vevers.

Bert and John just chuckled.

John climbed aboard the lorry and it drove out of the zoo onto the Outer Circle and off to St Pancras Station.

**

Somewhere out in the Multiverse

Zogfrith and Eldencrumb were having the equivalent of a debate over a beer. Not that they were drinking beer, although they could have if they'd chose (they'd had that discussion some time ago; Zogfrith being an Anglophile and Eldencrumb a Francophile).

"Look now that World War, your Frenchies performance was absolutely lamentable" espoused Zogfrith.

"Your RosBiffs weren't much better. They let my Poilus down so badly" countered Eldencrumb

"Pah your generals were useless; a monkey could have done better!"

"I'd like to see a monkey try."

Zoggie, as he was known to his friends, smiled slyly "And if one does what's in it for me, Crumbie me old mate?"

"I'll back off Marangie and let you have a clear field" replied Crumbie

"As if I need it. No no don't interrupt. You're on. I'll let the Brits have the monkey though – show you how it should be done."

"And if you lose?"

"Same thing, see if Marangie likes your advances then, eh?"

"Done"

Oh yes, thought Zogfrith, I reckon you will be!

**

Franzi stared through the holes in his crate at the buildings, people, and traffic passing by. Lots of buildings, people and traffic.

He could smell something though. The people were frightened. What was it Bert had said? That was it "War". What was "War"? Franzi didn't know. He turned the word over in his mind and had a long and satisfying scratch.

They reached the station and a team of men helped load Franzi's crate on to a flatbed wagon, securing it in place with chains.

St Pancras goods yard was packed with noisy shunters, wagons, freight engines. "Very interesting indeed", thought Franzi then "I need a cigarette". John perched on some sacks close buy trying to get comfortable for the journey. The weather was good today, it hadn't been a great summer so far. Franzi held out an arm towards him and whooped.

"I wondered how long it'd be before you asked," said John, reaching into his pocket and pulling out a cigarette packet. He lit one up and passed it to Franzi. Franzi grunted with approval.

"You deserve it though, it's all a bit strange for you, mate, isn't it?"

Franzi sucked his teeth in response and carefully took a long drag.

John could swear Franzi was much more intelligent than apes were supposed to be.

They both settled down as the train pulled out of the yard and set off towards Dunstable on the LNER line.

**

The train travelled north at a sedate pace. Smoke and occasional cinders blowing over Franzi and John making them both cough when they did so.

Just over an hour on and the train plunged into a tunnel.

The world shook.

Franzi was unhappy. His head was ringing and he felt sick. He wasn't sure what had happened. There'd been a "whistling" and then a bang, whoosh and it had all gone black, an even deeper black than the tunnel.

He awoke slowly and felt "different".

The train was juddering but eventually moved on and out of the tunnel.

Franzi looked across at John. He didn't appear any different from his usual self but Franzi was definitely different. That word came into his head again "War" and with it images of men, women and children, dead or horribly injured. Broken buildings. Explosions. Even a smell of death. And then he saw uniformed men marching, Swastika banners (what was a Swastika?), then other men still marching with a red sun banner and he felt anger building.

He wanted to do something but was unsure of what. Not like him, he thought, which wasn't like him either. He would have normally gone into a complete rage and smashed things, torn things apart. Now, instead of doing that, he was "thinking" and "remembering". Very, very odd.

"You alright Franzi?" asked John.

Franzi shook his head which caused John more concern as he normally wouldn't have got a "human" answer.

"What's wrong eh? Want another fag?" asked John, looking to do something normal to cover up his confusion and concern.

Franzi nodded but also gave his usual grunt.

John fumbled for his cigarettes and then made a complete hash of lighting the match.

Franzi reached over and gently took the cigarette from John's mouth and the matchbox from his hand. He placed the cigarette in his mouth and deftly extracted a match, struck it and lit up before blowing out the flame.

John's face showed stunned awe.

Franzi added to his confusion by having a drag and then passing the cigarette over to John whilst patting him on the arm.

John drew a big lungful of smoke whilst trembling somewhat. He calmed down after more drags whilst Franzi still patted his arm and made cooing noises as if comforting a young Orang.

"Well lad," said John shakily "what's happened eh?"

Franzi put his hands to the side of his head and "exploded" them away.

"Your head hurts?" asked John.

Franzi gave his grunt of affirmation and also nodded.

"I'll get the vet to look you over when we get to Whipsnade," said John "I'm sure they'd want to anyway. You alright till then?"

Franzi grunted. The nodding motion hurt his head a little and it wasn't necessary to communicate with John as he "understood" Franzi's normal communication.

"Do you want another fag?" asked John.

This time Franzi whooped in a more positive yes which seemed to cheer John up. On a whim, he handed Franzi the cigarette packed and watched, wide-eyed, as the Orang gently took out a cigarette and then handed the packed back.

Reaching down to where the box of matches had been discarded Franzi picked them up and went through the motions to light up his new cig before handing the box back to John for safekeeping.

"Bloody hell" whispered John to himself. If I tell anyone about this who's going to believe me, he wondered.

They sat companionably as the train chugged on until it reached Dunstable station where Whipsnade keepers waited with another truck to take them up to the Down's and their new home.

**

Captain Beal himself, the Zoo Superintendent, came out to meet Franzi and John.

"Ah so here you are," he said bustling up to the truck, "Safe and sound, John?"

"Well yes sir. Mostly."

"Mostly," said Captain Beal inquisitorially peering through his glasses at John.

"Well sir he seemed to have a 'funny turn'" said John still wondering how he was going to explain what had happened and what the Captain would think of him. Not exactly the best way of starting a new role at Whipsnade.

"A 'funny turn'. What do you mean?"

"It's very hard to explain, Sir. He didn't have a seizure or anything like that" replied John.

"Ah – if it's hard to explain let's get Franzi into his new home, temporary as it is, and you into yours. Have yourself a cup of tea and something to eat with the men and then come and see me this evening at 19.00."

"Yes Sir."

"Higgins, organise Franzi and John please" ordered the Captain "See you later John."

Franzi blew a large raspberry and knocked on the outside of his crate twice then pointed at the Captain and stared at him very hard.

"Ah yes, sorry Franzi – I was forgetting to welcome you to Whipsnade. I'll come and see you later before lights out eh?"

Franzi grunted his ascent and held up his right thumb to the Captain.

"My word you're a clever chap, aren't you?" said the Captain.

"You've not seen nothing yet," said Bert under his breath "not by a long chalk."

**

Franzi gave a long appraising look at "Whipsnade" and found it to his liking.

His crate was offloaded onto a trolley and John and Higgins began wheeling it off.

"Duke's Avenue" indicated Higgins.

"What've we got for him and Daisy?" asked John.

"Divided paddock for the minute. Not much in the way of trees but we're going to be putting in climbing frames and such. What you decide really. You're the Ape Man" laughed Higgins.

"What do you mean?" asked John.

"Captain said "John Baker has been designated 'Head of Apes'" replied Higgins "and you notice he called you by your first name."

"I did," said John.

"Status that is. We thought 'designated head of apes' was a bit long-winded so we came up with 'Ape Man'. Alright?"

"It'll do"

"So, these two Orang's, you been with them long?"

"Since they arrived at the Park"

"How's this one? The girl, Daisy, was a bit shy. Taken to hiding in her shelter a lot."

"Oh Franzi, well he's a bit different. Hold on a minute"

They brought the trolley to a stop.

Franzi had been looking around as they had moved away from the entrance. To his right he'd seen and smelt the wolves in the Wolf Wood. Then the bears. The late afternoon sun was warm and many of the animals were taking it easy. Even so there were numerous calls and cries and screeches from various inhabitants. He'd seen no people though, only a few men in keeper's 'undress' uniforms going about the business of keeping the animals happy and the park tidy.

He realised they'd stopped, and John was talking to the other man pulling the trolley.

"Franzi," said John.

"Ook."

"Want a fag now the Captain isn't about (he'd be sure to tell me off)" he asked.

Franzi nodded and gave his usual grunt.

Now, thought John, I wonder if I imagined it on the train. And so thinking he offered the packet to Franzi. As before Franzi delicately selected a cigarette and handed the packet back. He left his hand out and accepted the box of matches from John. Franzi nonchalantly took out a match, stuck it, lit up, and ostentatiously blew it out.

"Blooming 'eck'" exclaimed Higgins "Never seen the like in my life."

"I know," said John, "Amazing, eh?"

Franzi ignored them and enjoyed his cigarette. He thought for a while and then motioned at John.

"Yes Franzi?" asked John

Franzi put his right arm through the hole and offered his hand to John. Whilst John had a good relationship with Franzi it wasn't as close as Bert's back at the Park so he was somewhat hesitant in taking the proffered hand with his right hand. He needn't have been. Gently but firmly Franzi shook his hand and looked at him in a very solemn manner - before swiftly opening the door to the crate and hopping down to the ground.

"What ya" Higgins jumped back.

"Franzi" shouted John

Franzi patted John gently and shook his hand again.

"Shall I call the other keepers?" asked Higgins.

John looked at Franzi, who shook his head. John caught on and shook his head

"No mate. I think we're absolutely fine" he said, a smile coming to his face.

"If you say so," said Higgins somewhat nervously.

Franzi turned to Higgins and held out his hand to him. With a severe amount of trepidation, Higgins responded and the two formally shook hands.

"Ook," said Franzi, indicating the way ahead.

"Yes fella," said Higgins "That's the way"

And with that Franzi took up the rope and pulled the trolley and crate along as directed.

For a moment the two keepers stared, looked at each other and then "Hoi Franzi, wait for us!"

**

John and Higgins led Franzi to the large "pit" enclosure between the similar large lion and tiger "pits".

It had been divided into two and a small hut had been erected in each half.

Franzi saw Daisy peeking out of her hut. She was obviously still a little nervy about the move but was pleased to see him. He let out an encouraging whoop to her and she responded.

"Well that's better," said Higgins.

"She'll be fine now," said John.

Franzi thought "She's not too bad. Wonder if she'd be happier here with a baby to care for?"

He shook his head, far more important things to do first before "courting", as the humans called it.

Franzi "helped" the men get his crate down off the trolley and hauled it over to his hut.

"You alright, Franzi" called John.

Franzi turned and waved at John before settling down on the floor of the hut and reaching across to the food that had been already placed in there. To be honest all this brain work made him hungry.

He vaguely took in John and Higgins going off with the trolley as he munched on his fruit and veg. Looking around the hut he saw a large bucket of water. The rough hued timber of the hut walls and the thatch type roof.

"Adequate," he thought.

"Oh, now there's a thing, the floor".

Packed dirt.

Chewing on a particularly nice morsel he took hold of one of the end timbers of the wall and pulled off a six-inch splinter. Idly he drew it across the floor. Lovely, just the job. He had a lot of work to do before the sun went down and in the morning before John came to see to him and Daisy.

**

The hooter had sounded the end of the day and the zoo staff had gone to their homes. Some, the majority, to villages surrounding the Park. Others to houses in the Park.

Higgins took John one of the old army huts that had been built for the workers during the building of the zoo.

Now, in summer, these would have normally housed the extra staff needed to cope with visitors, as it was they'd all been packed off home whilst the Park prepared for war.

"Nothing fancy John," said Higgins as he showed John a bed and locker/wardrobe.

"I've had worse" replied John

"Ablutions through that door at the end. The kitchen of sorts in that room. Pantry, spirit stove, kettle and the like. My crib's that one over there."

"Right. Wash and brush up then grub?" asked John.

"Oh yes. Food over in the cafe in ten minutes. I've got to check on a couple of things so I'll see you over there"

Later John and Higgins and half a dozen other blokes sat outside the cafe having a communal smoke and yarn. Dinner had been simple but satisfying, eggs, bacon and bread. All sourced locally.

The cafe clock showed the time to be 6-45, a lovely summers evening.

"I've got to see the Captain at 7," said John

"For a chat about Franzi, eh?" said Higgins

"Yes," said John slowly. He wasn't sure how he'd explain about Franzi seeming 'different'. "What's the captain like?"

"He's a proper gentleman. Treats us all fair and square. Let's you know what's what if he's unhappy, but I reckon we'd all agree his bark is worse than his bite, eh boys?" said Higgins

Nods and "That's right enough" came from the other men.

"And you can hear his voice clear across the Park," said one

"His wife and kids are lovely," said another

"He's a veterinary, was the principal army veterinary officer on the Gold Coast. Knows his animals and loves them all. God help anyone, staff or visitor who hurts one" said Higgins.

"Does he listen?" asked John

"He takes everything in and considers it before acting if that's what you mean," said Higgins.

'I hope so' thought John. "Best be getting along to see him then"

"Right. Take that path there and you'll see his house in front of you. The front door is fine. Likely one of the children will answer the door, Laura or Billy. You'll be expected "

"Thanks," said John rising from his seat after stubbing out his cigarette.

**

The Superintendent's House had been the imposing farmhouse before the Park had been acquired by the LZS (London Zoological Society). It was a grand house, in John's view, as he made his way to the front door.

He knocked and the door was opened by a boy of about 12 years of age.

"Hello, you must be the 'Ape Man'," he said.

John groaned a little inside – even here then they'd taken up his nickname.

"Billy, mind your manners" came a female voice from inside "and show John into your father while I make some tea."

"Sorry," said Billy

"It's nothing lad," said John shaking Billy's hand "Nice to meet you, Billy".

"I'm looking forward to meeting the Orangutan's," he said, whilst ushering John into a hall and then knocking on a door.

"Come in" boomed a voice that John recognised as the Captain.

Billy opened the door and showed John into what was obviously the drawing-room.

"Ah John, good to see you. Punctual too. I've heard good things about you. Come in, come in and take a seat" said the Captain indicating a comfortable armchair.

"Good evening sir," said John as he sat down.

"No, no, now – everyone one just calls me the Captain – even when the big wigs are down from London. Ah here's Gladys, my wife"

John jumped up from the chair.

"Glady's this is John Aspall. Our new Head of Apes"

"Hello John, nice to meet you," said Gladys as she put down a tray of tea things and offered her hand.

"Nice to meet you, Ma'am," said John shaking her hand.

"No John, no ceremony. Just Gladys please. We're all a big happy family here at Whipsnade."

"Yes, Ma...Gladys" replied John.

"I'll leave you men to talk then," said Gladys as she left the room.

"Sit you down John. Tea?" asked the Captain.

"Yes S.. Captain," said John.

The Captain poured out two cups of tea and passed John the sugar and milk.

"So, settled in? Franzi alright? Daisy perking up?" asked the Captain without giving John time to answer.

"Yes Captain," seemed to serve for all three questions.

"So, what's this about Franzi and the journey?" inquired the Captain, looking for all like a cherubic schoolboy with his small round-rimmed glasses.

"Well Captain, it's not just the trip now. I mean he's done more things since we got here."

"Ah, what things?"

"He got out of his crate as Higgins and I were taking him to his enclosure then pulled the trolley and crate on his own before taking the crate into the paddock and settling down" blurted out John.

"He did WHAT?" boomed the Captain

"Got out of his crate after shaking my hand."

"We had an adult Orangutan roaming free in the park and no one sounded the alarm," said the Captain accusingly.

"Well", said John "He wasn't doing any harm and he did go where we showed him"

"Are you mad? We can't have that sort of thing. What would have happened if he'd made off? We've spent hours, days even, searching and re-capturing escapees here. Oh, I know there weren't any of the public here but it's not the point. It's not on John, not on."

"No Captain," said John, hanging his head. 'A great way to start a new job' he thought. "But, if I can ask you, Captain, have you ever come across an ape that can to things only a human is supposed to be good at, and can communicate with you?"

"I saw some interesting things in the Gold Coast with Chimps and the like but no, apes cannot do much else but the basic things a human can do, and most of that's learned mimicking us."

John looked distressed and the Captain gentled his words "Look, John, what's Franzi actually done?"

"On the train, Captain, he, well he lit a cigarette"

"You mean you lit one for him and gave it to him? I've heard he has some bad habits"

"Yes Captain, well no really" mumbled John

"Which is it, man?"

"He took a cigarette that I was going to light for him out of my mouth, took the matches, lit the cigarette and gave it back to me to smoke"

"Why would he do that?"

"Because I was shocked that he'd nodded yes when I asked him if he wanted a fag and was making a complete Horlick's of lighting up. An' his expression Captain, you should have seen it"

"I see" replied the Captain slowly. "Then this business with his crate and escaping?"

"I don't think he was escaping. He was helping. He shook my hand first and then whipped out of the crate. Frightened the life out of Higgins and me. He saw that though, Captain, because he then shook my hand again and patted me on the shoulder before going to Higgin's and introducing himself."

"And then he took the trolley to his enclosure?"

"He did, Captain. Walked in. Took the crate to the hut and waved us for Heaven's sake. He even gave you a thumbs up earlier, never done that before."

The Captain rose and poured out another cup of tea for himself and John before going to a dresser and fetching out a decanter and two crystal glasses.

"I think we need a large Scotch," said the Captain looking at John.

John nodded.

The Captain poured them both a generous measure and passed a glass to John.

"Well, let's you and I see what surprises Franzi has in store for us first thing tomorrow."

"Yes Captain," said John.

"To Franzi" toasted the Captain. "To Franzi" echoed John.

**

Whipsnade – Tuesday 27th July 1939

Early morning and all the inhabitants, animal and human were stirring in the Park. Franzi had finished his work and, after scrubbing it out several times and being frustrated overnight when the light faded, he was satisfied that it would have the desired effect. He hoped.

'Well no point in worrying' he thought 'If this didn't work he'd have to be more radical until something did.'

He'd remembered seeing a newspaper in John's things whilst travelling and hoped it was the correct date.

Daily Express, Wednesday 26 July 1939. The headline "PACT CERTAIN" was under the headline "Britain and Russia Reach Agreement".

'Oh my. Really?' he chuckled to himself.

So, he had his point of reference to use to bait the hook and get 'Their attention'.

His first of three 'worms', (he liked the fishing analogy, in fact he thought fishing might be a pleasant way of 'forgetting' some of the horrible things now in his head), comprised, in a fairly good hand, he thought, for an orangutan's first attempt at writing,

A gentle one to start for the Navy.

His second, upping the ante a little, for the RAF.

And lastly, to really hammer his point home, something 'Cryptic enough' to get some grey cells working and but bloody dynamite when it came to the notice of those who knew what it meant.'

Chapter 2

Whipsnade - Thursday 27th July 1939

The working day started early for the Whipsnade staff. Most were up and about at 0600 hrs, military time being the form insisted upon by the Captain. Those living on-site took their breakfast together in the café at 6-30 and were working at 7.

John and Higgins and the rest of the men were finishing up their teas when the Captain came in. They all stood and nodded to him. No saluting or touching their forelocks on a normal day. That sort of 'foolery', as the captain deemed it, was reserved for the days of formal inspections and when the 'Board' came visiting from London.

"Good morning, men" he boomed out "Lovely day again"

The men murmured back their greeting and assent.

"Lot's to do before the weekend and the Bank Holiday. So let's get to it."

The room quickly cleared as the men made off to their respective demesnes.

"I'll see you later," said Higgins to John, as he went off.

"Right" replied John.

"Now John," said the Captain, "shall we take a stroll to see Daisy and Franzi?"

"Yes, S.. Captain," said John.

**

The Captain moved quickly for such a large man. He was over 6-foot-tall and very well 'upholstered' thought John who had to walk fast to keep up.

"Good night's sleep, John" inquired the Captain?

"Good enough Captain. It was hard to get used to the quiet after London"

"Ah yes, the countryside of England. It's a little noisier in the Park though at different times of the year. The wolves howling is very atmospheric."

They reached the Orangutan enclosure and were surprised to see Franzi and Daisy sitting together as close as they could given the double wire barrier between them. Franzi had one arm through the fence and was gently grooming Daisy.

Daisy it was that saw the men first and raised a small 'whoop' of greeting to John.

Franzi patted her on the arm and then rose to come over to the enclosure boundary where John and the Captain were standing.

"Hello Franzi," said John "Thank you for looking after Daisy."

Franzi responded with an 'Ook' and looked back over his shoulder to see Daisy was retreating into her hut.

"Now Franzi," said the Captain "How was last night? You sleep alright?"

Franzi shrugged his shoulders and grunted.

"All seems well then, John," said the Captain "Nothing to get excited about."

"Yes Captain," said John.

Franzi let out a loud raspberry and beckoned at the Captain and John, indicating his 'hut'.

"Really Franzi?" said the Captain "Is that going to be your way of communicating with me?"

Franzi gave the Captain the thumbs up and again indicated his hut.

"What on earth does he want? Any idea, John?"

"No Captain, but I suggest we go and see."

"Is he safe? I mean I've seen the damage an enraged chimp can do when I was in The Gold Coast. Break a man into pieces and rip his arms and legs off quite easily. Franzi is much larger than an adult chimp."

"I think we'll be alright. He was very gentle with me and Higgins yesterday and after all he is inviting us in."

John looked at Franzi who nodded his head.

"Well let's do it" decided the Captain.

They walked around the enclosure to the secured double entrance. It wasn't as they had expected it to be. Both pairs of bolts on the outer and inner doors had been ripped off.

Franzi stared at them from inside and made a sort of chuckling noise when he saw their surprised look.

"What on earth?" exclaimed the Captain.

"Franzi, did you do this?" asked John.

"Ook" Franzi responded.

"Oh, for goodness sake," said the Captain "You didn't go out, did you?"

Franzi shrugged his shoulders, opened inner and outer doors and waved the men through.

They followed him slowly to the hut and wondered what other surprises he had in store.

On reaching the hut Franzi motioned them to stop.

Stepping to one side he pointed to the floor inside.

The Captain took a pace forward and peered down. His vision took a while to adjust from the bright morning sunlight to the gloom inside.

"Oh Wahala" he cried, "Oh Wahala" shaking his head.

"Captain, are you alright?"

"See for yourself John" he replied moving to one side to let John have a look.

Staring at the floor John saw, written in a large clear script,

Sir Dudley Pound will be made Admiral of the Fleet, 31 July 1939

1,300 aircraft will test Britain's air defences, 8 August 1939

Sir Hugh likes Bletchley Park

"Oh crikey, Franzi" blurted out John.

He turned to look at the Orangutan. "Did you write this?"

"Ook," said Franzi and nodded.

Franzi touched John on the arm and then did the same to the Captain and went into the hut.

Franzi turned grunted and signed for a cigarette.

John pulled out the packet and started to offer it to Franzi before realising what he was doing. He stopped and looked at the Captain for approval.

"By all means John. I think he deserves one" he said retrieving, with a shaking hand, his pipe from his pocket.

Franzi took a cigarette and passed the packet back to John.

John offered Franzi the box of matches.

Franzi repeated his lighting up routine but this time he also lit the cigarette that John had put in his mouth before carefully extinguishing the match.

The Captain paused in astonishment as he watched and then lit his pipe.

The three remained silent as they smoked.

Finally, Franzi finished his cigarette and ate the dog end.

He looked at the two men and retrieved his splinter stylus.

To leave them in no doubt that he'd written the predictions on the floor he then wrote,

"I must see Mr Churchill".

**

The Captain and John were seated in the study, both holding a large tumbler of whisky despite it only being just after 8 am.

The Captain took his glasses off and pulled a large handkerchief out to clean them.

"Captain, what's Wahala mean?" asked John.

The Captain carefully replaced his glasses before answering.

"Trouble, John. Big trouble." He said slowly and took a large swallow of the malt.

John nodded in agreement.

"How, well what.. I mean to say Franzi" muttered John, unsure of the words or even the questions to ask about Franzi and his knowledge.

"I don't know, John. I don't know" said the Captain "What I do know is we've got to keep this secret – just as Franzi asked us to."

"He seems to be very calm about it all," said John.

"It's bad enough that we have an Orangutan that can write and communicate on a human level, but then we've got to add in what he's saying about things that haven't happened yet."

"What if they don't happen? Asked John.

"Then we've got the most intelligent non-human on the planet here at the Park who makes up stories" replied the Captain "But, given what's happened do you think those things won't happen, eh?"

"I don't think I'd give money on it Captain," said John.

"The first two statements make a kind of sense, given what Britain is facing but what on earth does the third mean?" mused the Captain.

"What are you going to do?"

"What are WE going to do John – you're in this too"

"Yes, Sir," said John slipping.

"You are going to take Franzi this notepad and pencils and make sure no one else sees what he's writing" explained the Captain, pulling the writing materials from a desk draw and passing them over to John.

"Yes, Captain"

"And best make sure he doesn't just sit in his hut today, people will be wanting to see him and Daisy, visitors and staff alike."

"I'll work with him Captain. He seems to know his own mind though"

"Yes, that he does," said the Captain. "Off you go then. I'll think how and who to speak with to get his meeting with Mr Churchill."

John downed the last of his whisky.

"Best of luck, Captain," he said leaving the Captain alone to ponder his conundrum. 'Wahala, it certainly was.'

**

Franzi was quite pleased how they'd reacted. Obviously, it was quite a shock for them, but running a zoo is never routine and emergencies, large and small, crop up all the time.

The morning weather had taken a turn for the worse. None of the staff's children were braving the rain and the Park wasn't due to open until Noon. Franzi had peace and quiet to consider what to commit to the pad that John had given him. John had also left him a couple of fags and a box of matches with strict instructions not to burn the hut down.

Franzi had given John a big hug and scribed 'it'll all be fine John. Don't worry. By the way, you must get Bert and his family evacuated here'

Franzi's thought processes were somewhat confusing, Orangutan and human. So far that hadn't caused any problems, but he was sure that some of the information in his head would have to be communicated very precisely to make sure the stupid humans didn't muck it up.

He lit up a cigarette and considered the task he'd set the Captain. He hoped the Captain could devise a way to entice Churchill into a meeting.

Time was of the essence. Perhaps he should consider multiple approaches to Churchill and possibly other people who'd become key players in the unfolding drama?

**

Whipsnade - Friday 28th July 1939

The weather improved and visitors began to arrive.

The first people to see the Orangutans were children of the staff. The Captain and Mrs Beal's children, Billy and Laura, John Macdonald, the overseer's son, and Lucy Corbett, daughter of the resident engineer.

They were an excitable bunch, privileged to live in their own 'Africa' as they called it. The two boys were 12, Lucy was 10 and Laura 8.

Billy and Mac shouted at the Orangutans who were both engaged in mutual grooming through the separating fence.

"Oi" "You" "Come here then" were punctuated with whistling at the apes.

Daisy got up and scampered back to her hut. Franzi rose and wandered over to his toilet area.

"Stop it, stop it" Lucy cried. "Look what you've done" she pointed to Daisy's hut.

"Stop upsetting them" your fathers won't be pleased" she continued.

"I'll tell Father," said Laura "and you'll both be in trouble."

"Oh do shut up, girls, look the big ones coming over now," said Mac.

"Best shut up though," said Billy. "Look there's the Ape man," he said, pointing to the other side of the enclosure where John was wheeling a full truck of food down to the gate.

Franzi advanced to the edge of the enclosure closest to the children, slowly so as not to alarm them.

"Ha, see he came to me," said Mac as Franzi took careful aim and threw a carefully chosen turd at the boy which hit him in the face.

Mac screamed his disgust whilst the other children laughed at his discomfort.

"Serves you right," said Lucy.

"Poo you smell" cried Laura.

"Shut up!" said Mac

"Really, Mac – be careful how you talk to my sister," said Billy.

"Look," said Lucy "He's laughing too" pointing at Franzi

Franzi was hooting loudly at his joke.

"Children what are you doing?" asked John appearing at their side of the pit.

"Nothing" sulked Mac and he ran off back up the hill towards the staff houses.

"Billy isn't it?" said John.

"Yes sir."

"I hope you weren't upsetting Franzi and Daisy. I won't stand for it," said John sternly.

"Sorry Sir," said the children together.

"Now, would you like to meet Franzi?" asked John in a kindlier tone.

"Oh yes!" the girls exclaimed.

"Would I ever?" said Billy.

"Follow me then"

John led them round to the dual gates and called for Franzi.

"Alright Franzi if these three come in to see you," he asked.

Franzi replied with an "Ook" and the vigorous nodding of the head.

"So, children, Franzi says he's happy to meet you. Do you want to go inside and meet him?"

"I don't feel happy about that," said Laura, edging back a little.

"Erm, I'll stay here and say hello," said Billy seeing the powerful ape close too.

"I will," said Lucy

"You too stay there then. Lucy stay by me," instructed John opening the first door, closing it behind them and then opening the second.

Franzi moved back from the entrance and crouched down even though he wasn't much taller than Lucy.

As she approached Franzi held out his hand. She looked at John who said "It's fine" before holding out her hand and grasping the large ape's big hand.

They slowly shook up and down and Franzi gave out a low 'Ook, ook" before letting go and patting her on the arm.

"Oh he's so wonderful," Lucy said.

"He's a very special boy," said John "and I think he likes you"

'Ook' and a head nod.

"Can I come and see him every day?" Lucy asked.

"I'm sure that might be possible," said John leading her back to the gate.

"Goodbye Franzi," she said, looking back and waving.

"Ook" and a wave followed by a large raspberry from Franzi.

The children laughed and waved and blew raspberries in response.

'My' thought Franzi 'I think I've made a friend there'.

**

"Dr Vevers please," said the Captain.

"Ah, hello Geoffrey, Bill here"

"Fine, fine. Yes, I think we'll be prepared if the balloon goes up."

"Funnily enough I wanted to talk to you about Franzi and Daisy."

"No, nothing wrong. Daisy was a bit nervous but Franzi is settling in very well."

"I wondered if you're still in touch with Solly?"

"Yes, I'd heard he's working with the War Office."

"Do you think he could spare me some time to discuss ape behaviour?"

"No there's no problem. It's just that I'm interested in how Franzi and Daisy are interacting. We might be looking at a fruitful outcome if we handle it right."

"Do you think he'd help out with that?"

"Excellent. Just let me write that down. Oxford 1 2 9 5"

"Yes, I'll keep you informed. Goodbye."

'So this evening then' thought the Captain as he pushed to one side his copy of "Social Life of Monkeys and Apes" 1932, Solly Zuckerman, Fellow of the Royal Society.

**

Franzi paused and scratched his head with the chewed end of the pencil.

'This isn't going to be simple' he thought. 'Getting people to take him seriously was going to be tricky and once they did how did he want to take things forward?'

'Should he just leave it for them to act on his "revelations" or should he be more pro-active?'

He'd learnt that some humans could be trusted and that they could be quite creative. Others, he'd found, were right stubborn bastards even if they were competent.

His 'knowledge' included information on key people and their character as well as their strengths and weaknesses. How they'd react to him was a complete unknown. John and the Captain seemed to be coping with his new self quite well, but they'd really seen nothing yet. Perhaps he'd keep things simple with John and not burden him with too much. The Captain was a different matter, after all he was the Superintendent and could, if he chose, completely negate Franzi's efforts. He needed to fully win over Captain Bill Beale.

He returned to his list.

John had set up a sort of 'desk' for him, so writing was easier than putting the notebook on the floor.

Franzi had excavated a hole under the area that he normally slept in and covered it with two boards. On top of that, he'd made sure his bedding leaves and branches were piled to hide what was beneath. He was confident that hiding his work there was safe, after all, who was going to try and take something from a full-grown Orangutan?

He had several headings,

People to be encouraged

The Enemies

Warnings to prevent disasters

Technology

'Nice word that last one, it rolls around in the head and sounds GOOD'.

So many things inside his mind. And anger, ANGER, at the bad men.

Better get writing then – but in some sort of order or he'd make a right midden out of it, as Bert would say.

**

"Solly?" asked the Captain early that evening.

"Bill Beale, Whipsnade"

"Geoffrey gave me your number"

"All going well with the War Office?"

"Good, good."

"Well I wouldn't expect you to tell me that but a nod's as good as a wink to a blind man"

"I've got an odd request. I know you're up to your eyes in it but is there any chance you could come down here Saturday or Sunday?"

"Late afternoon would be best. I want to introduce you to one of our new 'friends' who's been evacuated from London"

"I'm sure you'll find it very worthwhile. I doubt you'll have seen anything like it in all your work on apes."

"Sure, we can put you up if you like. I'll ask Gladys to set the spare room up."

"So 1600 hrs? Yes, at 4 o'clock. Excellent. Til then. Goodbye"

**

John sat down with Franzi at the end of the day. Out of sight of people they shared a convivial smoke.

"So Franzi, what've you been writing today?"

Franzi held up a note pad and raised his thumb.

"Mind if I see?" asked John.

Franzi raised his hand palm outwards to John and shook his head then reached for his stick and wrote it the earth 'Best not' and 'Too dangerous'.

"I don't understand," said John

'Big secrets' wrote Franzi and then smoothed out the words.

"Government type secrets?" asked John in a low voice.

Franzi nodded.

"So, are those for Mr Churchill then?"

'Ook'

Franzi smoothed the earth and wrote

'Who are the children?'

"Oh, you liked them did you?"

'Ook'

"Even the one you threw poo at?"

'He was showing off to the others and upsetting Daisy'

"I bet his Dad will have words with me about it."

Franzi shrugged and chuckled.

"That one was John Macdonald, his father is the works overseer. The other boy, Billy, is the Captain's son, the younger girl is his daughter, Laura."

Franzi chuffed.

"And the other was Lucy Corbett. Her father is the park's engineer"

'What sort of engineer?'

"Mechanical and electrical, he makes sure the Park's pumps and machines all work as they should" replied John.

Franzi let out a long huff of understanding. Well that's what John thought to himself. He caught himself thinking. 'I'm sat here, discussing things with an Orangutan as if it's the most normal thing in the world. If I told anyone else except the Captain, they'd think I was mad as a hatter.'

Franzi was writing again

'Have you a plan of the Park?'

He knew fine well John had, he'd seen him referring to it a few times during the day as he was still getting his bearings and understand what was where.

"I do. Do you want to see?" asked John.

'Ook'

**

Franzi was stealthy when moving around the Park at night. There was little chance the two patrolling watchmen would see him even though it was still quite light, but he didn't want to disturb any of the animals. Firstly, it might scare some of the timid ones and secondly, alarm cries would alert the watchmen that something was amiss.

John had been helpful to a degree showing Franzi where things were on the Park map. Franzi had been careful not to show too much interest in Lucy's home.

He carefully checked around the garden and outside of the house before opting to pop over the fence. He swung himself up onto the outhouse roof and proceeded to carefully peer into the bedrooms on that side of the building.

The first room was empty. In the second room he saw Lucy sat up in bed reading a book. He tapped gently on the window. Deep into the story, she didn't respond. He tapped harder and risked an 'Ook'. Looking up Lucy screamed and dropped her book. Franzi swung up onto the roof out of sight.

"Are you alright Lucy?" shouted a woman

"Yes Mum," Lucy called back staring hard at the window and wondering if she'd imagined seeing an orangutan.

"It'll be time to stop reading and go to sleep soon" her Mother responded

"Yes Mum."

Lucy swung her legs down and got out of bed.

Slowly, as quietly as she could, she tiptoed to the window.

It was open to let cooling air into her bedroom on this balmy summer evening. She opened it further and looked out.

Franzi saw her head appear out of the opening and gave a long 'shush'

She jumped back in surprise but clapped her hand over her mouth to stifle the scream.

Franzi eased himself down onto the window.

He breathed on the glass and reverse wrote 'Hello Lucy. May I come in?'

Lucy's eyes widened in surprise. She stood back and let him in.

He held out his hand and she shook it, then he sat gently on the floor.

Franzi signed writing at Lucy and looked at her hopefully.

You want to write something? She asked

Franzi nodded 'Ook'

Lucy thought for a minute and then looked in the top draw of her bedside cabinet.

"I've got a pencil. No spare paper though, except" she paused "I suppose you could write in my diary" she offered.

Franzi shook his head and made a dismissive gesture with his hand.

"No?" said Lucy.

"It's a bit difficult for me to get some now. Mum keeps paper and envelopes downstairs and she and Dad are still up. They'd want to know why I needed it." She paused.

"I know. I have a slate and chalk I used to practice writing with"

Franzi nodded and raised a thumb in assent.

Lucy got up opened a cupboard and, after some rummaging, presented Franzi with a slate framed with wood and a chalk.

"Sorry it's only pink chalk, I haven't used this for ages"

Franzi quickly wrote in a neat small hand 'This is fine, thank you'

Lucy stopped and gave a little gasp of surprise.

"How come you can write?" she exclaimed.

'It's a pity I can't talk like you,' wrote Franzi.

"But apes aren't supposed to be able to write" she cried

'Shush, you must keep the secret, friend Lucy' he scribed

"I will, I promise. You shouldn't be here though either. How did you get out? How did you find me? And what do you want?"

Franzi winked at her and chuckled whilst writing

'So many questions '

"You're teasing me," Lucy said a little huffily

Franzi shook his head.

'Sorry child Lucy' he wrote. 'Will you help me?'

"To leave the Park," she said with concern?

He shook his head and wrote 'To send letters '

Lucy smiled, "I can do that, but who too?"

"Lucy," came a woman's shout from downstairs "who are you talking to? Time you were asleep young lady. I'm bringing you your cocoa now."

"No one Mum," said Lucy and then to Franzi "go" in whispered command

Franzi quickly moved across the room taking the slate in one hand tucking the chalk behind his ear. He swung one-handed out through the window and landed on the outhouse roof a little more heavily than he intended. An action that prompted a man, Franzi assumed Lucy's father, to shout "Bloody hell, what's that?"

"Language," said Lucy's mother.

Franzi wasted no time jumping over the fence and disappearing into the twilight.

**

The weather on Friday started as poorly as Thursday had done.

Franzi finalised his list of people to write to in the first instance. He wanted to ensure they were 'prepared'.

When John appeared with his hand truck of food Franzi helped him wheel it into his enclosure and drew him to one side in the hut.

'John,' he wrote 'Can I have sheets of paper please, as well as another pad?'

"Have you used the first pad up so quickly," asked John laughing. "What have you been doing with it? Not tearing out sheets to wipe your bottom," he joked.

Franzi blew a raspberry and laughed, pounding the ground with his hands before writing

'No John, my anus works properly, unlike Homo Sapiens!'

John punched him playfully on the shoulder and they had a romp until Franzi pinned him down.

"Good to see you're still fun-loving Franzi despite the 'change'" said John rubbing his bruised ribs as he struggled to rise. "Ok Franzi, I'll get you what you want."

'And envelopes' Franzi wrote in the dirt.

"Envelopes," asked John, looking at Franzi sideways. "What do you need envelopes for?"

'To keep things organised' scribed Franzi.

"Of course, silly me," said John sarcastically.

Franzi pounded him on the back, but not too hard, then ushered him, with the truck, out of the enclosure.

**

When the weather improved and the gates were opened to the public Lucy and her friends came to look at Franzi and Daisy.

Daisy was settling in nicely now, her nerves soothed by Franzi's attention. She really quite liked him.

Franzi wasn't sure quite what was happening to him, whether it was the 'event' or just normal orangutan hormones. It wasn't unpleasant but it was distracting when he had a war to win!

He made sure to go as near to Lucy and surreptitiously write in the dirt – 'later' before hurriedly scuffing out the word.

Lucy nodded at him and the other children were pleased, as were the visitors, to see him in 'entertainment mode'.

**

Dusk fell.

Franzi stole out of his enclosure and made his way to Lucy's house.

Lucy was waiting expectantly for him at the window.

She moved aside as he quietly swung onto the sill via the outhouse roof. This time, after putting down the slate and envelopes, he gave her a gentle hug. They both sat down on the floor.

"Franzi, I saved this for you, " said Lucy. She offered him a banana.

He considered it then shook his head.

'That's very kind Lucy', he wrote 'but you have it. There might not be many about soon.'

"Oh," she said, a little puzzled. She saw the number of envelopes and gasped. "So many letters?"

'Sorry,' he wrote.

"Well," she said post is 2.5d a letter and you've got... one, two three four five six seven eight nine ten. That's 2 shillings and a penny."

He looked downcast as he wiped the slate. 'Ah, yes, postage'.

Possibly I'm not so clever if I forget things like that.

'Ook' he asked?

"It's alright this time," said Lucy, "I've a postal order for half a crown from my grandma for my birthday. I can go to the post office and change it then post your letters."

Franzi chuffed and nodded.

'I will pay back the money, Lucy ' he wrote.

Lucy looked at him. "It's alright. I don't need it at the minute. I'll just tell Mum and Dad that I'm saving. Anyway, how could you get money?"

"Lucy," cried her mother from downstairs, "I'll be up in a minute with your cocoa".

Franzi chalked quickly 'You'll be surprised' then made his exit without crashing down hard on the outhouse this time.

**

After Lucy had her cocoa and the house was all quiet, she lit her bedside candle and scrutinised the envelopes. Franzi had neatly addressed each one in his fine hand,

Marcus Oliphant

Franz Simmons

Wallace Akers

Sir Wilfrid Freeman

Geoffrey de Havilland

Frank Whittle

Stanley Hooker

Tommy Flowers

Lt Cdr Charles F. Goodeve

R V Jones Esq.

**

Whipsnade - Saturday 29th July 1939

"Solly how the devil are you?" asked the Captain.

"Not too bad Bill, considering the ongoing flap, of which I can't speak' replied Solly laughing.

"Good drive down?"

"Very pleasant. I needed a break. Popping down here will recharge my batteries."

"If you leave your bags there I'll get Billy to put them in your room. Come through, come through" said the Captain ushering Solly into the study.

"Take a seat. Could I get you some tea or something stronger?"

"Well it is past 4 so I wouldn't mind a whisky and soda" replied Solly.

"Coming up. I much prefer brandy though, so I haven't got any fancy Scotch," explained the Captain.

After they'd exchanged general chit chat and the alcohol had mellowed them a little Solly exclaimed

"Come on Bill. What's the thing that makes it doubly worthwhile me coming here, on top of seeing Gladys and yourself."

"First a question for you. How many times have you seen apes communicating with humans?"

"Many times. I refer to it extensively in my boo, of course"

"Yes, I can see that" replied the Captain retrieving a copy from his desk. "But I mean really communicating"

"Oh some primates in close proximity or raised by humans are very communicative," said Solly. "Now tell me why the question?"

"Well you're pretty scathing in your book about behaviour anecdotally reported by laymen," said the Captain slowly.

"And I am still of the same opinion" Solly responded.

" I hope you wouldn't consider me in that category, " asked the Captain.

"Not at all my dear fellow" Solly reassured him.

"Good. Then I'd like you to come and meet one of our Regent's Park refugees who's exhibiting some quite remarkable talent."

"Do tell Bill, stop beating around the 'ourwoud'" said Solly.

"No, no. Wait and see." The park hooter sounded the end of the working day. "Ah there we are. Time to take a stroll."

Solly drained his glass and stood up "Now you've really got me interested" he commented.

**

They chatted companionly about the Park and its residents and the potential impact of war, if it came, as they strolled down to the orangutan's enclosure.

John was waiting for them at the gate. He'd been talking to Franzi whilst he waited for the Captain and Mr Zuckerman to arrive.

"Good evening Captain, Dr Zuckerman"

"Hello John," said Solly "how do you think you're going to like it here?"

"It's a treat to be out of the City and see the wonderful space the animals have here."

"John, how's Franzi today?" asked the Captain.

"On fine form. He entertained the crowds well and coaxed Daisy out of her shelter. I'm not sure what he was up to but he apparently got the crowd to throw him money for a performance he did."

"Oh yes? Doing what" said the Captain.

"Pretending to be Hitler, goose-stepping and saluting, so I'm told" laughed John.

"Wonderful, wonderful. Franzi" exclaimed the Captain.

On hearing his name Franzi put his pencil and pad down and hid them under some bedding before he emerged from his shelter.

He stared at the three men and gave an inward chuckle when he recognised the stranger.

Time for some fun.

He ambled across to the gate and gave a perfectly normal Orangutan greeting.

The Captain and John were somewhat nonplussed, but then again they'd agreed with Franzi that he wouldn't 'show off' in front of strangers.

"Good evening Franzi," said the Captain.

Franzi responded with a loud raspberry.

"Really Franzi, " expostulated the Captain!

"Perfectly normal behaviour for a happy Pongo pygmaeus" laughed Solly.

"May we come in?" asked the Captain.

'Ook' said Franzi. Then he performed a series of lazy rolls back to his hut.

"I take it this is a safe thing to do," said Solly.

"Oh yes sir," said john opening the gates into the enclosure to let the Captain and Solly in.

The three men walked over to Franzi's hut and squatted in a semi-circle at the entrance.

Franzi signed at john for a cigarette. The Captain nodded his agreement as john paused for a moment before passing over the pack.

Franzi took a cigarette and put the pack down then signed for a light.

John passed over the matchbox.

Franzi carefully extracted a match, struck it, lit the cigarette and blew out the flame.

He took a draw on the cigarette and gave a satisfied 'Chough' and a 'thumbs up'

"There you see, Solly," said the Captain.

"All very interesting but hardly startling. I expect this young fellow had a varied upbringing before the Society acquired him" said Solly.

The Captain beamed and gently prompted Franzi, "Franzi tell Solly something that you told us"

Franzi put a puzzled look on his face 'Ook?"

"Go on Franzi," said john handing Franzi the pointed stick and clearing detritus from the earth floor of the hut.

"Ook?"

"It seems clear to me that whatever you thought you had from 'Franzi' was just a fluke or oddly remembered reflex action from his past," said Solly dryly.

The Captain looked between Franzi and Solly unsure of what to say.

"How about we go back to the house and you give me a couple of scotches in compensation for this jape before what will be, as usual, a delightful meal from Gladys," said Solly, standing up.

"Franzi" muttered john sternly under his breath.

Franzi patted him on the arm.

He looked at Solly and blew a very loud raspberry whilst gesturing him to sit down.

Franzi picked up his stick and wrote

'Well Doctor Zuckerman you might know your Papio hamadryas and Pan troglodytes but you ain't seen nothing yet'

And with that Solly's jaw dropped and he sat down with a thump on the ground.

"Oh goodness me!"

Chapter 3

Whipsnade - Sunday 30th July 1939

Sunday breakfast in the Captain's house was an event.

All the family sat down together and today Solly joined them too.

Billy and Laura talked excitedly about Franzi and his performance.

The Captain smiled at them and said, "It's an interesting thing to draw in the crowds once word goes around."

"If the press gets hold of the story it then I'm sure the newsreels will be here pretty quickly", Solly remarked.

"Mum, we'll be in the pictures," said Laura.

"Wait and see young lady" her mother replied. "Now if you and Billy have finished you can help me with the washing up. Come along".

**

After the children and Gladys had gone Solly lit a cigarette and the Captain brought out his pipe. "So, what next Solly," he asked?

"Well Franzi told me to 'continue to keep at it' and 'don't let the bomber ghouls get their way'"

"Any idea what that means," said the Captain?

"There's been some talk about establishing a team to review the results of any bombing the RAF carries out, but how could Franzi know about that? And how could he know that I'd be involved, because that's not been determined yet."

"He seems to know a lot of things that I suspect no one knows about and what we're going to face soon," mused the Captain.

"It makes no sense," said Solly "But I agree with him that the fewer people who know about the source of these, erm, 'forecasts', 'predictions', I don't even know what to call them for goodness sake."

"I'm still shaken too," said the Captain "But we haven't had any proof so far on his first three pronouncements." He paused, "let's consider each of them".

"Dudley Pound promoted to Admiral of the Fleet. A rank that's in the King's gift" said Solly.

"Not an unusual or unlikely thing for the First Sea Lord to be so promoted," said the Captain.

"The Admiralty will probably release the information today, if I asked the right person" suggested Solly.

"May as well wait," said the Captain, "but what about this air force exercise?"

"I doubt we can get any information on that. Only certain RAF senior officers and Air Ministry fellas will be aware of what's planned" mused Solly.

"And this last one 'Sir Hugh likes Bletchley Park'" posed the Captain?

"Hmm," said Solly, "puzzling."

"The other thing is Franzi's request to see Churchill," said the Captain.

After a pause Solly asked, "And what would you like me to do?"

"I did wonder if you might have some line of communication to Churchill?"

"Not a one that I'd currently go to," said Solly. "Let's face it he's a bit of a sore point with everyone at the minute. Not that he's saying, 'I told you so' openly but it's clear he did, didn't he?"

"And now we have to pick up the pieces," said the Captain.

"There's still a chance the Russian pact will happen," said Solly "But I'd not trust Stalin as far as I could throw him."

"I'll have to think of something. Franzi is going through notebooks at a rate of knots and is quite insistent that he sees Churchill" said the Captain.

"Have you seen what he's been writing," asked Solly?

"No, no-one has. John told me that Franzi made it clear that they are 'dangerous' secrets'" replied the Captain.

"What's he doing with the notes?"

"Not sure, he won't let anyone, including John, near his hut though," said the Captain.

"Hmm. I wonder if you made it easier for him to write here whether John could search the hut?"

"In what way 'easier'" asked the Captain?

"Well, it's just a thought but have you heard the old one about 'if enough Chimps had a typewriter they might come up with Hamlet'?"

"I have indeed. Saw some things in Africa but I've never seen a chimp type though" chuckled the Captain.

"I'd wager Franzi would be able to - and jump at the opportunity, especially if it included a cigarette or two as a bribe."

"Splendid idea"

Solly slapped his forehead.

"What is it, man?"

"Well if this is all high-powered stuff then there's only one Sir Hugh that I know of that fits the bill" Solly responded.

"Yes?"

"Oh it all fits, clever Franzi" exclaimed Solly.

"Who man" demanded the Captain.

"Sir Hugh Sinclair, head of the SIS. Rumour has it he bought a place near Bletchley last year with his own money when the Treasury wouldn't cough up."

"Wonder what that's going to be used for," said the Captain.

"Best not to ask" replied Solly.

"I bet Franzi has an idea," said the Captain. "Speaking of whom let's find John and tell him the plan. Then offer Franzi a typewriter".

**

Whipsnade - Monday 31ˢᵗ July 1939

"Have you seen the paper, John?" asked the Captain when he called in at the 'store' where the animal food supplies were held and distributed.

"Yes Captain," John replied as he loaded up his trolley with fruit and greens for the orangutans.

"So Franzi got that one right," he said in a definitive tone.

"He did indeed Captain," said John.

"Can you bring him up to the House around 1900 hrs this evening and we'll show him the typewriter. Gladys was very suspicious; she knows I don't type unless really pressed to. And then only in a painful one-fingered exercise," said the Captain.

"Will do Captain," replied John. "It looks like it's going to be a beautiful day today so we should get lots of visitors."

"Yes, and the Press," said the Captain. "Someone's been telling them about Franzi. They rang me first thing this morning."

"Shall I tell him not to do it?" asked John. "It's showing off a bit and he said he didn't want anyone to know he's 'special'."

"Too late John, too late. The cat's out of the bag now. I wonder what he's done with the money and where did he get that cap from?"

"That's Higgin's," said John laughing "He was helping me out and Franzi pinched it and wouldn't give it back. Couldn't work out why at the time."

"Another thing for you to look for when you get the chance then," said the Captain, chuckling too.

**

It had been a long, busy, enjoyable day.

Franzi was pleased. The crowd were pleased as were the Press and photographers who'd snapped him performing his 'Hitler' skit. They particularly liked his humming, either of 'Deutschland, Deutschland über alles' or better still 'The Lambeth Walk'.

He'd made quite a bit of money in ha'pennies, pennies and the odd thruppenny bit and sixpence. With what he had from Sunday he could pay Lucy back and still have enough to post more letters.

Franzi considered the letters he'd written and then, pulling out the writing paper, commenced to write a few more. After all the more people in key fields he could stimulate and coach before the orchestra got its new conductor the better. What a pleasant simile he thought and began to hum. Dah dah dah dum.

**

Come evening, after the visitors had left, the hooter sounded and dusk was falling, John appeared at the enclosure gate. He called out and waved at Franzi before letting himself into the compound. Franzi quickly hid his current work and went out to meet him.

"Well my lad" John started" the Captain's invited you up to see the typewriter we told you about earlier. Are you ready to go?"

Franzi looked at John carefully. He didn't quite like his tone. John sounded 'stressed'.

Picking up his stick Franzi wrote 'Not tonight. Tomorrow.'

"There'll be a cigarette or two in it for you," coaxed John.

Franzi was sure something was amiss. He pointed to what he'd already written and added 'Tired. Busy day. John go now'.

"Come on Franzi," said John.

Franzi shook his head and pointed at 'John go now'.

John patted Franzi on the arm and Franzi gave him a hug.

'Alright, Franzi. I'll tell the Captain tomorrow."

**

Franzi watched John walk back up the hill towards the Park entrance and the Captain's house. Higgins joined John and Franzi heard him say "So I won't get my cap back tonight then?"

"Tomorrow," said John and then they were out of sight.

'Really' thought Franzi 'Do they actually think I'm that stupid? So they want to search do they?" Going inside his hut he went to his 'hide' and took out the notebooks and letters he'd written. Taking a sheet of paper he quickly wrote a message and put it in the hide with Higgins' cap before covering everything up with bedding once more.

He took his slate and chalk too, checked the coast was clear and set off, via a circuitous route, to Lucy's house.

**

John tapped gently on the back door of 'The House'.

The Captain opened it.

"John, ah. Where is Franzi," he asked as he peered into the darkness of his garden?"

"He wouldn't come, Captain."

"He what" exclaimed the Captain, "Why ever not?"

"He said he was 'tired' and that he'd come tomorrow," said John slowly.

"I see," said the Captain. "Well, I suppose that will have to do. Can't make a fuss over it."

"No Captain. I said there'd be some cigarettes in it but he still wasn't interested" replied John.

"Not to worry John. Perhaps he is tired, anyway tomorrow will do. Thank you for trying."

"I'll be off then Captain," asked John?

"Yes indeed. Good night."

"Good night Captain."

The Captain went back inside to his study, sat down at his desk and lit up his pipe. 'Odd' he thought. And then got on with Park paperwork, of which there seemed to be even more of in this queer period of tension between nations.

**

Monkey island was dark and deserted. Originally built to house the Parks Chimps it was now empty as they'd been moved on.

Franzi considered again – 'Would it be a safe place to keep his documents?' 'Probably, unless they got the chimps back or baboons or gorillas,' he thought.

'Chimps and baboons were right pains in the arse. When all was said and done baboons were just the thugs of the primate world, chimps, on the other hand, were full of themselves thinking they were really smart and clever with all their 'cute' antics for the humans. To be fair though that was mainly the young ones he'd come across.'

Fortunately, the small lake surrounding the island wasn't deep and Franzi was able to wade across. He wasn't averse to swimming but most of his kind avoided it if they could.

When he reached dry land he quickly found the shelter that had been marked on the Park map and hid his completed notebooks as best he could. It was only a temporary solution, but it would do until he'd persuaded Daisy to let him dig a pit in her shelter.

**

Franzi was still quite damp from the chest down when he got to Lucy's house.

He tapped lightly on her window. She glanced up from her book, threw it down and ran on tiptoe to let him in.

She stopped at the window, then raised her hands to prevent him going into the room.

"Franzi, you're wet, and you smell," she wrinkled her nose. "You can't come in here like that. Mother will have a fit if you stink my room out."

Perching on the window was difficult. Franzi had envelopes in one hand and his slate under the other arm, the chalk was in its usual place behind his ear.

He sniffed. Yes, he did pong a bit from the mud and ooze of the lake.

He pushed the envelopes and slate at Lucy then dropped back down to the ground before disappearing out of her sight around the corner.

Lucy lay the envelopes on the floor. Two obviously had coins in them. Both were quite heavy. The others were sealed and had names and addresses on them.

She waited anxiously, peering out of her window. It felt like an age but Franzi was back in ten minutes or so, this time only wet from the chest down. The smell, thankfully, was bearable.

She let him in as he looked apologetically at the water dripping from him onto her floor.

"Don't worry, it'll dry?" she said.

After a big hug followed by 'Hello's' and 'Ooks' they sat.

Franzi gathered the envelopes around him, picked up the slate and wrote, 'Friend Lucy, here is your money back' handing her one of the envelopes containing coins.

She emptied it out, it was full of sixpences, far more than the money she'd spent on postage.

"Franzi, this is more than half a crown," she cried.

'I know,' he wrote. 'Ten shillings, I think. Half a crown back and the rest is for you and to share with your friends.'

She smiled broadly and hugged him again.

'This one is for more postage' he scribed and handed her the second, heavier, envelope.

Pouring this one out she saw a few sixpences and a good number of thrupenny bits.

"Right oh," she said, "For these new letters?"

He nodded, 'Ook' and passed her the sealed and addressed envelopes.

Wiping his slate, he wrote 'I need a bag, a satchel or sack bag. Can you help?'

"Hmm," she thought, "I think so. I might be able to persuade Billy to let me have his old satchel."

'Ook'

"I can't promise but I'll find something," Lucy said, "He'll do most things for me."

Franzi chuckled. "I have more money if we have to buy one," he wrote.

"We'll see," she said.

'Must go now', he wrote 'Bye Lucy'. He gave her another hug then left as silently as he'd arrived.

**

The Captain pushed his chair back. The pipe sat unlit. The out tray quite full. The in-tray definitely not empty but a good start had been made.

He glanced at the clock. 2230. Time for a nightcap, check on the children and then take cocoa in to Gladys.

The Captain rose and then helped himself to a large brandy before sitting down in his favourite armchair. He eased his glasses and rubbed the bridge of his nose. He'd have to call Solly tomorrow and explain that there'd been a delay in intelligence gathering.

He jumped and nearly spilt brandy, his thoughts were broken into by a knocking at the study window. It was dark outside, and his desk light and standard lamp didn't illuminate much outside their own ambit, but he could make out Franzi's large face through the glass.

"Franzi," he said as he waved him in the direction of the back door.

**

Franzi sat himself in the second armchair in the room, his feet didn't touch the ground, well not in a way he was comfortable with, so he draped his legs over a chair arm and 'lounged'.

The Captain couldn't help but smile. "Happy, Franzi?"

'Oook' said Franzi then pointed at the Captain's glass of brandy and signed for a cigarette.

"Really Franzi?"

"Oook"

"That District Officer got you into some really bad habits. Oh alright," said the Captain.

He started to pour Franzi a small brandy until Franzi blew a raspberry, at which point he continued to pour until Franzi's glass was as full as his own.

A cigarette and lighter were next, Franzi coping unfazed with what the Captain would have considered a 'new' and unseen gadget as he lit up.

"So Franzi, John told me you were tired this evening?"

'Chuff. Oook,' Franzi replied.

He held up his glass and 'toasted' the Captain before taking a long slurp. He smacked his lips. 'Not as good as District Officer Whyte's malt whiskey but much better than Malay tuak he'd sampled sometimes,' he thought.

"The typewriter is over there," said the Captain. "Would you like to take a look and try it?"

Franzi shook his head and signed for pen and paper.

The Captain obliged and provided a book to rest on.

Franzi rearranged himself so he could write comfortably and penned

'Thank you, Captain, for inviting me into your home.'

"Don't mention it Franzi," said the Captain. "You can come anytime as long as Gladys and the children don't see you."

Franzi nodded. Then wrote 'Writing everything to communicate with you is long-winded.'

"Indeed. It must be."

'Been thinking. I know sign language. Need a signer that can be trusted'.

The Captain nearly choked on his brandy. He nodded "Yes, yes," he said, as he tried to recover his composure.

'Solly should help find,' noted Franzi.

"What a good idea. I was going to call him in the morning," said the Captain.

I bet you were, thought Franzi, hoping to discuss my notes. Outwardly he just nodded.

He started writing again. 'Can you get me a blackboard, two writing slates and chalks please?'

"I see no problem with that. It might take a couple of days though," replied the Captain.

'Ook'. Then wrote, 'Blackboard and one slate here, the other for me.'

"Very well," said the Captain.

'Goodnight Captain,' wrote Franzi 'Thank you. See you tomorrow.'

Franzi stood, finished his brandy and stubbed out the last of his cigarette in the desk ashtray.

Damn good manners for an ape, better than a lot of people he knew, thought the Captain.

"Goodnight Franzi, I'll see you out."

**

Whipsnade - Tuesday 1st August 1939

Next day the Captain called on the Park staff as usual, just after their breakfast before they began their work.

After greeting them and thanking them for their Bank Holiday efforts he took John aside.

"John, you'll be surprised to learn that Franzi came to the House last night after all."

"Really Captain? That's interesting," said John.

"We had a fruitful discussion about communication. He said he'd be back to see me this evening, so you'll have a chance to explore his demesne later," said the Captain.

"Yes Captain. I'll warn Higgins. Shall I bring Franzi up to the house around 2000 hrs?"

"Yes, perfect time," the Captain replied. "I've also had a thought, perhaps we should now remove the fence between Daisy and Franzi? Or do you think it a bit early?"

"I think that's a good idea. Franzi and Daisy seem to be getting on very well. I'll put it off until tomorrow, shall I? After we've had a look round Franzi's bit?" said John.

The Captain nodded. "Good. Until later then."

**

"Solly? Bill here."

"No, we didn't get a chance to search for the notebooks yesterday. Franzi refused to come up when John asked him."

"Yes, said he was tired. Odd thing though he turned up later at 2230 hrs."

"Yes, I thought so too. Sat and talked about communication and asked me to find him someone who could be trusted and who knew sign language."

"Agreed, it does sound a good idea. Do you think you could find someone through your contacts?"

"If you could it would speed things up somewhat. Hopefully we should be able to get our hands on the notebooks tonight. Franzi said he'd come and see me this evening."

"Right. I'll talk to you tomorrow. Goodbye."

**

Franzi spent a good part of the day with Daisy. He was sure she'd be happy with him entering her hut and tailoring it to his needs.

After what they'd read in the newspapers the public wanted a bit of a show and he gave them something to talk about but he didn't get the hat out today.

The Park closed and, in due course, John came to take Franzi to the House. Franzi put on a 'carefree' performance on the way and they were admitted by the Captain and escorted to the Study.

After pleasantries and Franzi being plied with brandy, large, and cigarettes, John excused himself and said he'd be back later. Franzi wrote on the new slate provided by the Captain, 'No need John. I'll go home on my own.'

John nodded at Franzi and the Captain then let himself out.

"So Franzi, I didn't tell you that your pronouncement about Dudley Pound was correct. His promotion was announced in the papers yesterday."

'Ook'. 'It's unfortunate that he's a sick man' he wrote. 'Perhaps it should only be a short appointment.'

The Captain looked at Franzi sharply. "What's that you say?"

'He has hip problems and doesn't sleep well and he's developing a brain tumour. By the way, Chamberlain is very sick with cancer of the bowel.'

"My God Franzi, where do these revelations come from?" exclaimed the Captain.

'I just know,' wrote Franzi, shaking his head.

"And what about me and my family? What can you tell me?" asked the Captain.

'I believe you'll have long and happy lives,' wrote Franzi.

The Captain was silent for a time. He looked into Franzi's eyes but gleaned nothing from the sage.

'May I type now' asked Franzi?

"Certainly," said the Captain indicating the typewriter and desk.

Franzi spent some time at the machine. He loaded new sheets of paper with ease and set the completed typing to one side as he went.

Eventually, he finished and said 'That'll do for tonight. Thank you, Captain. I'll see myself out.' And with that he was gone off into the night.

The Captain was intrigued. Franzi had typed but had not taken his notes with him. What on earth had he recorded that he didn't mind being seen?

He picked up the completed scripts and read the title 'Plans and Actions for Whipsnade Zoo Park in the event of War.'

**

Whipsnade - Wednesday 2nd August 1939

Early in the morning before the Captain had a chance to go and see his staff at the café John knocked on the front door of the House.

Billy let him in and shouted for the Captain whilst showing John into the Study.

The Captain had finished dressing but not yet eaten and he asked Gladys for tea for himself and John.

Shutting the door behind him he turned.

"So, what did you find John?"

"Well Captain, he had a hide under his bed."

"And?"

"Well there weren't no notebooks, writing paper or envelopes in it, only Higgins' cap and this," he said, passing the Captain a single sheet of paper.

The Captain turned it over then saw the cartoon of Chad and read "Wot No Secrets?"

Chapter 4

"Mr Oliphant?" The University porter called. "You have a letter, Sir."

"Just put it in with the normal office post," Oliphant replied in his South Australian twang.

"Can't sir!" called the porter at the receding back of Oliphant, "It's marked Private and Confidential, Deliver by Hand. You knows the rules, Sir."

Oliphant swung on his heel and returned to the desk.

"Alright, Hughes. Give it here."

He took the proffered envelope and retraced his steps to the stairs. As he made his way to the lab he scrutinised the letter. He noted that the address and instructions were written in pencil, albeit in a very neat and professional hand.

He sat at his desk and opened the letter.

'Dear Professor Oliphant,

I write to you on a matter of great urgency and secrecy. As you know war between Germany and Great Britain, including the Commonwealth and Empire, is very likely.

I can confirm that this conflict cannot be avoided and that by the evening of 3 September 1939 it will have begun.

Your role in it, and that of your team and colleagues is crucial.

I realise you do not know me, and I cannot, as yet, reveal my identity to prevent information falling into the wrong hands, be they German, Italian, Japanese or Soviet. What I can say is that I know a great deal of information about you and what you are working on. I can provide significant details of how to accelerate your successes and prevent your failures. This will ensure Britain has the tools it needs to fight and defeat the Axis of Evil in a short a time as possible thereby minimising the suffering of millions.

To give you some reassurance that I am not some crank I have detailed on a separate enclosure facts and equations relating to key developments you are working on. Please take especial note of what your colleagues, John Randall and Harry Boot are working on in respect of the Cavity Magnetron and cm length radar; and also tell Otto Frisch and Rudolf Peierls that their thoughts on atomic reactions are sound. (I have supplied a brief note to assist them in their work).

You will find enclosed in this letter a strand of hair. By this you shall know further communications come from me.

It is likely that my Government associates will contact you in due course as will I, they to reassure you of my bona-fides and I to provide more information.

Yours Sincerely

F Whyte'

Oliphant quickly scanned the other few sheets of the letter and found a piece of coarse, reddish-brown hair.

"Strewth!"

**

Stan Hooker sat at his desk in Osmaston and re-read the 'Private and Confidential Letter' that had been delivered that morning.

Its contents were stunning.

As well as stating it was from someone who was obviously, if he was to be believed, close to the Government. It set out categorically when the war that everyone had hoped could be avoided was due to start. It went on to extol the virtues of Stan and his Rolls Royce team and set out, with succinct descriptions and diagrams, what they should concentrate on 'immediately'. It spoke of some of the Chairman's 'less than optimum' decisions which had compromised the Merlin engine currently in production. The author suggested that Stan should use his 'freedom' of action within the company to set things in motion without reference to Ernest, actions, which in due course, would be confirmed as necessary by the Government.

He nodded his head at some of the statements of Merlin issues. The loss of power in negative G situations, the internal coolant leak and cylinder head problems. Obviously, he had lots to do but at least now he had a mapped out development programme that in some way matched his own thoughts whilst pointing out 'blind alleys' to avoid.

Contact was promised with further information and much more detail. The writer had enclosed a strand of rough, reddish-brown hair and stated that it would be present in all future communication.

He put the letter in his pocket and decided he and Albert Elliott needed a long talk over a cup of very strong tea.

**

Squadron Leader Whittle was depressed. He knew it, the team knew it. Power Jets WU was looking at financial disaster if the engine couldn't be engineered to behave and stop running out of control. He was a physical and mental wreck. He chain-smoked, took drugs, slept hardly at all and had multiple stress-related conditions. His weight had crashed to 9 stone and he looked, as he felt, a wreck.

But he had to succeed, he thought, desperately, especially if the rumours that the Germans were working on a similar engine were true. If only they'd seen what he was offering them in 1929. Such fools. And all the criticism, cynicism and behind the back laughter every year and continuing. No one to turn to and now his temper was becoming so short he was alienating his friends and team.

He lit another cigarette and opened the letter marked 'Private and Confidential'.

> *'Dear Squadron Leader Whittle,*
>
> *Before reading this letter let me state that I am aware that you have been through hell and continue to be denigrated by a great many people who do not have the intelligence or wit to see the great leap forward that you are proposing and developing.*
>
> *You do not know me, and I cannot, as yet, reveal my identity to prevent information falling into the wrong hands, be they German, Italian, Japanese or Soviet.*
>
> *What I can say is that I know of your struggle and what you are trying to achieve. I can provide significant details of how to accelerate your success, prevent you from failing AND ensure you receive the support, financially, scientifically and emotionally to do this without ruining your mind and health.*
>
> *I have included in the letter details of where you are now, what problems you are facing and a route to an operational engine.*
>
> *Stick with your centrifugal approach, yes it's not as good as an axial engine BUT the RAF need jet fighters sooner rather than later! Time enough for new engines when the war is going well. I've put down*

some information that should enable you to get a significant performance improvement over what you envisage. Don't worry about what the engines will be paired to, I have that in hand. I shall ensure that you have all the support you need once my Government associates endorse my recommendations and contact you to confirm my bona-fides.

You will find enclosed in this letter a strand of hair. By this you shall know further communications come from me.

Please take care of yourself in the interim.

Yours Sincerely,

F Whyte'

Whittle threw the letter down on his desk. The last thing he needed was some lunatic thinking he could help him. No one could help him. He stubbed out his cigarette and lit another.

Then he saw something on one of the enclosed sheets that caught his eye.

He commenced reading the sheet. Finished that and read the others.

After half an hour Whittle picked the strand of reddish-brown hair from the envelope and held it up to the light. 'Perhaps there was someone who understood what he was about?'

He started to cry.

**

It was interesting, thought Franz, that the letter in front of him was addressed in his 'old style' pre-anglicised form and not Frank Simons.

He'd changed his name when he and his wife had arrived in England, but he was aware through contacts back in Germany that he was still known to the authorities there, and on an interesting 'list'.

Still he and his wife were safe now and living in Oxford and his work went well.

So, he wondered' who was writing to old Franz Simmons?

When he finished reading he wasn't sure what to do. The information contained in the letter was very accurate about his current work and what he was trying to achieve. The wonderful thing was that it set out, in simple steps, how to separate uranium-235 by gaseous diffusion. He was still at the 'thinking' stage and here it was all laid out for him.

And the red hair? Who was this fellow?

He wondered if he could speak to Oliphant and Lindeman? Not about the letter, of course, but how he could now do the wondrous separation and create the most dangerous element on earth.

**

"Excuse me, Sir," Leading Seaman Hughes said. "Private and Confidential letter for you".

Lt Cdr Charles Goodeve looked up from the paper he was writing.

"Yes, Hughes?" he replied distractedly in his soft mid-Canada accent.

"Letter Sir. Private and confidential. Bit odd though."

"Why's that?"

"It's addressed in pencil."

"Hmm, crank letter maybe?"

"Wouldn't like to say, Sir".

"Not to worry, give it here."

"Sir," said Hughes passing it over and turning heel to leave.

"Hughes, I'll have a mug of tea, please. Two sugars, spare the milk," Goodeve ordered.

"Sir."

'Hughes was turning out to be quite useful, a reservist recently called up with a decent scientific background,' Goodeve thought. 'Just got to get him broken into a few of my foibles.'

Setting his notes aside he opened the letter. A coarse strand of reddish-brown hair fell out of the envelope. Goodeve picked it up and examined it. Not dog, a bit coarse for human hair, horse? He smelt it. Somewhat 'musty', no, not horse. A puzzle.

Hughes returned with the tea.

"Take this to Captain Bates please," said Goodeve, handing a file across.

"Sir."

On his own once more Goodeve unfolded the letter. It comprised several sheets, some with diagrams some all text. He commenced reading the top paper.

'Dear Cdr Goodeve,

I write to you on a matter of great urgency and secrecy. As you know war between Germany and Great Britain, including the Commonwealth and Empire, is very likely.

I can confirm that this conflict cannot be avoided and that by the evening of 3 September 1939 it will have begun.

Your role in it is critical.

It will fall upon you and your team to make weapons innovations not yet thought of which will enable the shortening of the terrible war to come.

I can assist you in determining what to pursue and what to consign to the waste paper basket.

I can, in further contact provide you with details of who you be working with and how their talents may best be used with the information I provide on weapons development.

I realise this is likely to be a surprise and shock to you, but I can say that you will be soon appointed to a new directorate.

I have enclosed some details of war-winning weapons for your perusal.

You will find enclosed in this letter a strand of hair. By this you shall know further communications come from me.

It is likely that my Government associates will contact you in due course as will I, they to reassure you of my bona-fides and I to provide more information.

Yours Sincerely

F Whyte

P.S. The Germans will deploy mines activated by the magnetic field disturbance of a passing ship. See page 1 of the enclosed notes. By the way, you'll get your hands on an actual mine in November.'

"Hughes!"

**

Geoffrey began to read the letter his secretary had presented to him.

'War inevitable.' Well, that's hardly news. 'September the third.' Hmm, a month to go then.'

'Aircraft, multi-role, twin-engined, version 1 then an upgrade.'

'Bin the pure fighter' - well that was only there as a sop to the Ministry anyway.

'Propellers, yes, if Fighter Command let me have aircraft to test on.'

He paused reading the letter. He couldn't resist looking at the technical sheets.

'Beautiful, beautiful,' he said. 'Charles will like this and Eric will be pleased. They'll dovetail nicely onto his designs.'

'So improved Merlin's. Oh, she'll fly, she'll fly!' The thought of his new 'bird' flying excited him now as much as it had when he first began to build aircraft.

He turned back to the letter.

'I will be ensuring that you have the full backing of the Air Ministry.'

That would be nice instead of their constant carping, criticism and requirements changes. I wonder how Wilfred will be persuaded to agree?

'I have taken steps to ensure that suitable armament should be available for the aircraft proposed.'

You will find enclosed in this letter a strand of hair. By this you shall know further communications come from me.

It is likely that my Government associates will contact you in due course as will I, they to reassure you of my bona-fides and I to provide more information.

Specifically, I will provide you with design details of an aircraft to be built as soon as practical to be designated DH99.

Yours Sincerely

F Whyte'

P.S. Please hold work on all other aircraft not detailed here.'

De Havilland re-read the letter and notes.

'Who is this chap I wonder? Obviously knows his stuff. But how is he going to stop the infighting between the prima donnas of the Ministry, RAF and aero companies?'

**

The Post Office Research Station at Dollis Hill looked for all the world like a large red brick school, including similar large windows to admit natural light to the working areas which Tommy thought extremely sensible. It helped when he was trying to assemble various pieces of equipment and test them.

The post came round every morning to his section about 9-30 am. The Messengers pushing a trolley loaded with internal and external mail dropping them into the in trays of the staff and taking away anything that had made its way to an out tray.

Today, Greenfield, the 14-year-old Messenger came over and proffered a letter.

"For you Tommy. Special one," he said in his broad Cockney accent. "'Arry says you've got to sign for it."

"Is that so Sparra?" replied Tommy in an accent almost as broad. Not surprising since he'd grown up in the East End. "Go on then." He pulled a pencil from behind his ear and scribbled his initials on the mail sheet.

"Sparra, get a move on. We haven't got all day," shouted the senior Messenger.

"See ya, Tommy."

Tommy smiled as the young lad made haste to catch up his mentor.

'So what's this,' he thought looking at the envelope? Not official so it can wait.

Now let's finish this switching board. He stuffed the letter, with some difficulty given its thickness, into his pocket and got back to work.

At lunchtime he and Frank Morrell met up and took their sandwiches out into the Station's gardens. Sitting on the grass Tommy brought out the letter and opened it up.

'Dear Mr Flowers,' it began.

'I have read about your work at Dollis Hill and heard about some of the interesting thoughts you have had in designing machines using vacuum tube technology.'

Well, I wonder how this chap knows that, thought Tommy. I've only played around with a few 'doodles' so far – I don't even know what you'd use such a machine for.

The letter went on.

'You are going to be instrumental in assisting in the breaking of key codes. Your machine, though others might scoff, will be the first of its type in the world.'

'I set out in the enclosed sheets how you might proceed and will supply further information in due course.'

'I realise this sounds most fantastical, and I can't reveal my identity at present due to security issues, but I can tell you that I am taking steps to have a special unit established as soon as possible by the Government, Post Office and the Intelligence Service.'

'I have enclosed a piece of red hair which will accompany further communications."

'Please keep this to yourself but you can share the information with Frank Morrell as he will be working with you.'

'Yours Sincerely,

F Whyte.'

"Well I never, " he exclaimed.

"What's the matter, Tommy, bad news," asked Frank?

"See for yourself," he said passing over the letter whilst retaining the additional sheets to study.

Frank read and then re-read the letter.

"Bloody mad man, I'd say," he said.

"If he is, he's a bloody clever one," replied Tommy, and passed over the first of the notes for Frank to read.

**

Air Chief Marshall Wilfred Freeman sighed. What a bloody mess. So many companies, so many different aircraft options. So many 'unknowns', unproven designs, failures to meet specification, delays with engines, weapons, and the absolute nightmare, changing operational requirements. It went on and on. Oh for the happy days' dogfighting German fighters at the Front.

How long did Britain have?

He shook his head. This was getting him nowhere. Tea, that's what he needed, tea.

"Corporal!"

His office door opened after an acceptably short delay.

"Sir?"

"Tea.. please."

"Right away sir," Corporal Hamilton replied. Proper Officer and Gentleman the ACM, he thought not like some of the brass hats.

He put the kettle on and spooned the tea into the pot.

"Morning Corp," said LAC McInnes. "Got his Nibs post. Any chance of a cuppa?"

"You make the brew while I sort the bumf," replied Hamilton.

"Right oh."

Hamilton carefully went through the pile, checking each and rating by importance and interest.

McInnes attended to the tea making as though his life depended on it. He knew what happened if the ACM's brew wasn't to his liking and he was sure he didn't want to be posted away from London to Machrihanish or somewhere worse.

"Ready Corp".

"You follow me in and make sure you don't spill it on him, I've got enough to carry with all this lot."

**

Freeman looked up from his work, "McInnes, I see you are carrying my mug. Does this mean you made the tea?"

"Yes sir," stammered the LAC.

"Brave. I take it you've got it right this time? What will it be? Five attempts to get it strong enough to stand the spoon in and not too much milk?"

"Yes sir. I'm sure it'll be to your taste," said McInnes reassuringly.

"I've got a posting form ready if it's not Sir," said Hamilton hiding a smile. He knew when the ACM was leg-pulling.

Freeman picked up his mug and tried a sip of the hot brew. He scowled.

McInnes looked nervous. Then the ACM smiled beatifically.

"At last McInnes."

He turned to address Hamilton. "Corporal, I think we can say McInnes is now an effective member of the team".

"Very good sir" replied Hamilton. "Off you go then now McInnes. "

McInnes came to attention and with a "Thank you sir" executed an almost perfect about turn and left the office.

"So Corporal, what have we this morning?"

"Something from COAS then pretty much the usual sir. One oddity, a letter marked private and confidential. "

"Put it beneath the COAS work and I'll get to it. Thank you, Corporal," said Freeman, dismissing Hamilton.

**

Sometime later, Freeman, after dealing with Sir Cyril's correspondence, turned to the strange letter. Handwritten, educated hand, in pencil. How strange. Not from an official source then, nor something from one of the aero companies with an attempt to special plead their case for this or that project.

'Dear Air Chief Marshall Freeman,

I write to you in confidence about matters pertaining to the upcoming war with Germany. It is now certain that there will be a war and I can confirm that by the evening of 3 September 1939 it will have begun.

Your time to determine the best way forward for RAF aircraft in peace is coming to an end.

You will play a pivotal role in the war to come. I wish to provide you with some guidance to assist in the provision of suitable aircraft for the RAF in time to make a difference. Later I shall be able to advise and aid you in the strategic campaigns to be waged by the Airforce.

I have included in this letter details of which aircraft developments and manufacture to expedite. Which aircraft should be stricken from service, the resources to be better used elsewhere and the production capacity to be redirected. I list whose proposals and developments should be rejected. I include brief reasons why my suggestions are made.

I realise that this may be difficult for someone in your position to accept, especially from an unsolicited and unknown source.

I cannot, as yet, reveal my identity to prevent information falling into the wrong hands, be they German, Italian, Japanese or Soviet.

I can assure you that others will be working to ensure that the targeted development of the RAF's aircraft will have engines that perform, designs that work and focused requirements. By these combined efforts Britain and its Empire will best ride out the storms of war to come and go on to an early victory.

You will find enclosed in this letter a strand of hair. By this you shall know further communications come from me.

It is likely that my Government associates will contact you in due course as will I, they to reassure you of my bona-fides and I to provide more information and support.

Yours Sincerely

F Whyte'

Freeman snorted loudly.

He'd been wrong. The letter was from someone trying to pursue their own agenda with special pleading.

He was going to put the letter to the waste paper basket but then considered an option. If, and it was a big if, someone had the approval or ear of Sir Kingsly Wood (Secretary of State for Air), Leslie Hore-Belisha (Secretary of State for War) and Neville, then it might just make his task a little easier. Worth a read over lunch perhaps.

**

Wallace Akers looked out of his office at the Thames and then turning his head further left, at the Houses of Parliament. He wondered how Chamberlain was going to pull a rabbit out of the hat this year and achieve a 'peace in our time' that lasted more than 11 months. Well ICI were doing fine out of the re-armament, but it was, to his organised mind, somewhat 'chaotic'.

Earlier in the day, he had received a most perplexing letter, purporting to be from someone who had connections to HMG. It discussed in vague terms, (to be excused as a security measure not only against the Germans, Italians and Japanese but also against the Soviet Union), a project which he would be called upon to run by the Department of Scientific and Industrial Research. A department he understood to be responsible for the encouragement and support of scientific research in universities and other institutions.

This 'project' was of such earth-shattering proportions that the 'world will never be the same again!'

Magnificent hyperbole. An enclosure listed several names from various fields who would work on the project. A further enclosure listed names of people who should never, on pain of death, be permitted to learn anything of it.

Well, he had enough on his plate to keep him busy and didn't need any distraction from an obvious crank, a crank who had such delusions of conspiracies that he had included a course piece of reddish-brown hair by which 'future communications from me shall be known.' Pah.

He'd consigned the entire letter, enclosures and hair to the bin without a moments further consideration. The only thing that stuck in his head was the name 'Tube Alloys'. How could alloy tubes change the course of a war?

**

RV was fed up. Moved about from pillar to post over the past few years. At odds with Lindemann, Tizard and Watson Watt his academic career was in tatters. Now just a civil servant in the Admiralty's Research Laboratory, he wondered where it had all gone wrong.

There was some talk about him going back to work for the Air Ministry but nothing concrete as yet. Having said that even if there was a move what would he actually be doing?

At least he'd kept up his contacts in the various research establishments and universities. He was well-liked by many of his contemporaries and they took him into their confidence even though the Official Secret's Act should have prevented them.

His work on infra-red detection had been side-lined once Lindemann and Watson Watt had 'decided' that radar was the way ahead. His thoughts on navigational and bombing 'beams' had been dismissed as fanciful. His ideas on 'jamming' radar detection just plain ignored. No, his life was miserable, except, of course, his personal life with Vera was wonderful.

"Post Mr Jones," said the naval rating who brought round the mail each morning.

"Thank you, Jarvis," said Jones.

He sorted through the memos and letters. One really cheered him up. He was tasked with going to a place called Bletchley Park to help set up a unit to provide intelligence on German weapons and scientific development. He'd never heard of the place and why on earth a unit had to be established in the wilds of Bedfordshire he had no idea. Well that's what the war panic did, odd requests to do odd things in odd places at a moments' notice.

This letter looked interesting. A pencil addressed envelope marked 'Private and Confidential'.

He opened it and read,

'Dear Mr Jones,

I write to you on a matter of great urgency and secrecy. As you know war between Germany and Great Britain, including the Commonwealth and Empire, is very likely.

I can confirm that this conflict cannot be avoided and that by the evening of 3 September 1939 it will have begun.

Your role in it, and your appreciation of the wide range of scientific possibilities open to Britain and her enemies, is critical. I would say, without fear of contradiction, if you are ignored the war could be lost.

You do not know me, and I cannot reveal my identity but in due course my associates in HMG will confirm my bona-fides.

In your work to date you have covered many aspects of technological advances that can greatly aid in the defence of this country or assist in the prosecution of war against its enemies.

I intend to support you in your role to be. To provide prompts and information to help you formulate ideas and solutions to operational requirements, known or currently unknown to the War Office and Armed and Support Services. To facilitate the development of equipment and speed it into service.

I can hopefully provide a shield to those who would block you.

I have enclosed some details of requirements and solutions which build upon your previous thoughts as well as some ideas on what the German's may be developing.

You will find enclosed in this letter a strand of hair. By this you shall know further communications come from me.

It is likely that my Government associates will contact you in due course as will I, they to reassure you and I to provide more information and support.

Yours Sincerely

F Whyte'

Jones looked up from the letter to see if anyone else in the room was looking at him. He scrutinised them. No, no one looked suspicious or was smirking.

Right. He picked up the phone and dialled his friend

"Gerald? RV here. Yes, well I got your letter. Very funny. You really got me going."

"What do you mean 'what letter'? The one where you tell me I'm going to be the equivalent of the scientific saviour of the nation if it kicks off with Germany. Ha-ha!'

"Don't give me that. It's got to be you. You know how much I need cheering up. Well, it's done the trick."

"So you're sure it's not you? Scouts honour?"

"Right. Not now. I'll tell you about it in the pub later. Once I've found out who the prankster is."

"No, I'm not annoyed. Not at all."

"Goodbye, Gerald."

He put the phone down. Curiouser and curiouser. He'd played enough pranks in his time to know one when he saw one.

Now, what did the enclosures say then?

He began to read.

After analysis he put the papers down and picked up the red hair.

Well well. Maybe not a hoax but he'd find out who'd sent this treasure trove to him, oh indeed he would.

Chapter 5

Whipsnade - Wednesday the 2nd of August 1939 continued

Franzi saw John on later that day after the hooter had gone.

John looked a little sheepish as he walked across to Franzi's shelter.

"Was it that obvious," he asked?

Franzi got up and gave and hugged John before laughing.

John laughed along with him.

"Alright then you rascal, you got us there. Where've you hidden them," He asked?

Franzi whooped and started a game of tag which got progressively more boisterous until John cried "Whoa, I give in."

Franzi let John up off the floor and beckoned him over to the doorway of the hut. Picking up his stick Franzi wrote, "That would be telling, John. Isn't it more fun for you and Higgins to try and find them, and the Captain to puzzle where they might be?"

"That's positively wicked Franzi," replied John. "You know the Captain will ask you later?"

Franzi just chuckled.

**

It was getting dark when Franzi accompanied John to the 'House'. The Captain opened the back door and ushered them quickly into his study.

Franzi made straight for the armchair he'd used the previous evening and got himself comfortable. "Ook," and then gave the Captain a thumbs up.

"Very good Franzi. Take a seat to John," said the Captain.

"Thank you."

"A drink, gentlemen," asked the Captain?

Franzi gave an affirmative 'Huff' and nod and signed for a smoke.

"Yes indeed," said the Captain. "John, help yourself and Franzi to a cigarette from the case there."

The Captain poured out three glasses of brandy and served his guests.

"Well Franzi, I don't know what to say," said the Captain.

Franzi shrugged and laughed. He signed for pen and paper.

"Ah yes, well here's something better," said the Captain retrieving a chalkboard and chalk from behind his desk. "Only managed to get this one so far. The other and the large blackboard and easel are being delivered this week from Dunstable," he explained. "And here's a damp sponge."

'You could have asked to see what I've been writing," chalked Franzi. He waved a finger at the Captain.

"Would you have shown us?"

'Some things, maybe. Others no.'

"Fair enough," said the Captain.

'I told John no to everything because the secrets are so dangerous in the wrong hands. I didn't want him to be in any danger.'

"I see," said the Captain.

After a pause Franzi wrote,

'Have you had any success in getting me a meeting with Churchill?'

"It is very difficult," said the Captain. "He's not well-liked and he's very busy in parliament."

'Not now,' wrote Franzi. 'Chamberlain has prorogued it.'

The Captain and John stared at Franzi, wide-eyed for the umpteenth time.

"Listen. I'll try everything I can. I'll even get hold of my old General from the Gold Coast. I know Solly is trying to find a way too, as well as finding you someone who can sign," said the Captain trying to placate a visibly agitated Franzi.

'Ook.'

"But you have to face it old chap, it might take a while."

'Oook,' said Franzi and wrote 'We don't have time to waste. I'll wait a week.'

He downed his brandy, gently put down the glass and left them, without the cigarette.

"Franzi," John called to the departing orangutan. To no avail, Franzi didn't even acknowledge him.

"I wonder what he meant by that Captain?"

"I've no idea John, but I can't see him quietly sitting here at Whipsnade. Can you?"

**

During the next days Franzi established a routine of sorts, especially when he agreed with the Captain that his typing was his and his alone to share or not as he chose.

The fence between Franzi and Daisy had been removed and Daisy had proved amicable to allowing Franzi to dig out a 'safe' under her shelter. Franzi considered this a 'just in case' option but, to be on the safe side, he had also created another one in the wolf wood.

Not only was he producing briefing documents about technology which would help in the war to come, but also writing papers on training, tactics, combined arms, asymmetric warfare and special operations covering land, sea and air. A draft of a suggested T.O.E. had also taken up a great deal of time.

Then he had the 'difficult' matters to deal with. How to provide intelligence of upcoming German operations and weigh up the consequences or 'butterflies'. He considered the initial major event that would cause 'ripples' would be the Norwegian campaign. Would Britain and France be able to stop the Germans? If they did, what would the German's then do?

Lucy had been a dear and persuaded Billy to let her have his old satchel so now Franzi could easily carry around his papers. He'd been careful not to show the Captain the satchel because he might recognise it, he was sure his wife would given it had been his son's. Perhaps he should ask the Captain for a proper briefcase?

**

The Park had seen large numbers of visitors brought out by the improved weather after the earlier summer had been so dismal. Many had heard about Franzi's parody of Herr Hitler. Franzi, John and the Captain had agreed to publish times of his performance so at least he wasn't being asked to perform all the time.

**

Whipsnade - Friday 4th August 1939

On Friday morning the phone rang in the Superintendent's study.

"Hello, yes this is Captain Beale."

"Yes, I have heard of Pathé News."

"We do, yes. Franzi our male orangutan."

"Would I mind? Well, I'll check with Doctor Vevers and the Board but in principle, it should be alright."

"Yes, I'll make arrangements for your crew to be admitted early on Saturday and get some of my staff to assist them."

"I'll confirm the details later when I have Dr Vevers' approval. Not at all. Goodbye".

The Captain replaced the receiver and then lifted it to make a call.

"Geoffrey? Bill here."

"Yes all's well. You saw Franzi in the papers after the Bank Holiday?"

"I agree. It was very good publicity, and free too."

"It's gone further now, as we thought it might. Pathé News want to film here on Saturday."

"I told them, tentatively, yes, subject to your and the Boards approval."

"Right, I'll let them know it's fine then?"

"You and a few of the Board and friends are coming?"

"Not at all. I'll make sure we've got the catering sorted out. Beer this time?"

He laughed "Well I'm sure they will. By the way, it's not a formal visit, is it?"

"Good. Pathé is turning up here at 0900. I suggest you try to get here for 1200 for some lunch then Franzi will 'entertain' at 1400 as usual."

"Goodbye."

"Gladys," he shouted, "It's happened. You can tell Billy and Laura they might get their wish. Pathé News is coming on Saturday to film Franzi!"

**

Whipsnade - Saturday 5th August 1939

The weather on Saturday morning wasn't promising. The Downs and Park were shrouded in low cloud and a fine drizzle was falling when the camera crew turned up.

Leonard Henry wasn't pleased. He was Pathé's man when it came to animal stories and when he'd been told about Franzi he'd decided to go along in person for the filming, after all everyone loves a day at the zoo, and poking fun at Herring Hitler. He'd struggled out of bed early, nursing a small hangover after partying late at the Savoy, to catch a lift with the crew director.

One compensation was the bacon sandwiches and tea in the cafeteria, and at least he didn't have to go out in the mizzle until just before the performance.

Franzi was up early too. He and Daisy had spent a comfortable morning eating breakfast followed by mutual grooming.

**

The previous evening the Captain had told Franzi and John what to expect. They'd gone over this and that and consequently Franzi hadn't typed but they'd enjoyed a pleasant hour or so drinking the Captain's brandy and smoking his cigarettes.

John had been excited, the Captain less so.

"The thing is Franzi, don't go over the top. Just your usual please," advised the Captain.

'Ook,' then 'But of course,' he chalked, then, 'I would like a comb please.'

"What on earth for?"

Franzi laughed, 'You'll see.'

"Please behave yourself Franzi, it's not just the cameras and public here, Dr Vevers and a number of the Board and friends will be too."

Franzi responded with a rumbling chuckle followed by a loud raspberry.

"Shush," pleaded the Captain, "not so loud."

"Bill, what on earth is going on," Gladys shouted?

"Nothing dear. John and I were just sharing a joke."

John laughed quietly, and Franzi gave a second, subdued, raspberry to ram home how amused he was.

"Right, enough from you too. You may as well go if you can't be serious."

They took the hint and departed. Outside they separated to go their separate ways to bed.

**

By 1400 the weather had improved, the sun lightning Franzi's performance area as well as putting the crowd, the Board, camera crew and Leonard in a good mood.

The Captain, Dr Vevers and Leonard stood together and watched as Franzi came out of his shelter with Daisy.

"Here we go then,"

Franzi patted Daisy on the arm and then forward rolled towards the crowd until he was at his 'mark'.

He stood with a flourish. The crowd applauded.

Franzi flicked his hair to one side and produced a black comb which he held, left-handed, above his top lip. Then commenced to "hum" Deutschland, Deutschland über alles. The crowd applause increased.

He looked about him, left and right, and then commenced goose-stepping up and down all the while continuing his rude accompaniment. The crowd roared with laughter.

He stopped marching after three passes and turned to look at his audience.

He then parodied a typical Hitler speech that the people had already seen on many occasions. His whoops and raspberries punctuated the mime to the delight of the crowd as did his final Nazi salutes before he fell on his back as if he'd been shot.

Tears of laughter ran down Leonard's face. "Wonderful, wonderful," he managed to say as he gasped for breath.

The Captain, Dr Vevers and the Board were laughing and applauding too.

The crowd were applauding, cheering, and calling for an encore and throwing money down into the enclosure.

John was beaming. Daisy was hooting her approval. Everyone was delighted, all except one couple off to the side. Herr Bruno Himmler and Frau Irma Gruhne, the German embassy's deputy security officer and his secretary. They were most definitely not amused.

**

Whipsnade - Thursday 8th August 1939

Each evening John and Franzi walked up to the 'House' at dusk to meet with the Captain. John came inside for a drink and smoke and the three of them had a chat. He left and Franzi got on with more typing.

By the evening of Thursday, the 8th Franzi was getting more anxious that there'd still be no news of any contact with Churchill, let alone him getting to see the man.

During that day the sky had been full of aircraft across the country. They'd even seen a number flying over the Downs.

John came down to the enclosure around dusk as usual but Franzi didn't go to the gate to meet him.

"Everything alright Franzi?" John asked. "Are you ready to go up to the 'House?"

Franzi remained seated in the doorway of his shelter.

'Oook,' he said, and shook his head. He brought out his chalkboard and wrote, 'Not this evening. I'm having a night off.'

"Oh, alright then," said John. "I'll tell the Captain."

'Ook'.

"Nothing wrong I hope? We all saw the aeroplanes today. You know the Captain and I believe you? And the Professor must have seen them too. I bet he rang the Captain this evening to talk."

Franzi shrugged.

"There might be some news about Mr Churchill or someone for sign language," said John encouragingly.

'Maybe I'll see the Captain later,' wrote Franzi.

"Alright then lad," said John.

**

Franzi wrote three letters. The first two he left by the enclosure gate. The third he quietly posted through Lucy's open window after he'd checked that she was asleep.

Then he took his satchel and went up to the House.

He hid the satchel in the garden before tapping gently on the study window to attract the Captain's attention.

"Hello Franzi," said the Captain, and let him in. "John said you'd likely come and see me."

They settled down with brandy's, a pipe and cigarette.

'Ook' said Franzi, and cocked his head to one side.

"Well, yes. Good news and bad news," said the Captain.

Franzi gave a resigned 'Chuff' and took a slurp of his brandy.

"Yes," said the Captain, nervously. "Solly has found someone who can work with you on signing, so we'll be able to communicate much more easily."

'When?' wrote Franzi.

"Not straight away, the young lady is the sister of a friend of Solly's. Trouble is she's working with the War Office at the minute so only able to come here at the weekends"

'Ook. And the bad news?'

"Erm, we haven't had a good response from Mr Churchill."

Franzi slowly rocked his head from side to side, a gesture the Captain hadn't seen before.

"General Giffard, my old commanding officer from the Gold Coast, sent him a letter explaining, in vague terms, that he had someone who needed to see Churchill urgently about the current crisis. He couldn't be very specific because you've not told me very much about why you want to see Churchill, so I couldn't tell him very much," said the Captain.

'Ook'

'Point taken,' chalked Franzi.

"So it was hardly surprising that Churchill's response to George was 'Sorry I can't spare the time at the minute. Far too busy. Remind me later.'." said the Captain.

He waited for Franzi's response. He was expecting some show of emotion, frustration or even anger.

Franzi surprised him. He laughed.

'Not to worry,' he wrote.

"Oh," said the Captain, "Have another brandy?"

'Ook'.

Sometime later the Captain, who was known for his ability to hold his drink, was, in Glady's eyes, somewhat 'squiffy', when he got to bed.

Franzi, on the other hand, wasn't. Fit and well and focused with the satchel, papers, chalkboard and chalk he was off on an adventure!

**

London

Earlier that evening Herbert von Dirksen, German ambassador to the Court of St James, had accompanied his deputy security officer, Bruno Himmler, to the cinema.

Von Dirksen was a rising star in the Nazi Party, a former Leutnant in the Kaiser's army, his family were new blood aristocrats. He had worked hard and tirelessly to support Hitler since 1925. His reward was to replace Ribbentrop as ambassador in London when he had been elevated to the position of foreign minister.

Von Dirksen detested Communists, Jews, and Poles alike and was scornful of the decadent effete British.

He wouldn't normally have been seen dead in a cinema in England but Bruno had insisted he see for himself. Himmler had reported the outrage of an ape parodying the Führer and the reaction of the crowd at Whipsnade. von Dirksen saw the cinema audience roaring with laughter and approval at the insult. He and Himmler hadn't waited to see the main feature.

Late though it was, von Dirksen called Himmler's namesake in Berlin. After a short conversation it was agreed action should be taken to show these English that it was unacceptable to mock the Leader and to teach the animal-loving fools a lesson.

Chapter 6

Birmingham University - Friday 11th August 1939

RV could have just picked up the phone to talk to Marcus Oliphant but by chance he and Vera had been invited up to Hoar Cross Hall to stay with the Meynell's for the weekend. He decided to call into the Physics Department at Birmingham and see the man in person.

It was late Friday afternoon when RV was shown into Marcus' office. Papers were strewn around the desk in various piles and the ashtray was full of cigarette butts.

"RV, nice of you to pop in. Staying at Hoar Cross again?" asked Oliphant.

"Yes, the Colonel and Lady Dorothy seem to like our company," said RV.

"And you get to enjoy a relaxing English country house weekend party," Oliphant teased.

"There is that. It helps me think when I go out popping game in the grounds. I can get things in perspective. Clear my head and sort out puzzles," he replied.

"I can see how that'd work. I wish I could spare the time, we're going full speed here."

RV nodded.

"You didn't just call in for a cup of tea, did you Mate?"

RV smiled. "You're right, I didn't."

"So sniffing intelligence or something specific to our work here?"

RV reached in his pocket and brought out an envelope which he laid on the desk.

Oliphant pulled it close and turned it so he could see the address.

RV noted a slight look of surprise.

"Yes?" said Oliphant, looking at him quizzically, "Am I to read it, bin it or light a cigarette with it?"

RV reached into his pocket a second time and produced a strand of coarse reddish-brown hair which he laid on the envelope.

Oliphant looked at him sharply. Said nothing but reached into the desk draw and produced a matching strand.

"So it was you who wrote to me?" asked RV.

"Bugger! I was going to say the same to you," exclaimed Oliphant.

They laughed.

"I'll tell you about mine, in general terms of course," said RV, "If you'll tell me about yours."

"Agreed," said Oliphant.

"Right. I've got a date for the kick-off and a promise to help me in a role that's not been established yet. Then technical stuff about radar and such."

"He's told me to hold certain work." said Oliphant, "To encourage the team to work on specifics, including radar, and given me some highly technical, and brilliant, pointers on how to proceed."

"And no idea who he is nor who his 'associates' or sponsors might be to make these things happen?" said RV.

"Yes, that's exactly right."

"Just the one letter?"

"Just the one so far," said Oliphant.

"Anyone else you know got one?"

"No, but I haven't mentioned it, even to the team. Why did you think I might have been brought into the 'plot'?"

"I think," said RV, "that this fellow is spreading a wide net to bring in people almost at the decision points but not quite at the top."

"I see."

"He specifically warned me off Lindemann, Tizard and Watson-Watt."

"That's interesting. Maybe he thinks they're too 'entrenched' in their own positions?"

"Sounds plausible," said RV.

Oliphant nodded, "In which case we've got to go softly and make sure we let this chap and his boss get all their programme and people sorted."

"I want to track the man down though, speak to him."

"You're always the one seeking intelligence, that's why you get the roles you get."

"True," replied RV. "Now where was your letter posted from?"

Oliphant produced the letter from his draw. He scrutinised the postmark. "Dunstable."

"Same as mine," said RV. "Don't you find it odd it's in pencil?"

"Very. I thought it was a crackpot at first until I read the technical stuff."

"I thought it was a practical joke."

"Well you are known for the ones you pull on others," chuckled Oliphant.

"True," replied RV. "I wonder who else has had one?"

"I'll do some quiet digging around."

"Me too."

**

Chartwell - Saturday 12th August 1939

Despite war being, in his mind, imminent Churchill only had his domestic servants to 'protect him'. Walter Thomson, he knew, had left the police and was, by all accounts, running his own grocery shop.

Clemmy was concerned for his safety. He was the most vocal and best-known politician to oppose Hitler and Hitler was known to take action against those he considered 'bedrohlich'.

Churchill was still seething about Chamberlain's proroguing of Parliament.

His information on the Russian mission suggested Stalin was playing some sort of duplicitous game. He couldn't blame him after all Chamberlain hadn't sent Halifax to add gravitas to the negotiations, let alone offering to go himself. It seemed as though he'd given up. The disappointment of all the efforts of appeasement coming to nothing.

The onset of night had brought with it a late summer thunderstorm which still rumbled in the distance as it moved off to the northeast. The wind hadn't yet dropped after the storm and the tall trees were complaining as they were buffeted about.

A crack, like a broken window, jerked Churchill's conscious back to the present.

None of the staff lived in the house and Clemmy was probably fast asleep.

He reached into his desk drawer and drew out his Webley & Scott automatic.

He checked the magazine and slid the safety off.

Switching off his desk light he rose and crossed the room to the door.

Listening carefully he thought he heard the floorboards creaking in the corridor.

He stepped back and took cover kneeling behind his desk.

The door handle slowly turned, then the door was pushed open.

The figure outside advanced cautiously into the room, gun in hand.

It was obvious that the man hadn't realised how big the room was as he glanced right and then left. His eyes widened as he saw Churchill's weapon pointed directly at his head.

"Drop the gun and raise your hands," ordered Churchill.

The assassin ignored the request and moved quickly, raising his gun.

Churchill's shot caught him in the chest, and he dropped. His gun fell and bounced harmlessly away off the wooden floor.

"Idiot," said Churchill, standing up and moving to the fallen man.

That movement saved his life. Two shots rang out, shattering the window by his desk and missing him by inches.

He moved quickly to the study door, out of the line of fire from the window. He was careful to stay close to the oak door and not move to the corridor window which would have given his assailant another clear shot at him.

From upstairs he heard Clemmy shout "Winston, are you alright?"

"Yes 'Kat'. I hope you've called the police?"

"Of course, and told them there's a gunfight going on," she replied in measured tones showing no sign of panic. "How many are there?"

"One less than when they started this game," he joked. "I wish I had my Tommy gun. I told you I shouldn't put it in the gun room."

Another shot rang out, shattering the hall window. The live assailant had stuck to his task and not run off.

Winston turned to cover the window.

There was a tremendous crash from the study.

Winston glanced inside.

He was amazed to see what appeared to be the attacker from outside sprawled on the floor, obviously out of action.

He entered the room and looked at the broken window.

'My,' he thought, 'how did a big chap like that get through such a small window?'

Two more shots rang out from outside and then his question was answered when a second man came hurtling through the broken window attached, as it seemed, to an irate orangutan.

**

Winston turned to greet the police officers as Clemmy in her dressing gown ushered them down the hall.

The inspector leading them spoke "Are you well sir? Have all the assassins been rounded up" he said, looking at the gun in Churchill's hand.

"I am indeed Inspector, and yes there are three in there. One has a gunshot wound in the shoulder and the other two are somewhat battered" he replied, turning to indicate the bodies strewn around the study.

The four armed policemen moved past him to secure their prisoners.

"My word, where's he gone?" Winston exclaimed.

"Who sir," asked the inspector?

"My rescuer, the er ....." he went no further, how could he tell them about an Orangutan when clearly they'd think it errant nonsense.

"Are you alright Winston?" asked Clemmy, "You look a little odd."

"Fine, my darling, fine. Just a little shaken."

" Well sit down and I'll get you a brandy. Inspector would you and your men like tea? Marjorie and Dennis have come up from the lodge. "

"No ma'am, thank you. We'll take these three away with us, the van should be here now."

"As you wish," she said, passing a large tumbler of brandy to Winston who'd collapsed into his favourite armchair.

"I'm leaving two if the lads here on guard for the rest of the night. I'll speak with the Chief Constable in the morning about further measures" he said to Churchill.

"Thank you, Inspector. I'll be speaking to the Home Secretary and the Commissioner first thing. I need Walter Thompson back right away."

**

After the police and prisoners had gone and Clemmy had a cup of tea brought in by Marjorie she gave Winston a sharp look.

"Now 'Pug', what happened? I know you shot one of those fellows but there is no way you could have beaten the other two, I doubt if you could in your heyday," she said.

"Well I say, my dear, that's a little harsh" she raised an eyebrow "but possibly very true." He smiled.

"So," she prompted.

"Of course; I had very timely assistance. Very able assistance" he paused, "And I have no idea how, or who, or where it's gone."

"It?"

He nodded.

"Surely who," she said.

"Well, no." He took a long gulp of his brandy and gave her his most serious stare "this is one of those secrets"

"Not a word Dear," she confirmed.

"I know this will sound as if I'm mad, but I was rescued by an Orangutan."

**

Chartwell - Sunday 13th August 1939

The next day after Winston had discussed the attack with Sir Samuel Hoare, the Home Secretary and Air Vice-Marshal Sir Philip Game, the Metropolitan Police Commissioner, and confirmed that Walter Thompson would be approached and asked to re-join Special Branch, he took a stroll with 'Rufus', his miniature poodle, around the 'estate'.

There was no sign of any Orangutan, not that Winston had much experience in tracking or finding an ape. Even Rufus failed to sniff out the ape, although he put up a couple of pheasants and chased a rabbit.

So far Winston hadn't mentioned who his 'rescuer' was to the authorities and they'd not yet raised it with him.

The prisoners were, he was told, going to face detailed interrogation. Winston knew that would be a gruelling experience for them, by turns cajoled then threatened, but at least there was no British equivalent of Gestapo 'questioning '.

He wondered what the questioners would make of the prisoners saying they'd been scragged by an Orangutan. He chuckled at the thought.

Walking back to the house from the lake he pulled up short when he saw the writing that defaced his masterpiece wall by the orangery.

'Mr Churchill, could you spare me an hour or so of your time this evening? I shall be at your conservatory doors at 9 pm. Your friend from last night. F Whyte'

**

Whipsnade - Friday 11th August 1939

Lucy woke early. The sun was streaming into her bedroom and her eye was immediately drawn to the envelope on the floor. She threw back the covers, jumped out of bed and ran to pick it up. She read 'Lucy' and knew from the handwriting it was from Franzi.

'This was new, why didn't he wake me', she thought? She opened the letter and read,

'Hello Lucy,

Just to let you know I've had to pop out of the Park for a couple of days to see someone important. Don't worry and make sure you and the other children look after Daisy.

See you soon.

Your friend, Franzi'

**

John and Higgins walked downhill to their respective work areas after breakfast. Talk was all about the probability of war and John was concerned how it might impact on the football season to come.

There was no sign of Franzi but Daisy was sat at the enclosure gate. She waved at John.

'She's picking up behaviour from Franzi,' thought John. 'I wonder where he is? Writing I suppose in his hut.'

"Hello Daisy, how are you today?"

'Ook' she replied then waved two envelopes at him.

A feeling of dread came over him.

"Where's Franzi?" he asked.

Daisy pointed to the countryside beyond the Park.

'Oh no,' he thought and grabbed the letters.

One was addressed to him. The other to the Captain.

He tore his open and read.

'Good Morning John. Just popping out for a couple of days. Don't worry. Give the Captain his letter. I'll be back soon.

Cheers, Franzi

PS. Look after Daisy.'

**

John put his head down and ran up the hill as fast as he could.

"You alright John?" shouted Higgins. John just waved, he had no spare breath to reply.

Nearing the 'House' he slowed slightly and composed himself. 'No point in getting to the Captain and being unable to speak' he thought, followed by 'Bugger that, he needs to know as fast as possible.'

As luck would have it the Captain and Gladys were coming out of the house as it came into view.

"Captain, Captain," he shouted.

"What on earth is it John?"

"He's gone sir, I mean Captain," said John breathlessly.

"Who's gone man," said the Captain, he felt a sinking feeling inside knowing that he was pretty sure of the answer.

John came to a halt in front of the Captain and Gladys and thrust out the letter.

"Franzi."

Gladys looked at the Captain and saw he'd turned pale.

"Bill, what's happening? Who's the letter from?"

Without thinking he replied "Franzi." And tore open the envelope.

'Dear Captain,

As you are aware time is pressing if things are to go better than they might. I'm just popping out for a couple of days to see what I can do. You might say, in a variation on one of your human phrases 'I'm off to see a man about a dog, – actually a few dogs, of war.'

Please don't raise any alarm. I'll be back quick as you like. You'll have to let the public know that my 'show' is cancelled for the moment due to 'a pressing previous engagement'. I don't think Higgins doing a 'stand-in' would go down too well.

If someone calls and wants to talk about me you can be open and honest if they quote the password "Copperknob".

See you soon.

Best wishes,

Franzi'

"Oh Wahalla!"

**

Chartwell - Sunday 13th August 1939 continued

Winston was in two minds whether to tell Clemmy about the appointment. He hummed and hawed all day, which was most unlike him, before blurting it out after dinner over the cheese and port.

"Kat," he began.

"Yes Pug," she replied.

"Err, about last night."

"Yes. About the thing we're not supposed to discuss with anyone."

"Yes. Well you know I looked around the gardens this morning?"

"You did, and you said you didn't see any orangutan," she said archly.

"That was perfectly true. But I did see the writing on my wall."

"We all hope to see that dear," she teased.

"Clemmy! Be serious."

"Yes dear."

"It, he, I mean the orangutan wants to meet me for a 'chat' this evening."

"Oh," she exclaimed. "So not only a bodyguard but an ape that's able to write?"

"Yes, it would seem so. Unless someone is having a wonderful joke at my expense," he said.

"When and where is this meeting to be?"

"9 o'clock in the conservatory. I'm to leave the door open."

"It's 8-30 now, Dear. You might have told me earlier I could have made arrangements," she admonished him.

"Like what?"

"I don't know. Possibly a drink and snack suitable for a wild man of the forest," she laughed, then stopped abruptly.

"It could be dangerous. Should I get one of the policemen on duty to be with you?"

Winston paused in thought before replying.

"Well if it is the orangutan from last night I don't see how I can be in danger but if it's someone else..."

"Yes?"

"Tell you what, I'll have my Tommy gun with me and you invite one of the constables in for a cup of tea. If things go awry then ride to the rescue, my Dear."

She gave him a sideways look, "Winnie you really are an incorrigible old swashbuckler."

He chuckled. "I'll go get my 'little friend' shall I? Oh, and make sure Rufus is kept out in the kitchen please. I don't know how he'll react."

**

Churchill lit two standard lamps in the conservatory. The sun had set but twilight had not yet faded.

The French doors of the conservatory were wide open as was the door back into the house. Inevitably moths were making their way into both the conservatory and the house which would annoy Clemmy. He wanted a clear and open line of retreat for himself and access for the police if anything went wrong with the meeting.

He wasn't sure what to expect. Someone, a keeper or trainer perhaps, possibly with the orangutan. He checked the Tommy gun, magazine full, safety off, spare magazine. Good.

Full glass of brandy, bottle, cigars and matches.

"Peace in our time. Bollocks!"

"What's that Sam?" he said.

Winston stood up and went to the parrot's cage.

"Dead duck," squawked the parrot.

He eyed the foul-mouthed bird within.

"Who do we hate eh?" to which Sam replied, "Fucking Nazis," in a passable rendering of Churchill's growl.

"Wonderful Sam, wonderful," he said.

Sam let out a loud screech of alarm, "Aaaark!" then screamed "Fucking Hitler!"

Winston jumped in surprise.

A loud and authoritative 'Ook!' made him jump again and turn, this time in alarm.

Winston and orangutan stood and stared at each other whilst Sam still shrieked.

The ape pointed at the parrot and laughed. He raised his right arm and gave a Nazi salute, then fell over backwards as if he'd been shot.

Winston couldn't help himself and joined in the laughter then covered up Sam's cage to restoring a semblance of sensibility to the meeting.

"Well sir," Winston said, "You gave me quite a turn there."

Franzi chuckled and blew a raspberry.

"Indeed. Will you have a seat?" said Winston, and indicated a large rattan sofa which was furnished with a number of soft cushions.

'Ook,' Franzi nodded. Before curling up on it as per his practice at Whipsnade he retrieved a chalkboard and satchel from by the door and arranged them close at hand.

Winston watched in fascination, obviously the ape was no stranger to furniture and making himself comfortable.

He shook his head and recovered the Tommy gun from where he'd left it. I would have been well and truly stuffed if 'Red' had been intending mischief, he thought.

He engaged the safety on the gun before placing it on a side table, then sat down.

Franzi pointed at the glass and cigar and chalked 'I could do with a drink and smoke.' Then, swiftly rubbing out that request he wrote 'But where are my manners? Good evening Mr Churchill, my name is Franzi. May I call you Winston?'

**

Franzi was comfortably furnished with both a large brandy and large cigar. He was enjoying both immensely. It might have been worth the journey for those alone but he had a serious job to do. He had to engage Churchill and convince him to accept facts, events, potential events, and suggestions which would dramatically reduce the carnage of the war to come AND, hopefully, ensure a better post-war world.

Neither man nor ape broke the spell of mutual enjoyment of alcohol and tobacco. The night sounds of late summer only served to enhance the magical and surreal feeling that persuaded Churchill not to question the presence of an orangutan in his conservatory.

'Thank you for seeing me,' chalked Franzi.

"Given what you did last night it would have been churlish of me to refuse," said Churchill.

Franzi chuffed.

"You are, I take it, the orangutan from Whipsnade that has been entertaining the crowds?"

'Ook.'

"I've had a number of people asking me to meet with someone 'special' as a matter of urgency, including General Giffard. Would that someone be you?"

'Ook.'

"I can agree that you are very 'special'."

Franzi waved his glass in agreement and blew out a large smoke cloud.

"Thank you for saving me last night. I doubt I would have survived without your intervention."

Franzi nodded in reply, 'Pure serendipity I do assure you.'

"One does wonder about such things," said Winston thoughtfully. "Given your obvious skill at entertainment, and writing of course, I have to wonder why you wanted to meet with me. Wouldn't a theatrical impresario or circus owner be more appropriate?"

Franzi wagged a finger at Churchill.

"Sorry."

'You are one of the critical people in history at the moment,' wrote Franzi.

"I am, am I? Sat here on the side-lines, baying at the moon, as some of my detractors would have it."

'A temporary aberration. They should have listened to you earlier.'

"And you know this how?" asked Churchill, his attention focused entirely on his new arboreal acquaintance.

'I know things, a lot of things. Things an orangutan normally wouldn't know.'

"So you come to me? Why not someone else?"

'You are the key for Britain, the Empire and Commonwealth and I live in England, for now at least.'

Churchill sat back and drew long on his cigar.

Franzi was frustrated. 'So much to tell, so much to do in a short time and all the while restricted to a chalkboard!'

He drank up his brandy, sat forward and chalked, 'Are you ready to be amazed? Are you ready to trust me, Winston?'

Churchill mirrored Franzi's stance, "I believe I am."

Chartwell - Monday 14th August 1939

Clementine Churchill breezed into her breakfast room and came to an abrupt halt.

"Pug, what an earth are you doing here?" she exclaimed.

Winston looked up from the paper he was studying, "I can't be in my own breakfast room, enjoying breakfast then?" he smiled.

"Well, it's just not you. We don't usually see you until around 11. What on earth is wrong?" she said as she took her seat opposite him.

"Nothing wrong dear, far from it. I've just been up all night reading papers and I have an early morning meeting."

"What papers? Who came? Did 'Mr Whyte' turn up? We didn't hear anything other than Sam squawking" she blurted out.

Winston laughed.

"And that's another thing," Clemmy said, "Why so happy? You've been ready to commit murder if any of Neville's cronies had contacted you."

"That, my Dear, was before my new colleague, Mr Whyte, explained a few things to me last night and left me this lot to study," he said, pointing to the pile of papers at his side next to an old school satchel.

"Oh. So a man then, not an orangutan? One of those spy types from Poland or France?"

"No Kat, far from it, an in the flesh, full-grown orangutan with a most extraordinary talent. Oh and by the way don't go into the conservatory without me, he stayed overnight."

**

Franzi was enjoying himself with Sam and Rufus in the conservatory. Sam would screech out "Fucking Nazis" and "Fucking Hitler" whenever Franzi goose-stepped and gave the salute. Rufus loved being stroked and having Franzi throw a ball for him to fetch out into the garden.

It had been a good night. The conservatory had at least been dry so he'd not been soaked in the overnight rain.

He decided he would get soft if he stayed here. Better to have his new friend Winston come up and see him either at or somewhere near the Park.

Yes item 1 on this morning's agenda, let the Captain know he was safe.

His stomach rumbled. He'd been on slim pickings since he'd begun his journey 3 days before. Have to put that right.

Item 2 on the agenda, food!

Then on to World War 2.

There was a tap at the door.

Churchill and Clemmy came slowly into the room.

"Fucking Nazis!" screeched Sam.

"Winston, that bird is too much!" said Clemmy.

Franzi blew a loud raspberry and gave Clementine a thumbs up.

She smiled, her nerves settling to a degree in the humour of the moment, "I'm glad you agree, Mr Whyte?" she asked.

Franzi reached down and produced his board and chalk,

'Franzi, madam. Please to meet you,' he quickly wrote then rose, crossed to Clemmy and shook her hand.

"Franzi," she repeated.

"Let's sit down then. Clemmy, can you bring us some tea, please? I don't think Marjorie is quite up to meeting Franzi at the minute," said Winston.

"Yes dear," said Clemmy.

'Oook'

"Yes Franzi?" asked Winston.

'I need food please. I am very hungry. If it isn't too much trouble?'

"Not at all. We'll see what we can do. I'm not sure we have much in to tempt you, what is it that orangutans eat anyway?"

'In the wild fruit, lots of fruit. Young leaves, shoots, bark, insects, honey and bird eggs. I'll take eggs, bread, lightly cooked bacon if you haven't got those,' wrote Franzi.

"I'm sure we'll find something for you and I'll get the gardener to collect up more fruit if you like?" said Clemmy as she let herself out.

"Thank you for your concise notes and appreciation of the current situation," said Churchill.

'I would like you to ring Captain Beale at Whipsnade please, and let him know I am alright.'

"Of course. Now?" asked Winston.

Franzi nodded.

'He won't acknowledge I'm missing but tell him you are 'Coppernob' and he'll hear you out.'

"Really?" said Winston "you've chosen that name for me?"

'Suited you at Harrow'

"I've got no hair now, well not much to speak of."

They laughed at the joke.

'Another thing,' wrote Franzi, 'I wrote to a few people whilst I was waiting to talk to you.'

"You did what? Who?" Churchill cried. "No one who can betray the secret I hope?"

'Key people, like you. I doubt they'll piece together who I am or where I am. I did include a piece of my red hair in each letter and told them to watch out for it in future correspondence or contact,' Franzi chuckled in his deep rumble.

"Red hair, or my lack of it is going to be a 'thing', is it?" said Winston.

'Oook, ook, ook' Franzi replied.

"You sir are incorrigible!"

**

Later that day a London Zoological Society van drove up the drive at Chartwell. It didn't pull up at the front or back doors but was directed by Dennis, the Churchill's handyman and general factotum, to a track that went down to the large pond by the copse on the edge of the grounds.

John parked and got out of the van.

'Oook, ook, ook,' Franzi burst from cover and rushed to give his friend a great hug.

"Franzi, you big daft, what are you?" said John.

Churchill emerged from the cover too. "Good afternoon, John, I believe it is?"

"Yes sir,"

"Good, good," said Churchill shaking his hand.

"I hope he's been behaving himself, sir?"

"Oh yes. A perfect gentleman."

Franzi responded with an outstanding raspberry.

"Very good Franzi, but you forget playing the simple ape with me isn't going to work now, is it?"

Franzi chuffed.

"I'll use the satchel to send you things, if that's alright?" said Churchill. "I wager there's only one such of those with that graffiti on it so you'll know the correspondence and papers have come from me."

'Ook'.

Franzi produced his board and chalk.

'Now Winston no more 'black dog. Remember you've now got the 'Red Ape'!'

"I'll try Franzi, I'll try. I think we've the trump to ace Herr Schicklgruber but it's still going to take some blood, toil, tears and sweat. Now be off with you, I'll see you soon."

Chapter 7

De Havilland Works - Monday 14th August 1939

Air Chief Marshall Freeman enjoyed getting 'out of the office'. He wasn't going far today, just a short trip up the road, but he was interested to see what reaction he got from the first manufacturer he'd been advised to approach by Mr Whyte's letter.

Geoffrey de Havilland wondered why he hadn't been summoned to the Air Ministry and why ACM Freeman had asked to meet at the works. He'd also asked to see Charles Walker and some of the design team for the DH98, as he'd named the aircraft he had been encouraged to focus on.

How on earth did Freeman know about the work going on for the multirole 'Wooden Wonder' that Mr Whyte had described in his correspondence?

Despite his concerns Geoffrey had laid on 'The Works' for Wilfred Freeman. A tour of the factory to look at the wing assembly lines which de Havilland had been 'granted' by the Air Ministry. Then a closed meeting to look at the DH98 drawings and plans as requested, Then lunch and then a session with just the ACM, his aide, Walker and de Havilland.

"Well Geoffrey," said Freeman, "I'm very impressed. You're still working away at the mundane wing assembly contract but you've taken your first thoughts on the development of the DH95 'fast bomber' and come up with something quite remarkable."

"Thank you for saying so Wilfred," said de Havilland, "we aim to please."

"Do I sense a degree of cynicism there Geoffrey?"

"As you recall, Wilfred, you were one of the chief detractors from the fast bomber concept, let alone an aircraft that could perform to a degree of excellence across a wide range of missions."

"Yes I agree I was. The bomber chaps wanted, still want to be fair, a large, heavily armed monster that can fly into the heart of Europe with a large bomb load and come home safely."

"So why the change of mind?" asked de Havilland.

"I could, on a slightly muted note, ask the same of yourself, given what went on before."

De Havilland nodded, "You could, but I asked first."

The ACM chuckled. "Yes you did. Well, to be honest, I had some input from someone who has obviously studied the probable RAF operation requirements in a most detailed way. He has also the ear of, if I am correct, the powers that be. He asked me to look at several options for aircraft development and gave me chapter and verse on what is and isn't going to work. I'm here to see if you fellows can provide what I was advised was going to be a winner."

De Havilland beamed. "Well, Wilfred, I'll be honest with you, we were asked to concentrate on this kite and given some pretty detailed input on the design including variants, armament, engines the lot."

"So it wasn't you who wrote to me by a third party then?" asked the ACM

"No it was not," replied de Havilland.

"Oh my, this is going to be interesting then, "said Freeman. "I thought I was just being lobbied by companies to ensure they got government contracts. I know the information provided was detailed and suggested something more complex than that but until I came here..." he tailed off.

"Who is behind it then?" asked de Havilland.

"I've absolutely no idea," replied Freeman. "The recommended aircraft development and suspension of certain production runs is just the tip of the iceberg."

"Yes?"

"It's been suggested that I somehow influence strategic thinking, sweep up parts and supplies of aircraft described as 'obsolescent' for other purposes and assist in the complete reorganisation of production and training."

"By whom?"

"A chap called Whyte."

**

Bruno Himmler used his connections to get in touch, discreetly, with a member of the BUF. The man, Alan Boylan, worked as a gamekeeper for one of Oswald Moseley's friends and had done some bully boy jobs for the Party.

They met in a pub in Luton and Himmler explained what was to be done.

"Kill it if you can, or maim it if you can't, I'll leave the details up to you," he said.

"Bit tricky walking in there with me rifle, I'll check if I can get a sight from outside. If not I reckon poison would work."

"Whatever. But soon. We want the public to remember."

"A week do you? "

"Eminently. "

"You what? "

Bruno sighed. "That will be fine. Here's £10 on account, the rest when it's done. Don't get caught. If you do you'll be taken care of so tell no tales."

"Whatever you say gov. "

**

British Army HQ Cairo

"Sarge, here's a funny one."

"Really Corporal Jones?" Sgt Bostock said in a bored tone.

"Well, I think so."

"Go on then. Make me laff," said the sergeant sarcastically.

"Something for the two mad 'uns."

"Jones you don't refer to Generals as 'mad 'uns', if the Captain here's you you'll be digging latrine trenches out in the great fuck all from now till doomsday."

"'E sez it too."

"'Es an officer, so he can."

"Not just 'im is it? Most of the staff don't like 'em" said Corporal Jones. "Why is it sarge?"

Bostock pushed his chair back and blew out his cheeks before explaining, "You see my son they have come from jolly old Blighty with new ideas, and them new ideas are upsetting the old types here. The ones who know what's what about soldiering."

"What do you mean?"

"They want to stop the infantry and the artillery and, most of all, the cavalry doing what they've always done."

"As in?"

"Well with the infantry it's marching, digging, shooting and occasionally charging, the artillery firing off and the cavalry.."

"Yes sarge?"

"The cavalry? Well, that would be ponsing about all over the place, searching out the enemy, charging at 'em all 'hell or nothing' and then coming back to the mess and bragging what great fun it was."

"So these chaps from England don't hold with that anymore?"

"No my son. They say that's not what's going to win against the Iytie or Jerries."

"And are they right sarge?"

"Blowed if I know corporal, I'm only a sergeant clerk. Now then what do you find so funny?"

"They've both got letters.."

"No? Really. God help me," said Bostock looking up at the ceiling. "Who'd thought it generals who've got letters from England."

"'S true, from the same person it looks like, see 'ere," said Jones offering up two large envelopes to the sergeant.

Bostock adjusted his glasses. Sure enough, the writing on both envelopes was in the same hand, and in pencil too. Very odd. Properly addressed though.

'Major General R O'Connor GOC 7th Division, Mersah Matruh'

'Major General P Hobart, HQ, Cairo'

**

Barnes Wallace was pouring over blueprints and reports of the latest 'tweaks' to the Warwick prototype. He was sure, as with the Wellington, Vickers would have another winner. An aircraft that could fulfil a number of roles in a better than adequate way.

He sighed. Well, it would if Napier could deliver the engines they'd promised on schedule and with all their glitches ironed out.

The first test flight was due and that always made any aircraft design team nervous.

The competition to meet the Air Ministry's specification was fierce. Avro had got their Manchester off the ground in July. It was comparable in bomb load but reports had it that it was faster. Still, it was early days.

"Letter for you Mr Wallis," cried the mail boy as he dropped an envelope onto BW's desk.

**

Roy was a happy man. The 'Manchester' had flown well.

Now his latest design was safely off the ground he was content, first hurdle over.

Time for a break. He got up and went to the window.

"Amy, can you get me a tea please?" he shouted.

"Yes sir," came the sweet reply.

He scratched his head and looked out onto the industrial panorama before him. Chadderton, well Avro's new works in south Chadderton, were quite pleasant, for a factory.

Smoke belched over Chadderton proper from a number of cotton mills. Not as many as there'd been before the Depression but even so plenty of smoke to fill the sky daily. The streets were grimy. Buildings darkened after years exposure to the 'muck' in the air.

He was used to living in the 'grim' north. He'd grown up in Widnes before going on to study at UMIST in the centre of Manchester. Occasionally he took his family off to the moors north of Chorley or even on holiday to Blackpool. He was a man of his locale and era even though he was working on the most advanced aero technology of the time.

He wondered about the opposition and how they were progressing. Barnes Wallace's team hadn't yet flown the Warwick but it was supposedly imminent. He caught himself thinking whether multiple companies competing to deliver to Air Ministry requirements and specifications was the best that could be done, especially with war on the horizon. Oh what he'd give for a crystal ball, perhaps he should take the family to Blackpool at the weekend and consult with one of the seafront fortune tellers?

"There's your tea sir," said Amy, "and the post."

He eased his shoulders and returned to his desk.

Good strong tea perked him up a treat. Only a couple of hours to go and he'd pop home for lunch.

As he sorted through the correspondence an unusual letter caught his eye. His name and the address were handwritten in pencil but that wasn't what stopped him in his tracks. Whoever had sent the letter had drawn the most wonderful aircraft on the back of the envelope. A huge, four-engined bomber – and underneath was written 'Lancaster'.

**

'Stuffy' sat at his desk and sighed. The reports he was receiving about the ADA weren't encouraging. Their aircraft were, when compared to the Germans and RAF, somewhat 'lacking'. The Dewoitine D500 might be compared with the Gladiator. Their most numerous type, the Morane-Saulnier MS406 might be on a par with the Hurricane. They didn't have anything, so far, that compared to the ME109 or Spitfire although the Dewoitine D520 showed promise. Strangely it wasn't the aircraft that concerned him so much. It was the organisation and morale that worried him. Would they be able to sustain multiple sorties a day? Would they be able to find the enemy or escort their bombers effectively? How would they react to casualties and setbacks?

By comparison to the French his plans for Fighter Command were well along. Progress wasn't as good as it might be but as long as they had time all the elements he'd worked so hard on since he became AOC should give the RAF a fighting chance to deploy on the Continent as required and protect home.

"Excuse me, sir. Do you have a moment," asked Sq Ldr Evans, Dowding's ADC, as he entered the room?

"Yes Evans. What do you want?"

"There's been a letter sir."

"From?"

"I'm not sure sir. I took the liberty of opening it given how busy you are," said Evans somewhat nervously.

"I see."

"It's marked private and confidential but it's written in pencil. I thought it was some crank..." Evans went on.

"But?" said Dowding raising an eyebrow.

"I think you'd best read it yourself sir. It's rather startling."

Dowding opened the letter and began to read.

War imminent. 3rd September. Hmm.

Advice and intelligence.

Further communication.

Red hair. "Evans where's this red hair?" he asked.

"Here sir," said the Sq Ldr handing it over for inspection.

Dowding nodded then turned to the enclosures.

Evans hadn't read them. He almost hopped from leg to leg in his eagerness to find out what they contained.

He watched Dowding's face but 'Stuffy' gave away nothing.

Eventually he looked up at Evans.

"You never saw this letter," he said in his usual dispassionate way.

"Pardon sir?"

Dowding repeated very slowly, carefully annunciating each word, "You never saw this letter. Understand?"

"Yes sir. Of course sir."

"Get me a full list of Squadron's operating Defiants, Gladiators, and Blenheims."

"Sir."

**

Dagnall - Wednesday 16th August 1939

Boylan felt sure that one or two rounds would be more than certain to put the ape down, especially since he'd cross grooved the 303 bullets.

He had been to the Park twice now and considered what could be done and how he could earn the rest of the £200 he'd been promised for success. The first time, Monday the 14th had been a waste of time. The orangutan hadn't been out. Boylan had asked about and been told that the ape had been ill and not seen since the previous Thursday. He'd gone back the following day and been rewarded by the sight of the 'Hitler skit' in the afternoon. To be honest he had found it quite funny but he had his orders.

Boylan considered poisoning the orangutan's food, but that looked far too difficult, no, the best way was to come from the outside, the downhill side, over the fence and move until he could take his shot at dusk with the sun setting behind him.

The following evening he parked on the outskirts of Dagnall village. When no one seemed to be about he got out of his van, pulled his cap low and set off down the road to a gateway he'd seen which gave access to a field leading up to the chalk Lion.

He could have taken the lane up the hill to the west of the Lion but he thought it best to avoid the road. He could work up the hedge line of the field and come out to the east close to the Polar Bears.

It was a steep climb and he wasn't as fit as he'd once been. By the time he got to the top near the boundary of the Park he was blowing quite a bit. He paused at the fence to get his bearings and his breath back.

Getting into the Park was no problem, he guessed it was only a boundary not meant to keep things out or in.

Boylan tried to keep off the Avenue and slowly made his way through the copse separating Tiger and Lion Pits then out onto the path that the visitors used to look down on the Lions.

At the end of the path he had a clear view of the orangutan's enclosure. Bingo, both apes were sat by one of the two huts inside.

He crouched down and pulled his rifle from the kit bag. He checked the mechanism. At which point he almost jumped out of his skin as one of the lions gave a thunderous roar.

'Bloody hell," he exclaimed, as he glanced into the Lion Pit. A large male was very close to where he stood. Fortunately it was a good few feet below him so there was no chance, he hoped, that it could leap up and take him. It clearly didn't like the look of him and two more lions were coming over to see what the commotion was about.

Boylan shook his head. Best get on with it before someone comes to see why the lions are upset. He turned back to the orangutan enclosure. No apes! What the hell was going on? He moved closer. They must have gone into the hut, but which one? He needed a clear shot and then to be on his way. He couldn't afford to blind fire into both huts.

Suddenly, in the failing light, he caught a glimpse of a dark reddish-brown 'something' disappearing into the trees off to his left by the main avenue. It surely couldn't be one of the orangutan's, could it?

The lions were still unhappy and his nerve was failing him. He thrust the rifle back in the bag and made a dash back the way he'd come. 'Bugger this for the Fuhrer.'

He was by the Polar Bear pit when Franzi hit him full on from the side. To be fair Franzi was just trying to stop him but Boylan's momentum and the extra boost the hit gave him helped him clear the safety rail around the pit. As he did so he dropped his bag and fell headfirst into the water. He scrambled to the surface and tried to swim but his heavy boots dragged him down. He reached down and tried to rid himself of his footwear and then heard two loud splashes.

He managed to kick off the boots and rose to the surface. 'Thank God' he thought just as the two polar bears closed on his struggling body.

**

When the keeper had arrived at the polar bear pit the next morning the Park staff had gone a little crazy. The bears had made short work of the trespasser. The man was obviously dead (as evidenced by his head being some distance from his body). The authorities were summoned and the Captain called Dr Vevers to explain what had been discovered.

Initially, the bag and rifle were missed, they'd sunk to the bottom of the pool. At length, a sharp-eyed member of staff had spotted the bag and arrangements were made to recover it.

**

Franzi had pondered the incident through the night. The man's screams hadn't been nice, thought Franzi later. He hadn't meant to hurt him, just stop him and find out. 'But find out what,' he thought?

He chuffed loudly and Daisy stirred in her hut. All in all it had been a stupid thing to do. He'd been angry when the lions had raised the alarm and he'd spotted Boylan with the rifle. Good job they had given warning or he, or worse Daisy, might be dead.

He resigned himself to another evening of questions from the Captain. He'd had enough the evening he'd arrived back from Chartwell.

"What on earth were you thinking Franzi?"

"How did you get there?"

"What would have happened if you'd been spotted?"

And on and on.

He'd brought the questioning to an end by writing, 'Churchill has to know about the bloody war!'

It was the first time he'd been rude to his homo sapiens friends and the Captain, noting the tone and underlying anger, stopped his criticism.

Taking a breath he went on, "Well at least he does now. Is everything as you wish it now? Or are you going to go off again without telling us?"

Franzi blew a loud raspberry and motioned for a refill of brandy.

"Alright Franzi, alright," said the Captain, "but you do realise you are the Park's property, don't you? And we have to care for you and make sure the public are safe."

Franzi almost stormed out of the study. Then thought. 'Oh yes, under the human's laws he was property.'

'Must have a word with Mr Churchill and get that changed once he is Prime Minister!'

**

Bruno Himmler was summoned to the Ambassador's office.

"So Himmler, what have you to say about this," said von Dirksen, as he threw a copy of the Express across the desk.

"Sir," Himmler stuttered as he read the headline on the page.

'Gamekeeper killed by Bears'

He quickly read on.

'John Boylan was found dead in the polar bear enclosure at Whipsnade park'.

He went a little pale.

"So I am right in thinking it was on your orders?"

"Yes sir," Himmler replied in a firm tone.

"Gone wrong hasn't it?" said Dirksen.

"It appears so sir. I'll arrange for someone else to carry out the task," he continued.

"Enough. No time for that now. We have to make arrangements to leave London. Ensure there are no security lapses as we pack and that our agents in place have all their instructions."

"Zu befehl! Heil Hitler!"

Chapter 8

Whipsnade - Thursday 17th August 1939

It wasn't the first time there'd been a fatality at Whipsnade on the Captain's watch. In 1934 a member of the catering staff, Stanley Stenson, had been mauled to death by a lion. A visitor had thrown his hat into the lion enclosure and Stanley said he'd get it for "five hundred quid". The hat's owner had agreed. The lions were dozing peacefully after feeding at some distance away when Stanley began to climb down. Unfortunately he slipped and efforts to haul him back up before he fell the forty or so feet to the ground had failed. Not only that they'd alerted the lions so that when Stanley did fall and hit his head on the ground one of their number, a known man-eater, had reverted to type and attacked the unconscious Stanley. Keepers had rushed in and driven the lion off with pitchforks but by that time it was too late. No blame was attached to the Park for the incident, after all it was an employee who'd chosen to put his own life at risk.

Five years on the police were quite understanding. At first sight it appeared as though the man, a gamekeeper, had been after one of the animals. Special Branch brought up the fact that he was a member of the BUF and that brought into question whether he was really at the Park to do some harm to the star anti-Nazi, Franzi, and if so was he working under orders?

**

"That was a close call Franzi. If that chap was after you as Special Branch seem to think," said the Captain after they'd settled down with brandies that evening.

'Very,' Franzi wrote.

"I wonder how he came to fall in to the polar bear pit?" The Captain fixed Franzi with a stare and waited for an answer.

'That must have been an accident.'

"I see. An accident. Did you happen to see the man?"

'He was by the lions when they got upset. I saw the gun and his with Daisy when he was distracted.'

"He was clearly scared by something. He must have run full tilt into the rail above the bears or he wouldn't have gone over," said the Captain.

'Oook'

"Ah well the police seem satisfied it was an accident. They are looking into the man's background, friends and contacts."

'Ook'

"And they tell me he had some interesting fascist friends who probably disliked your Hitler performance a great deal. Enough for them to order you shot."

'Ook' Franzi responded and then chalked 'Perhaps I'll stop that then?'

"It might be a good thing," said the Captain. "By the way, I had a call from Mr Churchill asking if you were alright this afternoon."

'Ook'

"He'd like to meet with you at the weekend. He's coming here. It could be interesting because Solly and the young lady who can sign are due here too."

'Thank goodness. That should make things much easier,' wrote Franzi, and then 'Can I have another fag and brandy now please?'

**

Friday 18th August 1939

Jane Weiss was feeling uncomfortable. Solly Zuckerman was a nice man, a lovely man really, but more like a 'brother' not a boyfriend. She was uncomfortable specifically because she didn't know if he wanted to be more than a 'big brother' or not.

He'd sought her out in the typing and clerical pool at the satellite office where he worked and invited her out for a cup of tea.

To be fair he'd not tried anything on with her, as her mother would say, in fact he'd seemed to be more interested in the fact that she was proficient in sign language than her looks or personality. He had stressed he had something 'very secret' he wanted to share with her but she couldn't think what it might be. He had something to do with the Air Ministry but he wouldn't, or shouldn't tell her anything about that. Finally, he'd said he'd a friend who needed help. He needed someone expert in signing and also someone who could keep secrets.

Signing was second nature to her. She'd been doing it for her younger brother since she was 8. Poor Aaron had been born deaf but he had taken to signing and lip-reading like a duck to water. He, like her, had a very sharp mind, and her parents had wanted their children to do as well as possible in their new country.

Isaac and Rebecca Wiess had quit Germany in 1933 as Hitler rose to power. They were moderately wealthy, in their community's terms, from their business in gems and gold. They had contacts all over Europe and further afield where gems were mined and it had taken them a while to decide where to relocate. Finally though they'd chosen England.

They settled in London within the large Jewish community of the East End and successfully continued their business.

Jane had enrolled in a secretarial college after school and joined the War Department when she was 18. She'd moved to Oxford a year ago.

She shifted in her seat to try to relax. To be honest Solly's sports car wasn't built for comfort. It wasn't quiet either, the engine was noisy as was the wind with the top off.

"You alright Jane," Solly shouted?

"Yes," she nodded.

"Not far now," he said.

'Thank goodness,' she thought. Even though it was 7 o'clock on an August evening she was cold and damp from an earlier shower. Thankfully she was wearing a mackintosh and her hair was trapped beneath a scarf. She wished she'd brought warm gloves though.

Fifteen minutes later they arrived at Whipsnade Zoological Park. It was the first time she'd been but she and her family had been to Regents Park Zoo many times.

She loved animals. Leaving their dogs and cats in Berlin when they fled had been very upsetting.

'That was another thing,' she thought. Solly had been most interested in her views on animals, whether she liked them, whether she got on with them and whether she had any phobias about them.

Well a German Jewish girl from Berlin didn't get to see that many animals, except for the wonderful zoo, and certainly she didn't get to 'meet' them. Spiders though, she didn't like spiders. She doubted Solly was going to take her to an insect house, that was even if the Park had such a thing. Surely they had animals that liked the outdoors? She'd seen a very amusing article in the paper about an orangutan there.

"Here we are," said Solly as he brought the car to a skidding halt on the gravel in front of a large house. He 'beeped' the horn twice before jumping out and running round to her side to open her door.

As she climbed out she saw a large, bespectacled man and a matronly woman and two children coming to greet them.

"Hello Solly," boomed the man.

"So this is Jane? Pleased to meet you my dear, I'm Gladys" said the woman as she gave her a hug. "And this is my husband Bill, superintendent of the Park."

"Very nice to meet you, sir," said Jane.

"No no my dear, Bill or the Captain," said the Captain shaking her hand.

"And these are Laura and Billy," said Solly alternately swinging both children off the ground.

"Come in dear," said Gladys, "I'm sure the men will bring in the luggage. You're probably starving. Laura go put the kettle on and make tea please."

**

After the children had gone to bed the Captain drew his wife aside.

"Now Gladys," he began, "I'm sorry to say I've been keeping a secret from you for the past few weeks." He paused, waiting for some sort of admonishment.

Gladys said nothing and waited until he went on.

"Er.. Well, we have a very important and special individual in the Park..."

"Yes?"

"Yes. He came to us at the end of July. He may be critical to England and the Empire's resistance to Hitler."

"So why is he here and why are you telling me now?" she said.

"It's pure chance he's here, well that's what he says. To be honest I am totally flummoxed. As to why I'm telling you now, well I'd like you to be with Jane when they and we are all introduced in," he looked at the hall clock, "about five minutes time."

"Bill Beale we have been married for many years now. We've been here, there and everywhere and had our share of adventures. You must know I'll do whatever is needed for you and England," she said reaching up to give him a kiss on the cheek.

"Come on then," he said, "Let's join Jane and Solly in the Study."

**

Jane and Solly were seated comfortably in the Study when the Captain and Gladys joined them. The fire had been lit to take the chill off the evening and they'd helped themselves, as invited, to a drink.

"Well then," said the Captain, "I've asked Gladys to join us this evening so Jane isn't overwhelmed by too many men."

Jane smiled and Solly laughed.

"We're just waiting for our friend to join us but I must explain, Jane, that Glady's hasn't met him either, so it'll be a first for you both."

Gladys glanced at the Captain sharply, "But I know all the members of staff," she said.

"Ah yes, well," said the Captain, "who said it was a member of staff my dear?"

At that instant a quiet knocking was heard at the window.

"Here he is now," said that Captain rising to his feet. "Er, Jane, please could you take that other chair, he particularly likes the seat you're in."

Jane shrugged her shoulders and moved to the seat the Captain had indicated as he went to answer the knock.

"Why are you smirking Solly," asked Gladys?

"I'm afraid, Gladys, and Jane – I have that sort of sense of humour," he replied.

They heard the Captain open the door and ask the visitor in. "Yes come in, come. They're all in there. Try not to upset anyone with your antics please."

The Captain came into the room first followed by, to the amazement of both women, an orangutan, and worse, no keeper.

The Captain stood back and allowed the ape to cross the room towards the seated guests.

The orangutan nodded to Solly and then crossed to Mrs Beale. She sat, transfixed, as he bowed his head then took her hand and shook it. That done he moved to Jane. He stopped at arm's length from her and signed, 'Good evening. I hope you and I are going to become very good friends.'

Automatically she replied 'Hello. I hope so too.'

**

Once the ice had been broken it was a lively social evening. Franzi no longer had to resort to his chalkboard and the 'conversation' flowed well, ranging over subjects that surprised everyone. Franzi, it seemed, knew so much about so many things.

He deliberately didn't mention anything about the coming war but entertained his friends with stories of his time in Borneo before he'd come to London Zoo.

Jane and Gladys were entranced. Franzi was a natural raconteur, supremely intelligent but with a wicked sense of humour. He ragged Solly and the Captain something rotten, gently teased Jane, and even risked a joke or two at Gladys' expense.

"Turning to a more serious matter," said the Captain. "I didn't mention this before but Mr Churchill is coming to see Franzi tomorrow evening, and, if you're willing Jane, I think it would be useful for you to be there."

'Oook,' agreed Franzi.

"I..," said Jane

"Bill," exclaimed Gladys, "more surprises? You're overwhelming the girl."

"Apologies Jane, and to you Gladys," replied the Captain, "but things are moving at a pace where surprises are going to become the norm."

'No time to lose,' signed Franzi. 'We must prepare as quickly as we can for what is to come.'

Jane translated and then said "That's fine Franzi, Captain. I'm happy to do what is needed."

'Ook,' said Franzi and gave a thumbs up after signing to jane 'You'll be fine. I'll look after you.'

She smiled back at him and nodded.

"Where on earth are we going to entertain Mr Churchill and keep it a secret?" asked Gladys.

"Oh, his visit isn't a secret. He goes to Regents Park quite a lot. He says being with the animals, like his pets, helps him think and put things in perspective," said Solly.

"I see. But his meeting with Franzi? It'll be nigh on impossible to keep that quiet if he comes to the House."

"Franzi and I discussed that," explained the Captain. "One of the old blocks used by the builders will do. There's one that will keep the water out if it rains and I'll get John to put a paraffin stove on to warm it up if it's a cool evening".

"I see," said Gladys. "That will have to do then. Are we finished here now?"

All eyes turned to Franzi for an answer.

'All's good. Thank you. I'm sure we'll all be able to work well together. Thank you, Gladys and Jane, for meeting me this evening,' signed Franzi. He gave both ladies a hug, turned and blew a raspberry at the Captain and Solly before signing 'I'll show myself out. See you tomorrow.'

**

Saturday 19th August 1939

"Good to have you back Thompson," said Churchill as he shook the hand of his old friend and bodyguard.

"Happy to be back sir. I was getting a little bored with the grocery work."

"I can imagine weighing out potatoes would become somewhat tedious after all the adventures we've had."

"I'm sorry I wasn't here when those chaps attacked you at the weekend."

"Not your fault. The powers that be had decided I didn't need protection as a simple MP."

"Foolish decision. You've made so many enemies over the years an attack was inevitable, especially in these times," said Thompson with venom. "I read the report and saw you were fortunate to have help on hand. I must say though, sir, I didn't recognise the man you described as someone you'd helped before."

"Ah yes," said Churchill, "Let's get off and I'll tell you about him on the way to Whipsnade."

"As you wish sir," replied Thompson.

Thomson and the detective driving sat in the front whilst Churchill worked on papers in the rear.

Even though Churchill had promised to reveal information about the 'rescue' he seemed more concerned with his work for most of the journey.

At last, as they neared Luton, he leaned forward and tapped Thompson on the back.

"I omitted some details from my statement for security purposes. Safe to say the chap who saved my bacon had actually come to see me about matters pertaining to the international situation. It was fortunate he arrived when he did and that he is a master in unarmed combat," said Winston with a mischievous glint in his eye.

"Yes sir, very fortunate," said Thompson with a smile. He knew Churchill of old, his mercurial moods and sense of humour. Something 'interesting' was going to be sprung on him although he didn't know what.

"In fact," Winston carried on, "I'm not sure if he's ever used a firearm."

"I see sir."

"You'll understand fully when you meet him this evening, " said Churchill sitting back in his seat once more.

**

They arrived at the Park just after 4 pm. The weather was pleasant and it was still busy.

A member of staff directed them to park up near the café where the Captain and Solly came to meet them.

"Good to see you Mr Churchill," beamed the Captain.

"Pleased to be here," Churchill replied.

"Can I offer you any refreshment or would you like to see some of the Park before the early dinner my wife has planned for us?"

"I would like to look at where those polar bears ended that poor man's life. A horrible way to die no doubt, even though I hear he was a fascist."

Solly and the Captain looked closely at the politician. Obviously he'd been doing his homework.

"Indeed Mr Churchill," said the Captain. "This way if you please."

"I wonder what he was after, eh, Dr Zuckerman?" continued Churchill as they began to walk down the hill.

"Well, sir," began Solly, "We were hoping it wasn't about our mutual friend."

"Don't believe in coincidences myself, do I, Thompson?"

"No sir."

"We know he must have upset a few people with his antics," said the Captain, "but to order someone to come and shoot him..."

"It's what we're up against Captain. A heinous regime that will stop at nothing."

Most of the visitors were by now being rounded up by zoo staff and shepherded to the exit.

By the time the Captain and party had reached the polar bears they were on their own.

They looked over the railings into the pit. The bears looked up at the four men and began to growl and pace menacingly.

"After more meat, I shouldn't wonder," speculated Churchill.

"Actually they didn't eat very much of the man," said the Captain, "just ripped his head off."

"Shows good taste if you ask me," said Solly.

"Indeed. Fortunately, on this island few of us can stomach fascists!" laughed Winston.

The others, except Thompson, joined in the laughter.

"So where is this amazing orangutan who does the Hitler performance?" asked Churchill, winking surreptitiously at the Captain.

"This way sir," indicated the Captain, "but I have to tell you he's not done that act since the man was found dead."

"Really?"

"The crowds have been very disappointed."

"I bet they have."

They made their way along past the tiger and lion enclosures to where Franzi and Daisy were housed.

John was finishing off delivering a new supply of food and bedding to the apes. When he saw the Captain and Churchill he came to pay his respects.

"Mr Churchill you've already met John Baker, our Head of Apes, and I would say one of Franzi's family," said the Captain as he introduced John.

Winston stuck out his hand and shook John's hand vigorously. "Very good to see you again John."

"And you too sir," John replied.

"Can we meet with your charges John," asked Churchill?

John looked at the Captain for approval. The Captain nodded.

"Come this way gentlemen," said John.

He led them to the gate of the enclosure. As they walked down to the entrance the men saw that they were being watched by a small group of children and a striking looking young woman.

"It's Jane with your children and their friends," said Solly.

"I think they've been here for most of the day," said John, "except at mealtimes."

"Franzi, Daisy," he called out as he opened the gate to the enclosure.

Thompson, ever vigilant, noted that the gate had not been bolted nor padlocked.

He instinctively checked for his automatic. Churchill saw the reflex action. "No need Walter, we're among friends here, even the animals."

Thompson relaxed, as did the others.

Franzi and Daisy responded to John's call and wandered across to see the visitors.

Well Daisy did. Franzi couldn't resist putting on a performance. He goose-stepped over, oomph oomphing the German newsreels favourite military march before coming to a halt in front of Churchill, giving the Nazi salute followed by an enormous raspberry.

"This is Franzi," said the Captain.

"Very pleased to meet you," said Winston as they shook hands. "Walter, this is the chap who saved my life."

Thompson's jaw dropped. Franzi turned to him, winked and shook his hand too.

**

Later that day, after dinner, Churchill, Franzi and Jane were in the old army hut at the northeastern edge of the Park.

The Captain had provided them with table and canvas chairs, refreshments and an oil lamp. John had brought down the large easel and blackboard at Franzi's request. Franzi had insisted he be provided with different coloured chalks 'for maps', and a board rubber.

Outside, John stood with the detective constable some way up the path to the zoo to stop anyone coming along. Thompson stationed himself by the hut door and occasionally patrolled around the building.

Franzi stood at the board before Winston and began to sign for Jane to translate.

'Winston, when we met,' Jane's eyes widened "they'd already met," she thought becoming distracted on how that could have happened.

'Oook!' said Franzi sharply, she'd obviously missed what he'd signed next.

"Sorry," she said.

"Never mind my dear, it is quite a lot to take in. I'll tell you about our first meeting someday, if Franzi doesn't," said Churchill.

Franzi blew a raspberry and signed 'Yes don't worry Jane but can we get on please?'

"Of course," she said.

He resumed. 'When we first met we spoke in general broad terms about the conflict to come.'

Churchill nodded.

'I'd like to inform you about specifics that are likely to happen between now and Christmas, things that you, in your likely role, will be able to have an impact on.'

"Am I not to continue as an MP," queried Churchill? "I can't see Chamberlain offering me anything useful to do if we go to war. Sorry, when we go to war."

Franzi nodded and then said 'Let's not get ahead of ourselves or we will lose the plot. By the way I will have this written up for you so you don't forget anything.'

"Pah, as if I would," responded Winston taking a sip of the brandy that the Captain had thoughtfully provided.

Franzi wagged a finger. 'I know how much time you spend on polishing your speeches and even then you forget things sometimes. You can't afford to do that during the war to come.'

"Point taken Franzi, point taken. I'll make sure I've got excellent aides, assistants and secretaries."

'To continue...'

Franzi laid out the major political and military events that were, as he said 'likely' to happen up until the 3 September.

Churchill growled like a bear when he heard of Stalin's duplicity and shook his head sadly when Franzi explained how Poland would be defeated and carved up between Germany and the USSR. Not only that, Russia would take the opportunity to re-acquire the Baltic states and then go on to attack Finland.

'And France and Britain cannot help any of them,' said Franzi.

"So then," asked Churchill?

'Then,' said Franzi 'Chamberlain will form a national government, Conservative in all but name since there'll be precious few people in the cabinet from the opposition parties. You will be appointed First Lord of the Admiralty.'

"What," cried Winston? "Back to the Navy? Wonderful."

'Yes and no,' said Franzi.

"What do you mean?"

'The Royal Navy isn't what it was, Winston. A lot of its power is quite illusory.'

"Come now," Winston began.

'A great deal of the information and advice I'm going to give to you is likely to upset and annoy you. It will challenge, in some cases, your previously held ideas about friends, countries and advisors.'

"I see," said Churchill huffily.

'Be a realist Coppernob, I 'm here to help you win a war, and win it in a way that will stop a great deal of suffering,' said Franzi looking at Jane and her Star of David pendant. 'So are you in?'

"When you put it like that I've no choice, have I?"

The pause and silence between the man and ape was thunderous and significant. Jane was shocked. She knew Churchill by reputation, but she had just seen him put firmly in his place by an orangutan, and what's more she'd voiced the words!

Franzi approached Churchill and offered his hand. Churchill stood and they shook hands before embracing.

Churchill stood back, his eyes were glistening.

'Oook, break out the cigars Winnie and fill up the glasses Jane!'

**

The meeting went on for some time but, by the end of it, Franzi had set out a programme of measures that Churchill could take. They should help to mitigate failings and mistakes of men, strategy, tactics and equipment within the RN. To a small extent they would have a positive impact on the Army, RAF and country in general until such time as Winston was appointed Prime Minister. On that matter Franzi steadfastly refused to commit himself to a date.

Chapter 9

Monday 21st August 1939

Sir Charles Craven, Chairman and Managing Director of Vickers Armstrong, was perplexed.

Some bloody fool called Whyte had written him a letter and given him a headache as a result.

He could understand what was going on in the world, Britain was re-arming as quickly as funds and manufacturing capacity would allow. Whether or not what they produced would do the job remained to be seen.

Whyte made suggestions regarding ship and aircraft that the company might wish to concentrate on, modify improve etc; that made sense. Vickers Armstrong produced aircraft and ships. To a much lesser extent there were tanks, but the companies tank heyday was now in the past. So why was he asking for them to undertake some preparatory work on a mongrel tank design? And why was he saying that in due course the Admiralty, not the Army, would fund the work?

**

"Chief, can I get this straight? God, AOC Fighter Command, has said we're to collect up all the Merlin engines we can and strip the ones off the aircraft he's now withdrawn from operations. Then we have to send them to where?"

"Flight, just get your lads on it," said the WO2 engineer. "It makes no sense to me either but you've got to agree those Defiants wouldn't even stand up to a Gladiator never mind an Me109."

**

Stan Hooker had made the most of the freedom Albert Elliot, Rolls Royce's Chief Engineer to pursue his own projects. He had an inkling what was amiss with the current Merlin and with that, and the information provided by Mr Whyte it had been a relatively easy 'fix'. Now he was keen to look at the supercharger option that had been dropped into his lap!

**

Barnes Wallis had been somewhat miffed when he read Mr Whyte's letter. He was very happy, thank you, working on aircraft designs. Now Mr Whyte had suggested that he should look at providing the RAF with some new bombs. He'd nearly thrown the letter away but then he'd read some of the detail and looked at the drawings. Oh my, what wonderful, effective, cruel and terrifying ordnance Mr Whyte had suggested. He was hooked. Bugger aircraft for the time being.

**

RV had inquired discreetly amongst his friends in the military scientific community to try to determine who else had been contacted by the mysterious Mr Whyte.

Reports came back of odd and out of the ordinary 'happenings' but nothing that could be pinned to any particular source.

Marcus Oliphant hadn't had any further contact but he had shared more of what his team were working on and what Mr Whyte had suggested might be 'interesting'.

Rumours had, somehow, reached Lindeman, Tizard and Watson Watt that someone was orchestrating scientific research direction and they hadn't been consulted. As a consequence the War Office had started some enquiries of their own.

It was early in the process but no one had come up with anything concrete.

**

ACM Freeman had started the process of rationalising aircraft research and development, not without a lot of fuss from some companies. He was expecting to be called in to explain himself to Sir Kingsley very soon. He hoped he'd have some more information from Mr Whyte and his patron or patrons with which to fight his case.

**

Tommy and Frank had been 'tinkering' in their spare time. Admittedly they'd been 'borrowing' GPO equipment and parts to enable their 'hobby' but they didn't consider it stealing as it was still at Dollis Hill, just not where any of the management might think to look.

The information and diagrams provided by Mr Whyte was enabling them to progress well but they were reaching the point where they'd appreciate more input from the 'genius'. Every day now Tommy hoped there might be further information to help him understand more fully what he was creating.

**

Geoffrey was cock-a-hoop over the 'Wooden Wonder' as Mr Whyte had described it.

He'd had a new batch of Merlin's sent over from Rolls Royce courtesy of Stan Hooker. To his delight Hooker's assertion that the new engines had been 'fixed' was, according to his engineers, true.

Geoffrey had given orders to produce and stockpile the new propellers.

Other news had been promising too. Work was progressing faster than expected on the 20 mm cannon the knowledgeable RAF types had been crying out for and they were just the thing for his 'Mosquito'.

**

Frank was a much nicer man to work with now. The whole team agreed he was much more chilled than he had been a couple of weeks ago. He was eating properly and appeared to be rested and refreshed when he came into work.

His vision on the engine design seemed to have crystallised and the problems they'd been experiencing with vibration and power surges had been remedied.

Strangely team members had caught him surreptitiously looking at a sheaf of papers that had come in a letter at the end of July. Odder than that, he'd been seen stroking a lock of reddish ginger hair and smiling.

**

Whipsnade - Tuesday 22nd August 1939

Franzi missed Jane. They'd parted with hugs on Sunday evening and Solly had promised to bring her back on the following Friday. She still had her work in Oxford until Churchill was appointed First Lord of the Admiralty, at which time he would re-activate the WRNS and have Jane enlisted and commissioned as soon as decently possible. In the interim Winston had asked Thompson to get her file from the War Office and check on her security status. She and her family were aliens and soon to be 'enemy aliens' at that. He'd have to ensure nothing interrupted her role as Franzi's 'mouthpiece' nor let anything distract her. That meant he had to look after her family too. Thinking about it they might be very useful in themselves. They had contacts throughout Europe in the precious metals and gems sector who might be able, with the right assistance, to provide valuable information.

**

The Captain had been a little grumpy on Monday. The news broke about the Nazi-Soviet Trade Agreement and he thought Franzi should have given him a tip-off. Their meeting last night had been less convivial than normal. It wasn't helped because Franzi had to revert to the chalkboard to communicate.

Franzi needed to have a talk with the Captain this evening and clear the air. He also needed to discuss arrangements to have a permanent 'office' of his own setup. He hoped funds could be found to refurbish the old army hut and put some sort of barrier in place to stop people wandering in. It may well be that more effective security would be needed but he'd work that out in a joint meeting with Winston and the Captain.

As soon as dusk fell he was off to have a brief chat with Lucy and then on to the 'House'.

Lucy had taken to Jane and vice versa. All the children liked her.

He climbed in through her open window and they greeted each other, as usual, with a big hug.

Lucy gave him an apple and then said, "Jane was talking to you, wasn't she?"

Franzi shrugged his shoulders.

"She was, I know it. I saw your hands and hers yesterday."

'Ook' 'Well,' he chalked 'you got us. It's a big secret though.'

She smiled. "Like those letters I bet?"

'Ook' he nodded vigorously.

"I've not told anyone. Don't worry," she said in hushed tones.

'I never thought you would,' he replied.

"Do you think she could teach me so I can talk to you like that?" she said, excitedly.

Franzi tipped his head to one side and considered.

'What a brilliant idea!'

**

Franzi took a long draw on the cigar that the Captain had provided. He'd noticed his orangutan friend preferred them and had scrounged a number from Churchill before he departed late Saturday night. The local tobacconist in Dunstable didn't have anything approaching the quality that Churchill smoked but the Captain hoped Franzi would be happy if that was all he could get.

Franzi was standing at the big blackboard, he found he had more room to write before his train of thought was interrupted by having to wipe the board clean.

'Cap,' he wrote, 'sorry about the Trade Pact. I've decided that, if Mr Churchill agrees, I'll give you notice of imminent developments. I know you've not asked me but I need someone I can trust to talk to here and now. What do you think?'

"Franzi, I'm not sure I should be privy to secrets," said the Captain.

'They're not secrets if they're going to be in the newspaper tomorrow, eh?'

"Point taken," said the Captain. "I'm happy to be of service however it helps."

'Good. Well, tomorrow people are going to be very excited because Hitler and Stalin are signing a non-aggression pact."

"Oh Wahala!" cried the Captain.

**

Whipsnade - Wednesday 23rd August 1939

Franzi took a day off just to enjoy being with Daisy. He needed to clarify ideas in his head and just fooling around with her or indulging in mutual grooming was calming and conducive to contemplative thought.

He'd typed up as much as he'd dared about 'things to do' and sketched what he could to start the development of better equipment. He gave the orangutan equivalent of a sigh, but there's only so much you can with a pencil and A5 notepad.

He planned to ask Jane to talk to Lucy about learning sign language, hopefully, they could provide her with a simple book on the subject.

People came to see the orangutan that made fun of Hitler but went away disappointed. Perhaps, Franzi thought, when things had changed and the country was locked down and needing a morale boost he might reprise his act.

As the sun beat down he and Daisy sought shade and retreated to their respective huts. Gentle snoring from inside her shelter told him she'd dozed off. He'd quite like to himself but something was troubling him beside the provision of advice on weapons, organisation and tactics. Yes, they were all things that needed to be addressed and, when Churchill became PM, he was sure he could guide him to put things motion. In the interim he had to make best use of the Admiralty. Ships. Aircraft. Men. All to be made as effective as they could be before April 1940. Prioritise AA capability. Refit certain vessels. Beach unsuitable commanders.

Franzi chewed on a tasty branch, considered a cigarette and then dismissed the idea. Although he had a good supply he liked the cigars better. Now where was he? Oh yes, supply. If departments and companies didn't do what they were asked to do it would be a nightmare. Winston had to have the right people in place to push through the new designs and production. Heaven forbid that they didn't produce enough .303 ammunition or produce too many obsolete tanks, anti-tank rifles and guns or that too many 2 in and 3 in mortars would be made, but not the bombs they used. Worse still that they'd continue turning out unsuitable death trap aircraft which had then to be found roles to fulfil to ensure backsides were covered (but only after many brave men had died proving the point). An all the while not telling Winston what was really going on.

No, he'd have to ensure that his knowledge of people either to put them in the right place or moved them if they were cocking things up – and faster than Churchill might otherwise have the information to act.

He felt another list coming on and reached for his notebook and pencil.

**

"Nothing yet about Hitler and Stalin," said the Captain to Franzi.

Franzi luxuriated in 'his chair' in the Captain's study and took a sip of brandy before chalking, 'If you were in Whitehall at the minute you'd see them running around like headless chickens wondering how they'd got it wrong.'

"I bet," agreed the Captain.

'Now to business,' wrote Franzi. 'I need more room to work, more room and drawing boards, pencils, pens, rules, geometry and design tools.'

"I see," said the Captain a little puzzled. "Why, exactly?"

'I have to have the content ready to coach the people who need help.'

"But surely you're just passing information to Mr Churchill so he can get the government to act?"

'Yes and, er, no.' scribed Franzi before cleaning the slate.

"Franzi, what are you up to?" asked the Captain sternly. "Who else have you been upsetting?"

Franzi blew a small raspberry.

'Cap you don't have to worry. I've not done anything to get myself found out or bring anyone here.'

"But….."

'Too secret, can't tell you. Winston knows anyway. Told him you see?'

"Right. So what is it you're after?"

'Well if Winston and you agree and we can get the funds and kit together, my own office, so to speak.'

"For heaven's sake…"

'I know it's not going to be easy but it'll be fine when he's First Lord of the Admiralty on the 3rd of September.'

The Captain opened his mouth to express surprise at the revelation then quietly mouthed 'Oh Wahala' before downing the remaining contents of his glass.

**

Whipsnade - Thursday 24th August 1939

Churchill responded to Franzi's request for a meeting the same day.

By 6 pm they were ensconced in the old army hut once more and ready for business.

Winston had pulled a few strings and Jane had been collected from Oxford by a Special Branch officer and driven to Whipsnade in time for tea with the Beals.

She took up her position in the room so she could see Franzi and address Churchill.

Thompson and a police driver accompanied the Boss and took up their guarding positions with John Baker after he'd accompanied Franzi through the Park.

"So," signed Franzi, "You've had time now to think on what we discussed before and the 'plan'. Any thoughts?"

"I think the thrust of our strategy is good. I'm concerned that you don't think we can get the French to up their game and stop the Germans. Being kicked off the Continent makes it so much harder to strike back," rumbled Winston.

Franzi bobbed his head sagely. "I know," he said, "but where would you begin?" They have to block or counter the German thrust through the Ardennes. The study they themselves commissioned said in 38 that it was possible to move an armoured force through the forest. They sacked the author and posted him off to the sticks. Do you think they'll take notice of you?"

Churchill sipped his brandy. "I suppose you're right. So you still think the best we can do is get our Expeditionary Force out intact and some French troops?"

"I do. Intact and with equipment after giving the Germans a bloody nose," said Franzi. "That's not why I asked to meet today though."

"Ah. More information? Or advice?" asked Churchill.

"Both. First though can we ask Captain Beal to join us to address some domestic arrangements?"

"By all means," said Winston and then shouted, "Thompson, ask Captain Beal to join us please."

**

After pleasantries had been exchanged, glasses filled or refilled and cigars and pipe lit Franzi began.

"The Captain and I discussed my needs in respect of a design office yesterday. It is not something the Park can address on its own. I need specialist materials to create designs and plans. I need someone to help me and to ensure security is as good as it can be while ever I work on such things here. The Captain and I both agreed it needs your involvement and input."

Churchill looked at both ape and man and slowly nodded before responding.

"I can see that you have far more in that head of yours than just general information about the war to come and what we need for the sake of

Freedom, to make it available to everyone who needs it. However, we mustn't compromise your security."

The Captain sighed, just what he'd told Franzi himself.

"I see this as perhaps a temporary measure until you are Prime Minister."

"Ah yes, and when will that be again," asked Winston?

Franzi produced a corking raspberry, "Good try Copperknob."

Jane blushed as she watched Franzi enact the signs for the nickname and she translated.

The Captain chuckled as he watched ape and statesman exchange insults and wondered who had the wisest head.

Churchill chuckled too.

"I thought you might establish a small Royal Marine training establishment here on the 4th of September. At least then I can work on their training and they can guard me," said Franzi.

Churchill looked at the Captain. "What do you think?"

"It's certainly possible," he replied. "We have plenty of room in the area."

"And what about this 'office' set up?"

"If you can supply funds and some willing hands I can't think of any objections. I'm sure Solly can source the materials and equipment Franzi has asked for."

"Good, that's settled then," signed Franzi. He reached for an envelope and passed it to Winston.

Then signed, "Specifics about the German fleet when war starts.

You don't need to worry about Admiral Scheer, she's in port having a refit.

Admiral Hipper is in the Baltic on gunnery trials.

Scharnhorst and Gneisenau aren't ready for sea.

Graf Spee and Deutschland and U-Boats have been ordered to take up their wartime positions. From there they'll begin their cruises."

Churchill and the Captain's eyes widened. This was very detailed information.

"And whilst you're taking that in I have to tell you that Pact Hitler and Stalin signed yesterday isn't just about 'non-aggression'. It is a full-blown military agreement. Poland is to be carved up and the Baltic States taken back into Mother Russia!"

**

London - Friday 25th August 1939

Halifax cornered Churchill in the Members Bar at lunchtime before the sitting for the day began.

"I'm surprised Winston, that you weren't here last night to vote on the Emergency Powers Act," he said slyly.

"Indeed Edward," Churchill replied, "I had it on good authority that it would breeze through. Which it did, of course."

There was no love lost between the two politicians. Halifax had been a principal supporter of Chamberlain's policy of appeasement. His change of heart was recent and Churchill distrusted his motives with every fibre of his political being.

"Now that's out of the way and are hands are not tied by any legislation we can get on with really preparing the country," said Halifax.

Churchill considered his response. Franzi had briefed him on the wrangling that was going on within the Conservative Party and how the Opposition Parties, although in a weak position, were prepared to use their clout with Tory 'hawks' (as Franzi termed them) to bring about a National Government. He knew that his appointment to the Admiralty was a 'sop' to these interest groups so he'd better not bugger it up by annoying Halifax too much now.

'Bide my time,' he thought. 'Revenge will be sweet when I'm PM.'

"I agree Edward but," and he couldn't resist a small dig despite himself, "it would have been better not to have soiled our Worldwide reputation by letting Czechoslovakia down eh?"

Halifax hardly reacted to the jibe.

'So skilful a snake,' thought Winston.

"Time and tide Winston, time and tide. We're much better prepared now," replied Halifax. He went on, "On that note, there is a feeling your services might be required. Would you be interested?"

'Steady boy,' thought Winston, 'not too eager now.'

"I think that I'd be honoured. In the right role of course. Any idea what Neville's considering?"

"Not really."

'Lying bastard,' thought Winston.

"Well let me know when you can. I'm staying up in town for the present so I'm available any time."

"I'll call you when I know anything," said Halifax. "I've got to pop off now and see Clement."

**

Lucy came to see Franzi and Daisy every day. Most evenings Franzi dropped in to see her. He'd begun teaching her signing. She was a quick learner. She was looking forward to being with Jane and learning more.

The staff and families of the Park were a mixed bunch. Local country people, Londoners and some people who'd worked overseas. It was a harmonious group where people fitted into their various roles without much debate.

Captain Beale had received a letter from Dr Vevers asking him to make preparations to house more people in the event of war. The Board had decided that they should look after their staff and families and evacuate as many as possible to the Park. Old huts were to be repaired and made habitable and new ones were promised. He made a mental note to make certain none were put near 'Franzi's HQ' as Gladys had Christened it when he'd told her about the plan. He also had to ensure there was a path from it to the land that he believed might be suitable for the Marines Camp. He must ask Franzi how many Marines were going to be needed to 'guard' him.

The work was growing by the day as Franzi came out with more 'revelations' on how conditions in Britain were likely to be during the war and that the coming Winter was due to be a 'bad one'.

**

Whipsnade - Saturday 26th August 1939

Solly and Jane arrived at lunchtime on Saturday. They'd spent the morning in Oxford buying some of the materials Franzi had requested for his office.

After lunch John had led Franzi, to the thrill of the visitors, around the Park before sneaking away through the House's back garden and down to the HQ.

Franzi was delighted to see Jane and Solly and the equipment they'd brought.

'It's all taking shape now,' he signed to the Captain and the visitors.

"Glad you're pleased with what we acquired," said Solly.

"You seem to have got most of the things Franzi asked for," said the Captain.

"Couldn't get some of the things in the jalopy. I wondered if John might be able to drive back to Oxford tomorrow afternoon in one of your vans and collect the big drawing boards?"

"I can't see why not," replied the Captain.

'Good,' said Franzi, 'Now that's settled can you all buzz off please and leave me to my typing?'

"Yes Sir! Of course Sir!" said Solly laughing. "Be careful though it's not a new typewriter."

"And the previous owner said it had 'foibles'," said Jane.

"I'll get John to stand guard Franzi," said the Captain, "We'll be back around 1700, if that's alright with you?"

Franzi's only response was a loud raspberry as he pulled a piece of paper from the folio and loaded it up.

"Well we'll be going then," said the Captain.

"See you later Franzi," said Jane.

**

Franzi was pleased with his work. He had more information for Churchill that could be sent to London so that Fleet dispositions could be optimised and work begun on the Marine Commandos, their training and equipment. He wondered whether he'd gone over the top with his small 'training and guard' force. Perhaps 400 men was a little ambitious but he wanted some of them to be ready for an operation in October and the others to be operational by April.

Hm, he thought, best get Churchill working on the secondment of officers from the Army too and to set up his 'toyshop' initially as a naval operation.

Busy busy, and communications were so damned slow! How long did it take to get people back to England from Egypt by boat if the RAF wouldn't play ball? Now there's a thing, could he swing some Sunderland's from Coastal

Command? They were very touchy about their relationship with the RN. Winston would have to use some charm with Frederick Bowhill. It should help that the Air Chief Marshall had been in the RNAS but... Failing that it shouldn't be too hard to get hold of a couple of Short Empires. At least they could move troops around faster than normal. Their range of just over 600 nautical miles was a limitation and it wouldn't be possible to fit more than 16 troopers and their gear aboard after adding some defensive capability. He wondered how Imperial Airways would react to Churchill requisitioning aircraft?

He sat back from his typing and considered his next moves with his 'correspondents'. They were due some more prompts and also a letter from Winston dated 3 September to assure them they had support and access to Admiralty funds if they couldn't get their normal 'masters' to allow them to pursue the R&D needed. Now that would ruffle a few feathers thought Franzi, and lead to the inevitable conflict with the Prof!

Chapter 10

Whipsnade - Thursday 31st August 1939

Franzi and the Captain were in a sombre mood. They sat in their usual chairs in the Study, brandy glasses full, pipe and cigar lit, and considered the news on the radio. Stuart Hibberd spoke, as always, in his measured tones, about the mobilisation of the Royal Navy and the call up of the Army and Royal Air Force reserves. He continued, "the government today has issued an order to evacuate civilians from cities and towns that are likely targets for enemy bombing."

"Well that's it then," said the Captain.

'Oook.'

**

De Havilland Works - Friday 1st September 1939

De Havilland was open-mouthed. He had mixed feelings. How could someone have got hold of the current plans for the 'Mosquito' and then how had that someone produced an amended set. Here were full details of performance, drag, speed, wing angle tweaking, undercarriage changes (with reasons why they were necessary) tailplane problems and the solution, slots and wing-root fairings fitted to the forward fuselage and leading edge of the radiator intakes to reduce, the annotation said, vibration. Another page covered the cannon and machine gun installations and operational issues, whilst another addressed bomb loading, internal long-range fuel tanks, and torpedoes. Torpedoes for heaven's sake!

He picked up the tuft of reddish-brown hair and the note that had come in the large package. This note was typed and the signature in ink with a postscript handwritten in ink.

'PS. I have taken the liberty of contacting ACM Freeman, Phillip Gant at the Ordnance Board, Barnes Wallace at Vickers, and Stan Hooker at Rolls Royce and suggested you all get together for a project meeting. I'm sure ACM Freeman will be able to expedite production of the revised aircraft as per my information to you and the other gentlemen detailed above. We must ensure the orders are placed to enable at least four squadrons are fully operational by April next year.

Yours sincerely,

F Whyte.'

"Peggy," he shouted, "please ask Charles and Eric to come and see me after lunch. Get Geoffrey and John to join us too."

"Yes sir."

"And get me Air Chief Marshall Freeman at the Air Ministry please?"

**

Whipsnade, Saturday 2nd September 1939

Franzi's HQ was now full of office and design paraphernalia, so much so it was crowded with only three people in it. The Captain had commented to Gladys that far from being 'a study' for Franzi it had become a full-blown command centre. All it needed now was a telephone exchange and despatch riders!

Given the restrictions on room and the fact that Churchill had informed him that there would be two more attendees at the 'Council of Pre-war' the Captain had set up his Study for the meeting.

**

Winston had pondered the question raised by Franzi for some time. Who could act as the conduit between Franzi, the military, and scientific worlds?

When it came to scientists and their ilk Winston had deferred to Franzi and his knowledge. That individual had already been contacted by Franzi.

The military choice was a bit of a headache. He and Franzi drew up a shortlist, considered some people, dismissed them and then started again.

Whoever they chose had to be senior enough and experienced enough to command respect with the three Service Chiefs and their respective commands? Several candidates were already committed to their Service roles in the build-up to war, including Bertram Ramsey, Alan Brooke, and Arthur Tedder. Franzi and Winston were eventually agreed that only one man would do, and rank would be no problem at all!

**

Winston had taken a gentle approach with their military choice, he was excitable, enthusiastic, opinionated and brilliant. What Winston didn't know was whether his view on the world could safely encompass an orangutan who seemingly possessed more knowledge than the Delphic oracle and didn't talk in riddles. Thank goodness he wasn't a bible basher or tea-totaller but he did still smoke those awful Navy Cut cigarettes rather than a civilised cigar!

**

Franzi knew who was expected and had made briefing notes accordingly. He wanted to touch on the key elements of the war to win and how they'd use the Admiralty to take the first steps to do so.

He didn't want to scare them or Winston. He wasn't sure exactly what Winston thought about him or the full potential of his 'Red Ape'. He'd let the man get his feet under the table first back at the Admiralty and then prepare him for the role of PM and Commander in Chief by degrees before the Nazi hammer fell on Norway and Denmark.

As an act of kindness Franzi had fully briefed Jane on who was coming to the meeting and what their roles were to be. She was not as flustered as she might have been before meeting Churchill and Franzi – nothing much could surprise her after that.

**

The Captain greeted the visitors at his door. Churchill, RV Jones and an older man dressed in an immaculate suit. After introductions were made and hands shaken he showed them into his study. He stood back to shut the door behind them.

"No, no Bill," said Winston. "It's your house, and I'm sure there's no harm in you hearing today's plans."

"If you are sure Sir?" said the Captain.

"Indeed I am," said Winston smiling, "and I'm Winston, not 'Sir'."

The Captain nodded and followed them in.

"Plus," said Churchill," If Jane is signing we need someone to keep the brandy flowing eh?" he laughed.

**

Both of Churchill's invitees stood stock still as they caught sight of Franzi when he moved from behind the large blackboard and easel. Their mouths fell open but neither showed any fear.

It had been a calculated move on Winston's part, in agreement with Franzi, that neither should be told who they were going to meet and be working for. The chances were high that they might have thought Churchill had lost his sanity if he'd explained how he was taking counsel from an orangutan who just happened to have travelled independently to Chartwell and stopped three IRA assassins from killing him.

Franzi stood still and opened his arms wide before signing,

'Welcome Admiral Keyes. Welcome RV. My name is Franzi Whyte. Please come in and take a seat. Rum Admiral? Gin sling RV?"

**

'Thank you for accepting our invitation to this meeting,' signed Franzi as he gestured towards Churchill.

Roger Keyes raised an eyebrow at this and looked to his friend for confirmation that he and 'Franzi' were equal partners in this endeavour.

Churchill nodded and smiled.

Franzi went on, 'I know RV that you've probably been puzzling over my correspondence and the information it contained. I hope you've had enough time now to confirm the broad thrust of the scientific strategy it set out?'

"I certainly have Franzi," replied RV. "I found out you'd written to Marcus at Birmingham too."

Franzi laughed, 'I thought your inquiring mind would start trying to piece together who was involved. Did you discover which other scientists and engineers I've written to?'

RV shook his head, "Not yet, but I suppose I can stop searching now?"

'You can. You and I will discuss that separately.'

"Thank you."

'Admiral, or may I call you Roger?' asked Franzi.

A broad smile broke across the craggy face of the old warrior.

"Since you're on first name terms with this old reprobate," he said, indicating Churchill, "I can't see why not."

'Ook.'

"See here Roger, not so much of the reprobate please," said Winston.

"You don't object to being called old then?"

"Sadly, Roger, that is a fact of life for both of us. We've got the scars to prove it. We've also got the experience needed to steer the Empire through the coming storm."

"If we can get into power and convince the fools to follow us it might not be too late to salvage something from the mess," replied Roger, "they've not listened to us so far."

"Franzi, please explain to Roger the mystery of knowledge you've brought us at the eleventh hour," said Churchill sombrely.

'Gentlemen, and lady,' Franzi began as he crossed to the large blackboard and took up his chalk. 'Germany will not leave Poland now they have invaded. They trust that we and France will back down as Chamberlain and Daladier did last year.'

A growl of disapproval came from Churchill and Keyes.

Franzi paused for a moment and looked into the eyes of both men and nodded.

'A shameful thing to do,' he said. 'If they had stood firm Hitler would have backed down. That being said if Britain and France had shown backbone over the Rhineland Hitler would not have continued his territorial demands. He may well have been brought down by more reasonable politicians and generals. As it is now he firmly believes he is the great strategist and architect of the Third Reich, infallible, unstoppable.'

'He is wrong about Britain and France backing down this time. You did not know this for certain when you came here today. You may have hoped it would be the case or wondered if Chamberlain might have caved in. I can tell you, with certainty, that at 11 am tomorrow Britain will declare war on Germany.'

A sob caught in Jane's throat as she ended Franzi's sentence.

He signed to her, 'It'll be alright.'

He hoped that would be true for her and her family. He couldn't guarantee that. He couldn't guarantee that by some fluke or twist of fate that all of them in the room would not survive the conflict.

"But we will prevail?" asked the Captain.

'Nothing in the multiverse,' "Have I got that right Franzi?" asked Jane.

He nodded. 'Nothing in the multiverse is ever certain. BUT I know the knowledge I have should stop the Nazi and Red Monsters from hurting this world in the way that they might otherwise do if I was not here. Knowing what I know, with the people in this room, we should change the future.'

Silence fell on the meeting.

Then Franzi made them all jump as he let out a tremendous raspberry.

'We'll beat the bastards hollow. Now fill the glasses Cap, and I'll set out the plan!

**

Keyes and RV sat quietly through the presentation. Churchill added his comments as Franzi painted the broad approach to defeating Hitler. How the aim was to implement a cohesive strategy that worked, improve tactics at all levels of the armed forces, improve weapons currently deployed, ensure the research and design of new weapons was focused, set production targets and implement changes in manufacture, management and labour practices to match new techniques to maximise the output of effective equipment. He detailed changes needed in training, in organisation, in all arms collaboration in operations and the interdependency of air and ground forces. The necessity to ensure the men and women on the sharp end had the highest morale and commitment to the new ways.

He touched briefly on how the Admiralty was going to spearhead the changes in the armed forces.

'This won't be easy,' he said. 'Vested interests in the Navy, Army and Airforce are going to fight like hell to stop us. They'll use every trick in the book – and some that aren't, every contact they have with influence to block our way. We have to be as stealthy as a python creeping up on a wild boar. We must use a cloak of deceit until we can't be stopped and the political situation changes next year.'

"And," said Winston, "we need to get together a team of all talents to make this happen.'

'Ook,' nodded Franzi and went on, 'Roger, I need you to smooth the way with the Joint Chiefs to ensure we get what we need from them.'

Roger cleared his throat. "You're saying I have to be as deferential as a new middy eh? Not easy for me as you must know," Franzi blew a raspberry. "Yes quite. But if it gets us what we want and stops Hitler it's fine by me."

'Precisely. I won't be easy I know. Maybe no surprise entrances in full dress uniform eh?'

Keyes and Churchill laughed.

"That really put the wind up the politicians," commented Winston.

'To continue,' said Franzi, 'It'll be hard poaching some resources but in a lot of instances the people we're trying to recruit aren't liked by their own service. Equipment may be harder as they'll be trying to hang on to everything.'

"Don't worry gentlemen, I'll make sure we get what's needed," said Keyes.

"And me, Franzi, what am I doing in all this?" asked RV.

'A thankless task,' said Franzi. 'You know the personalities and prima donnas in the scientific fields of Britain and the Empire.'

"I do. I've suffered at the hands of a number of them."

'Well, they'll have to be brought on board or side-lined. The latter can't be done until next year in any effective manner. With respect to the former, the team I've chosen are quite formidable. I believe I can mentor them, with your help. I know I can show up any detractors as absolute fools if they try to derail our plan.' Franzi looked at Winston, 'Including the Prof, despite him being one of your main supporters during your time in the wilderness.'

Churchill nodded. "You opened my eyes fully concerning the Prof. I wouldn't like to see him humiliated though."

RV looked at Franzi and Winston. 'Well,' he thought, 'if the Prof is under control it should be the same with his other tormentors.'

'You've also got to continue your own work,' said Franzi, 'so I suggest you pick a couple of capable assistants.'

"I have some people in mind," RV replied.

'I'm sure they'll be fine. However, despite the highest level of security clearance certain individuals have, I have to break it to you that currently, some people aren't what they seem to be,' said Franzi.

Churchill gave Franzi a shocked look. They hadn't discussed this before.

"Nazi's or sympathisers?" he asked.

'Nazi's and Stalin's spies.'

"Good God man," Keyes exclaimed.

'Don't worry,' reassured Franzi, waving his arms in a placatory manner. 'They can't do much harm where they are now. And I've got a list here which can be given to the Director of Naval Intelligence after your appointment tomorrow Winston. The problem after that is how we deal with or use them.'

"I see," said Winston. "Roger, can I leave that matter in your hands tomorrow, please? I might be rather busy"

"Winston, I have no position or standing in the Navy. What's happening tomorrow apart from war breaking out?"

"Ah yes, didn't tell you that. Franzi informed me I'll be appointed First Lord of the Admiralty just after midnight tonight. So don't worry about being appointed as something or other on my staff."

Keyes jaw dropped once more at yet another surprise.

"And that reminds me, young lady," said Winston turning to Jane, "You'll be called up to the WRNS when they're re-established in the morning. Duty base Whipsnade Shore Establishment."

**

The Toyshop Team - Monday 4th September 1939

"Lt Macrae letter for you sir," said Corporal Arkwright.

"Thanks for that," replied Stuart Macrae. "Official or private?"

"Looks very official sir. And Major Curtiss has asked you to report to his office once you've read it."

"Right oh."

Macrae pushed his sketch aside and tore open the envelope.

'Interesting, now what could the Admiralty be wanting with him?'

**

"Milli the Colonel has asked if you can report to him at once," said Lieutenant Gray.

"What's eating his nibs today, James?" asked the Major.

"No idea sir. He did sound a bit tetchy though, muttered something about 'proper channels'."

"I'd best get along sharpish then."

..

"What's this all about Jefferis?" demanded the Colonel.

"Pardon me, sir, but to what are you referring?"

"Bloody Admiralty requesting your services. You've been seconded and without a by your leave. Who've you been talking to? Eh?"

"I'm sorry sir, you have me at a disadvantage. I don't know of anyone in the Admiralty or the Andrew but since yesterday prior knowledge of what someone did before can be a little outdated."

"So you've not asked for a transfer or been talking to anyone about your 'odd ideas' for weapons and such?"

"No sir. I wouldn't do anything like that without discussing it with you first," said Jefferis trying to keep a straight face. Inside he was delighted, to get away from his GSO2 duties and the Colonel would be wonderful.

"Quite right, quite right. Well I've no say in the matter, nor, it seems, do you? You're to report to Bletchley Manor on Wednesday at 0800," said the Colonel, waving an order chit.

"Does it say to whom sir?" asked Jefferis innocently.

"See for yourself man," said the Colonel throwing the missive at the major.

"Thank you, sir," said Jefferis as he scooped up the letter. "I'll shoot off and hand over my work to Captain Tomkins."

"Indeed."

"It's been a pleasure to serve under your command sir," said Jefferis trying not to sound smugly satisfied.

**

"Sir?"

"Yes Hughes," replied Lt Cdr Goodeve.

"Special delivery from the Admiralty sir, by despatch rider sir."

"I see," said Goodeve taking the envelope and tearing it open straight away.

He quickly scanned the order, Report Bletchley Park 0800 Wednesday 6 September. Ensure you bring all you research papers you are currently officially working on and also your papers on miscellaneous projects you're working on unofficially."

He looked up and noticed Hughes was hovering. The right thing to do would be to chew his ear off for hanging about when he had work to do but Charles wasn't that sort of officer.

Hughes looked at him expectantly.

"I'm summoned," said Goodeve. "I'll need your help to pack all my papers. Start with those files on magnetic fields and degaussing. I'll go along and see Captain Keith and see if he's had a signal too."

"Will you be wanting me to come along too sir?" asked Hughes.

"Not this time Hughes, thank you,"

"Are you being posted sir?"

"Your guess is as good as mine. I'll let you know. If I am I'll see if there's a need for you there."

"Thank you, sir, that's very kind."

**

"Here's a thing, Neville,"

"What's that Charles?"

"Letter from the Admiralty."

"Ah, they've taken notice, have they? I said they would."

"Well yes and no. It's nothing to do with the torpedo."

"Really, then what?"

"A curt summons to report to Bletchley Park tomorrow at 8 am and meet with Admiral Keyes and a number of other experts."

"Admiral Keyes?" asked Neville.

"Yes, that one Zeebrugge and all that."

"I suppose you'll be going then?"

"I suppose I will," replied Charles Burney.

**

Cairo, Egypt - 4th September 1939

General Officer Commanding-in-Chief Middle East Command, Archibald Wavell, sat and scrutinised the signal he'd received from Ironside, CIGS, and sighed.

In one way it solved a problem yet in another it created two more. Sending O'Connor home was a mixed blessing. He'd done wonders with the 6th Division in Merah Matruh. He did have an annoying habit of coming up with radical proposals for the defence of Egypt and taking the war to the Italians if they took advantage of Hitler's bellicose attitude to the Entente. O'Connor also got on well with Hobart, as well as anyone could with the weird Fuller enthusiast, and they both plotted and planned about using an all-arms approach to war.

Gort proposed sending Montgomery our to replace the two Generals and advised that, in his view, such a move would 'ginger up' the troops in Egypt even more than they had been.

'It might all be for the best,' thought Wavell as he reached for a signal chit and shouted for his ADC.

"Edwards, get this sent off to O'Connor and Hobart at once. Arrange for a flying boat to pick them up and get them back to England as soon as possible. Priority one."

"Sir."

**

Beauly, Ross-shire - 4th September 1939

"Shimi, I've an odd one for you and I'm minded to let you decide since it's a request, not an order," said The Honourable Archiebad Leslie- Melville, CO of the Lovat Scouts.

"Who's it from Archie?" asked Simon Lovat.

"No less a person that Admiral Keyes VC."

Shimi let out a low whistle, "What have I done to deserve his attention?"

"I've no idea, but see for yourself. This arrived first thing by despatch rider from Invergordon."

Simon read through the signal and then turned to Melville, "Well, who'd have thought the RN would want specialist combat instructors?"

"Aye, and for land operations."

"Maybe it's just for raids?" Shimi ventured.

"Not much call for ghillie suits and stalking in raids. Snipers, well maybe."

"It is interesting though."

"You see it's not just you they're wanting to second but instructors too?"

"Yes. I'm game, if only to find out what they're intending to do. What do you think?"

"Ach well I can't see much harm in it at the moment. I can always put pressure on to get you back. Leave me the best instructors though."

"I will. I'll take a couple of the mad corporals we seem to have, Rob Mac Feegle and his brother Billie."

"And now you've proved to me that you are indeed smitten with the Lovat curse of madness," laughed Melville.

"They're wonderfully useful though," said Shimi, "Rob 'Anybody' is the greatest scrounger and improviser I've seen. And who would take on the 'Big Yan' in a fight or trial of endurance."

"You're right man, but you're welcome to them," said Melville as he continued to laugh. "Get yersel off and them too, to the Zoo Park at Whipsnade I see."

Chapter 11

Whipsnade - Tuesday 5th September 1939

Marines, lots of marines were arriving at Whipsnade. Six trucks disturbed the tranquil village. The men's banter and singing causing raised eyebrows and much tut-tutting from certain villagers.

Fortunately, they didn't seem to be staying and the convoy drove off toward the Zoo Park. Word soon came back to especially cheer the heart of one man in the village, Thomas Watson, Landlord of the Chequers Inn. The rumour was the Marines were setting up a permanent camp. Better give Benson's Brewery a call and get more beer in!

**

The first marines debussed from their trucks and followed the orders bawled at them by their corporals and sergeants to 'Fall In!'

"Cloughie, would you look at that," said Marine Flanagan out of the side of his mouth in his 'rich' Fermanagh accent. "I've never seen so much gold braid on a uniform."

"Flanagan, will you shush man, that's the bloody Admiral himself," replied Lance Corporal Clough.

"Attention!" barked Colour Sergeant Bourne.

Keyes stood on a small mound on the hillside and addressed the marines.

"You have been chosen as the best of the best of the Royal Marines. Your time here at Whipsnade Camp will see if that's true. You will have the best the Navy can give you to prepare you for your role. It will be very hard, make no mistake many of you will be returned to your unit. If you pass out from this training and that which you'll get afterwards you will be 'Royal Marine Commandos'. The first of your kind. Able to take on any enemy, anywhere. Your Officers," said Keyes looking at the assembled Majors, Captains and Lieutenants, "will be expected to be as good as you in all roles as a combat marine. They will have the same training you have, the same rigours, no special treatment for leave or passes. They will use the same weapons you all will use and be as proficient as an ordinary marine. If they fail, like you, they will be returned to their unit. Until they pass out from training they will drop one rank."

An audible sigh went up from some officers. Smiles plastered the faces of a number of other ranks.

"No man's record will be adversely affected if he is returned to unit from Commando selection and training," said Keyes to reassure the assembled marines.

"So, your first task is to establish HMS Whipsnade by building it. Until you complete it you will live in tents as if on a field exercise. You have one week until the balance of the 400 marines arrives."

"One week," groaned Flanagan, "and us to build for 400 men. I bet that Admiral isn't staying with us here in a tent."

"You there," said Keyes, pointing at Flanagan.

"Now you've gone and done it," said Clough.

"Me sir?" said Flanagan.

"Yes, you Marine."

"Sir!"

"Repeat what you just said to the Lance Corporal."

"I'd rather not sir," said Flanagan.

"But I insist," said Keyes.

Flanagan gulped, "I wondered where the Admiral might be staying whilst we build the camp."

"Close enough, I suppose," said Keyes. "To answer your question, I'll be staying here with you all, in a tent, on the same rations as you."

"I always said you were a proper gentleman and hero," replied Flanagan.

"Quite," said Keyes, with a smile playing on his lips. "Major Palfrey?"

"Sir?" responded the senior Marine officer at Whipsnade.

"Extra rum ration all around for the men tonight."

∗∗

'Roger, have there been any problems with the 'Toyshop' Team being released,' signed Franzi to Keyes.

Keyes shook his head, "None at all. No one is quite sure what's going on. Some 'optimists' are hoping that the Poles can pull something out of the bag or that we'll make peace once the dust settles."

'Unfortunately, that's not going to happen.'

"I agree."

'RV, are you now happy I can come with you to Bletchley tomorrow?'

"I wouldn't say 'happy', nor is Winston but we can both appreciate your reasoning. You can field the tricky questions that your notes don't cover," replied Jones.

'I'll be listening where they can't see me and note down responses you can have when you take a break.'

"You're such a valuable asset you should be hidden away behind so much security and 'smoke' that your existence and location is as mysterious as Atlantis," said Keyes.

'Oook ook ook,' laughed Franzi, 'it just so happens I could tell you where that is, if you're interested?'

"Franzi please, we've enough with getting on with the war," replied Keyes.

"Maybe after the war," said RV.

Keyes looked at RV sharply, "Don't encourage him RV please," he pleaded.

It was, to Keyes mind, an odd setup but in the two days they'd been working together they'd meshed well as a team. The hours had been very long and he'd spent some time back in London at the Admiralty sending missives hither and yon to pull together the people Franzi said they needed. He'd also set in motion the use of properties the length and breadth of the UK for the use of their military and scientists.

Winston had ensured the Fleet dispositions were optimised in accordance with Franzi's information.

Poor Jane was very tired. She'd kept pace with Franzi for most of the time but when she couldn't keep her eyes open Franzi had reverted to the blackboard.

RV and Keyes kept going on copious cups of tea and an occasional coffee.

Jane stayed in the House with the family and Gladys had made it plain to them all, including Franzi, that Jane needed help.

Priority one – find at least two more proficient signers who wouldn't go into a 'flat spin' when confronted by a genius orangutan.

Security was less of an issue now the Marines had arrived. There was still a problem about explaining the comings and goings of Franzi to his HQ with the Admiral, the wren, the civvy and the small flag staff that Keyes had agreed with Churchill was all he needed.

'Look,' said Franzi, 'just show me to the booties and tell them since they're at the zoo I'm their mascot.'

Keyes was sceptical, "Maybe."

'Roger they'll start asking questions before long," said RV

"Yes," Keyes agreed, "better to give them something before they invent their own story."

'Thursday then,' said Franzi, 'at morning parade.'

**

James Palmer was not pleased. He'd been given no option to refuse, an order from the Rothschilds was an order. Like it or lump it. He'd lost a prime field where he grazed his beasts and sheep. From Frog Corner along the road adjacent to the Park and thence just the other side of Bison Hill was now in the hands of the Navy. The Navy, for goodness sake! Why couldn't they make do with land around the coast and ports? He'd write to his MP, or maybe not since it wouldn't do much good. He'd do something, see if he wouldn't. Farmer Palmer was angry!

**

Wednesday 6th September 1939

The marines had worked long into the evening. Forty twelve-man tents were arranged in neat rows across the field. Food had been provided by the Zoo, rum by the Admiral. No-one was allowed off camp and no one tried to make a quick trip to the Chequers which had been spotted on the way in.

Dawn saw a gentle mist rising from the ground and a surprising absence of wind on the exposed hill.

The men paraded at 0700 today in full kit, ready for battle.

Keyes was please with what he saw.

The marines were well turned out, shaved faces told him there had been no personal short cuts taken, uniforms were neat and tidy, boots and brasswork gleaming, weapons apparently spotless.

"Parade attenshun!"

"Parade ready for inspection Sir!"

"Thank you, Colour Sergeant," said Keyes.

Keyes inspected men and officers with a keen eye. He found nothing to displease him.

He returned to the little hummock that served as his rostrum.

He nodded to Bourne.

"Parade stand at ease!"

"Well men it's been a fine effort so far. It is early days. Four weeks here will be followed, for those of you who survive, by a much more gruelling training regime in the wilds of Scotland. Major Palfrey?"

"Sir?"

"You may now carry on. Enjoy your run."

"Sir! Colour Sergeant."

"Sir. Parade, attenshun."

Thud thud.

"Parade left turn."

Thud thud.

"Parade. At the double, forward march!"

And off they went, out of the gate, turning left onto the road and then right into the Park. Once there they were ordered to run.

12 and a half miles of descents, ascents, woods, streams and a small river awaited them, with a final steep climb up the escarpment back into the Park and thence back to camp for breakfast.

"Remind me, Flags," said Keyes, "How long is it supposed to take them?"

"As per Mr Whyte's notes sir, no more than an hour and three quarters," replied Lt Bill Roper.

"A challenge, would you say?"

"Yes sir, even though they're only in combat order. Most of the marines have only been engaged in normal PT before today."

"Mr Whyte assures me that they need to be marching 30 plus miles in full kit at the Light Infantry pace before they move on from here."

Roper opened his mouth, but before he could respond they were interrupted by the local policeman ringing his bell as he rode up on his bicycle.

"Excuse me, sir," said Constable Morris, as he skidded to a halt on the grass.

"Yes constable," said Keyes.

"Were those your men I saw going off into the Park just now?"

"They were indeed."

"Well sir I informed the Major at the front of the column that they were breaking regulations."

"About?" said Keyes.

Roper held his breath. He'd seen Keyes explode on a number of occasions and all the signs were there.

"Not carrying respirators Sir."

"And what did the Major say, constable?"

"He didn't say anything. He just held up two fingers and kept on going."

"Quite right. I have it on good authority that there is no need for respirators, not now, nor the entire war. Now be a good chap and GO AWAY!"

**

Bletchley - Wednesday 6th September 1939

Bletchley Park was a hive of activity and getting busier by the day. Sir Hugh Sinclair, Admiral Sinclair, head of the SIS, had been prevailed upon by Churchill and Keyes to provide a secure location for the meeting of the 'Toyshop Team' as Franzi termed it.

The main house and site didn't lend itself to a discreet meeting, but the newly requisitioned Elmers School was not yet fully occupied by the traffic analysts. It benefited from a private entrance through which the LZS van, driven by John, Franzi's friend and keeper, could enter.

A pair of adjoining first floor classrooms had been set up for the meeting. Their internal windows had been blacked out and their doors were guarded by marines.

The connecting door between the two rooms was ajar. One room was set up for Franzi and Jane, the other for the military boffins.

Keyes welcomed the attendees when they arrived at the school. They had met at the Park and been provided with refreshments. Introductions were made all around and now they were itching to find out why they'd been plucked from their previous posts.

"Gentlemen be seated please. Smoke if you must," Keyes began. "Thank you for reporting promptly here today. I am sure you are keen to know what we require from you."

Heads nodded and the men settled in behind their desks.

"I have been reliably informed that you fellows have a number of ideas regarding inventive and destructive weaponry."

His audience eyed him with interest.

"I'm also told that you've not exactly had the best of luck getting the authorities to take notice of you, or getting funding to help you along."

"Very true," said Burney.

"Exactly," said Jefferis.

Goodeve and Macrae both nodded in agreement.

"Well gentlemen, I can tell you that such barriers will now be removed. You are now members of the Admiralties new 'Special Weapons and Science Office. The Office's sole task is to develop and deploy battle changing weapons and devices as soon as practical, first to the Navy and Marines and then to the other Services when possible."

"When do we start sir?" asked Goodeve and Jefferis almost in unison.

"Commendable keenness gentlemen," said Keyes. "You start today. Transport has been laid on to take you to a large house with grounds and plentiful outbuildings near Aylesbury. Winston has prevailed upon the owner to let us have the use of it."

"Excellent."

"Macrae, you look sceptical," said Keyes.

"Well sir, in my short experience of the military there's always a catch to something that looks too good to be true."

Keyes nodded. "There is a catch, if you could call it such, you won't have exactly a free hand in your research and development."

A groan rose from his audience.

Keyes waved his hand at them "But I think you will find that the guidance you will receive will build upon your productive and inventive talents to cause maximum discomfort to Hitler"

"Go on then, sir," said Burney. "Enlighten us."

"RV would you like to set out the programme please."

"Certainly, Admiral."

**

Lunchtime saw no break for them. Sandwiches and tea were brought in.

RV produced a large file for each man.

The programme was broken down into projects.

Charles Goodeve opened his file and took a sharp intake of breath. A tuft of reddish-brown hair fell silently onto the desk. Each man was too busy to notice the Lt Cdr's reaction. He scooped up the hair and put it into his pocket.

Some projects required collaboration with others on the team, some with people currently not part of the Toyshop.

So many things to work on. Navy, Army, RAF equipment. Each was set out with a detailed timetable. Some projects were follow-ons from their current work or their thoughts about potential research. Others looked like serious leaps in science and capability.

The team was relieved to see that 'known' projects which were reasonably understood came first. But the deadline for those was March 1940.

"With regard to specifics gentlemen, there will be more of that in time," said RV, "However, if there is anything that you can't wait to be answered I'll try my best."

**

A short break for tea, toast and cake mid-afternoon, as per any officer's mess, was followed by a short final session of questions and answers.

The team debated some points and had clarification from RV on several matters. They also determined who else needed to be brought into the enterprise.

They'd thought it odd that RV noted down their 'difficult' questions and then disappeared into the adjoining classroom. He reappeared with detailed answers. There was a strange 'musty' smell which wafted in from next door.

A woman's voice whispered things they could scarcely hear. Strangest of all was the occasional 'huff huffing' that sounded for all the world like laughter.

Keyes did his best to keep the team distracted at these times but there were raised eyebrows and furrowed foreheads around the company all the same.

He finally brought the discussions to an end and summed up, "So we have covered improvised weapons, anti-tank weapons, armour, camouflage, mines, torpedoes, anti-submarine weapons, and anti-aircraft solutions."

They all nodded in agreement.

"Good. Thank you for your efforts today gentlemen. Transport is laid on to take you to your new home. Staff will be waiting for you. Marines are providing security."

"Thank you sir."

"I'll be up to see you tomorrow," said RV.

"Goodbye and good luck gentlemen," said Keyes in dismissal.

**

Whipsnade Shore Establishment - Thursday 7th September 1939

"Do you know what he wants us to get now, and damned quick too?" said Keyes to RV over a cup of tea in the tent that was his HQ office and bedroom. Admittedly it was a large tent, but he hadn't 'roughed it' like this since Peking in 1900.

"Go on," said RV.

"Half a dozen tanks."

"I thought that he meant much later or that he was joking."

"Yes well, it gets worse. He wants Matilda Mark 2s."

RV raised an eyebrow. "Aren't they a little in demand by the tank chaps?"

"Yes," agreed Keyes. "What makes it worse is that he's agreed with Winston that they be shipped off to Armstrong Vickers on Tyneside to be 'modified'."

"That wouldn't have anything to do with the task we set the Team of coming up with an antitank shell for the Naval 12lber would it?"

"Oh it gets better. By some 'magic,' ACM Dowding has been persuaded to donate a number of Merlin mk3 engines, and they're to be shipped to Newcastle too."

"Aren't Vickers working on a new tank to replace the Matilda?"

"I believe that work is going on in Birmingham with Metro Cammell."

"Odd then?"

"If Franzi's ear-shattering raspberry was anything to go by I don't think he likes the new tank."

"How on earth are we going to get him half a dozen Matildas? Let alone ship them to Newcastle without anyone catching on."

A loud cough from outside, followed by a rapping on the large wooden pole supporting the front of the tent, made both men jump.

"Enter," said Keyes.

The flap of the tent was lifted and a short wiry figure sporting fresh stripes of a sergeant on his arms appeared.

"Excuse me, sir, ah happened tae be passing an overheard ye spiking tae this chiel aboot a sma problem ye hiv."

"I beg your pardon could you say that again, please? I didn't quite catch the meaning," said Keyes.

"Ye were spikkin tae this gentlmen aboot a problme gettin a tank."

"I think," said RV that the sergeant overheard our discussion regarding procuring six Matildas."

"Aye aat s fit ah said sir," said the sergeant nodding his head.

"Hold on one moment. Did you arrive yesterday with Captain Lovat?" asked Keyes.

"Ah did sir."

"From Scotland?"

"Aye, sir. The captain, masel, ma breether an the piper."

"That explains it. Now then might I trouble you to get the Captain and ask him to join us here?"

"Aye sir ah'll ging find him ah won't be gye lang," said the sergeant and was gone.

"Did you understand any of that, RV?" asked Keyes.

"Nary a word, sir."

"Don't you start, the Kings English please."

**

Within 10 minutes Lovat accompanied by the sergeant were back at the Admiral's tent.

"Lovat," said Keyes.

"Yes sir. You sent for me sir."

"I did indeed. It seems your sergeant here…"

"MacFeegal, sir," said Lovat.

"Yes. Well, MacFeegle said he was passing and heard Professor Jones and I talking about a problem we have."

"Yes sir. He told me about it on the way over here. You're needing six Matilda 2s and want to get them to Newcastle."

"Succinctly put," replied Keyes.

"Ah well, sir Rob here is your man. Sorry, Serjeant MacFeegle."

"Really?"

"Yes sir. He is the best damn scrounger I've ever come across, and that's saying something given the laddies we have in the Scouts."

"I think he was going to make me an offer, weren't you sergeant?"

"Ah wis sir, ah'll get ye fit ye wint an mak siccar they get tae their destination."

RV and the Admiral looked at Lovat.

"He said he'll get them and make sure they get to Newcastle too, if you give him permission, of course sir."

"Wasn't aat fit ah jis said, Shimi?" said MacFeegle.

"Is this one of those things that I don't ask how it will be achieved?" said Keyes.

"Best not sir. The sergeant here isn't known as Rob 'anybody' MacFeegle for nothing."

Chapter 12

Admiralty Buildings, Whitehall – Friday 8th September 1939

"So," said Admiral John Godfrey, Director of Naval intelligence, slowly after reading the 'note' from the First Lord. "I've got to get an agent into the Sandoz laboratories in Basel. Where they've got to 'acquire' or copy research work by a chap called Albert Hoffman on something called 'lysergic acid diethylamide'?"

"That's right," said Keyes.

"And it seems Winston is happy with this 'adventure'?"

"Positively so. He has a scientific advisor who believes it could be very useful. If we can get out hands on it," explained Keyes. He didn't bother to add anything about the likelihood that Franzi's odd plan was a longshot at best. To be fair Franzi had gone over the pros and cons with Winston, RV and himself. After considering the benefits and the low risk, of phase 1 at least, they'd decided it was worth the trouble.

"Not only am I expected to agree to this plan, but Winston says there's a man for the job?"

"Yes, John," said Keyes, soothingly. "It's not just a smash and grab raid. We need someone with finesse. Dr Hoffman, apparently, doesn't quite know what he's got and is working on other research. A little 'digging' or subtlety might be necessary to achieve success."

"I see. So one of my scientific chaps then?"

"Oh know. That's much too obvious, and why would he be in Switzerland, eh? No, in this instance we'd like someone who can keep a clear head whilst seemingly having a very good time drinking and playing cards with the Doctor."

"For heaven's sake who?" asked Godfrey bluntly.

"Your assistant, Lt Fleming."

**

Egypt - Friday 8th September 1939

Hobart boarded the RAF Sunderland at Alexandria and a launch ferried O'Connor out to the aircraft at Mersah Matruh as it waited outside the harbour.

He was as surprised as Hobart when they recognised each other.

"You're not going home too Dick?" asked Hobart.

" 'Fraid so Hobo," said O'Connor.

"Whose orders?"

"Gort's."

Hobart frowned.

"You too?" asked O'Connor.

"Yes," said Hobart in a growl.

"Donkey Walloper plot, do you think?"

"Seems likely. Do you know my brother in law is coming out?"

"Ah. That makes some sense. Is he good with tanks and sand?"

"He'll have to be if the Italians decide to join the party."

"So it's to Marseilles, then the train to Paris and onward to Calais and Dover?"

"The Flt Sgt told me it's a direct flight to Marseilles, no stopping off at Malta."

"Someone wants us home quick."

"I wonder what for?"

Nearly 8 hours later the flying boat touched down flawlessly in the outer anchorage of Marseilles and the two generals were met by a Royal Navy Captain.

"Good evening General Hobart, General O'Connor. I am Captain Bush. The First Lord has asked me to pass on his greetings and to hand you documents which will start to explain why you have been recalled to England."

"You mean, Churchill, do you Captain?" asked Hobart gruffly.

"Yes sir."

"Bloody Hell," said O'Connor, "someone really doesn't like us if they're letting the navy have us."

"Have you any idea, Captain, what is in these orders?"

"No sir. But I know the change of plan. We're to fly directly to England. I have a car waiting to take us to the airport and an RAF transport is ready to take off."

"And once in England?" queried O'Connor.

"As fast as we can to the Admiralty."

**

Whipsnade - Friday 8th September 1939

Keyes returned to Camp after a convivial lunch in town with Churchill.

Winston was pleased with the progress being made with the 'Commando' but he took a deep swallow of brandy when Keyes presented Franzi's latest 'requests'.

"Is this ever going to end Richard?" he asked.

"Well, the genie is out of the bottle. On giving these things fair consideration I feel Franzi has some good ideas."

"But we've had no concrete success so far from his information. He seems to be concentrating on building his own private army courtesy of the Admiralty. There's only so much I can do without annoying certain people who want to bring me down a peg or two just because I'm WSC."

"Franzi did provide you with general information on the surface raiders. Has there been no success there?"

"A sighting of a ship identified as an American Heavy cruiser in the Canaries but the weather closed in. Cumberland is still searching."

"I'm sure we'll catch Graf Spee soon enough. Please God before she sinks too many merchantmen."

"Getting back to this lot," said Churchill indicating the paperwork on the table with his cigar. "You think we just accept what Franzi wants, men, material, training sites?"

"I do."

"Present me with the details and I'll get the orders in motion and give you the support you need in the inter-service arguments that will undoubtedly break out."

**

RV met Keyes at the HQ tent when he arrived back from town.

"Good meetings?"

"Generally so."

"Tea? Or should we take that with Franzi? He's asked to see us both. An idea about how he can 'work' with the men."

"Well then, by all means, let's go see Franzi."

**

RV and Keyes could hear Franzi busily bashing away at his typewriter when they entered the hut.

Jane was stuffing papers into transit envelopes and then placing the envelopes into a dozen out trays labelled variously 'Science 1', 'Science 2', 'RAF 1', 'RAF 2', 'RN 1', 'RN 2' etc. etc.

"Good afternoon Sir," she said when she noticed Keyes. "Dr Jones said you might be popping in for tea. Shall I let Franzi know you're here?"

"If you would please Jane," said Keyes.

Jane tapped politely on Franzi's door and was rewarded with a loud 'Ook'.

"The Admiral and Dr Jones to see you," she said as she opened the door.

Franzi abandoned his typing immediately and with a loud whoop met both men as they entered his inner sanctum. Ignoring the hand that Keyes proffered Franzi embraced the admiral warmly and then repeated the gesture with RV.

"Well yes," said Keyes, "good to see you too Franzi," as he re-arranged his uniform before dropping down into a chair.

Franzi signed at Jane.

"Alright. So long as you can manage," she said. "I'll have the tea with you in a minute."

Franzi crossed to a large blackboard and wrote 'Everything going well gentlemen?'

"It is with the Toyshop boys. They're like kids in a sweetshop on Friday afternoon," said RV.

'Good'

"My trip to London was successful," said Keyes, "although Winston's eyes watered when I presented him with your wish list."

'I'll see him soon. I'll go to town if he's not got the time to come here.'

"I think the very thought of you in the corridors of powers will make him drop everything and come immediately," said Keyes chuckling.

Franzi and RV joined in the laughter at the thought of an ape in the Admiralty.

Franzi wiped the board.

'I've been thinking about the men here.'

"Yes?" asked Keyes.

'Meeting them. I've got a plan."

RV smiled.

Keyes groaned.

'When do the other marines get here?'

"Tuesday."

'Do you think the ones here could do some construction work before then?'

"I'm sure that could be arranged. What do you have in mind?"

'Something suitably strenuous,' chalked Franzi, 'if they could build.......'

**

Marseille - Friday 8th September 1939

The taxi drove with the usual gay French abandon through the streets towards Marseille Provence Airport on the Etang de Berre.

"Doesn't seem to be much of a war on here," said O'Connor.

"Life goes on, as usual, it seems," commented Hobart.

"Is it like this all over, Captain?" asked O'Connor.

"From what I've seen sir, yes. The flight down showed that there's not much of a blackout and Paris stood out like the Blackpool Illuminations."

"They must be confident then," said Hobart.

"Seems so, Sir. They're making a push into the Saar, or rumour has it."

"Do you think they're up for it Hobo?"

"I don't know Dick. They certainly gave their all 14/18. I haven't had a great deal to do with them since the intervention ended."

"I know Lydell Hart and Fuller have some fans here but it seems to me they're looking to fight this one like the last."

"It won't do, Dick. It just won't do. We're having the devils own time educating our people, especially the donkey wallopers. I know the Germans have played around a lot with the all-arms approach to warfare, especially supporting the tanks with infantry and 'air' artillery. If they've got it even partly right and we're not on our game there will be hell to pay."

"Here we are," said Bush, as the taxi pulled into the airport.

They were met by an RAF Flight Lieutenant who saluted the generals, "If you'll come this way please sirs, we are ready to take off."

3 hours later after an uneventful flight over a brightly lit French countryside, the Hudson descended slowly over blacked-out London and landed safely at RAF Hendon.

**

Glasgow – late afternoon, Friday 8th September 1939

Sgt and Corporal MacFeegle sat comfortably in the office of Thomas MacFeegle, movements controller, LMS, Glasgow. They drank tea suitably fortified with a wee bit of the 'water of life' and smoked whilst Thomas worked rapidly on special orders for re-routeing the train.

North British Locomotive's Hyde Park Works, Glasgow through to Vickers Armstrong Elswick Works, Newcastle.

Orders complete Thomas made a series of calls to ensure the changes would be correctly handled along the new route.

"Whoosh," he said taking a large gulp of whisky, "well that's done. You could have given me a wee bit more notice lads. Phoning when you did really put the wind up Doris. She holds that no good Christian should be up beyond 10 o'clock, never mind using the phone. She thought someone had died."

"We didn't ken we nott tae fash ye until hinmaist nicht," said Rob.

"What's the hurry anyway? The schedule has the train going down south in gentle stages."

"Ye ken fit the army is like," said Rob.

"Fortunately, no. But I'm learning. Are you sure Vickers are prepared," Thomas asked?

"Ach aye Shimi Lovat ah'll hiv caad the min aat Vickers."

"Well there you go," said Thomas handing over the papers to Rob.

"Mony thanks kizzen we ll send ye some mair o the fuskie seen," said Rob firmly shaking Thomas' hand.

"Bide safe ye rogues. Aire'll be hell tae pey fin the authorities find their trains gang astray," said Tomas chuckling.

"Yer bliddy richt, we were only supposed to take a dozen," said the Big Yan as the brothers MacFeegle left Thomas to his whisky.

**

The 'Lanarkshire Yeomanry' was ready to roll. Behind it sat 12 trucks each carrying two Matilda II tanks.

The engineer, Euan, and fireman, Gregor, MacFeegle looked at Rob. He smiled and nodded. Euan turned the regulator and after a hiss of steam, the locomotive slowly gathered speed.

Another epic tale in the legend of Rob MacFeegle had begun.

**

London – Dusk, Friday 8th September 1939

The RN staff car hurried through the gloom as the rain began to pour down on Finchley Park Way.

There were not as many vehicles about as pre-blackout but even so London had not changed greatly. Pedestrians crossing the road didn't help.

"Why the Devil can't they wear something white," Hobart shouted winding the window down? "IDIOT!"

O'Connor chuckled. The long journey had made his fellow general even more irascible than normal and he was known to be a short-tempered fellow at the best of times.

"Hobo, give them a chance, it's only been a few days after all."

"Mark my words Richard there'll be many deaths in the blackout before this war is over."

"At least no-one is saying 'over by Christmas' this time."

"Compared to the first time we are woefully unprepared, as you know."

"Here watch out," screamed Captain Bush as a lorry spun on the greasy road surface ahead of them.

The RN driver tried his best to avoid the collision but failed.

Time seemed to pass slowly for those in the car. All four men watched as part of the lorry's load shifted and two panels sliced neatly through the staff car door next to Bush and Hobart.

"Oh bugger," said O' Connor as he watched blood gushing from the wounded general and captain.

**

The Admiralty – Friday 8th September 1939

"Excuse me sir," said Churchill's ADC. "I have General O'Connor on the phone for you."

"I thought he and Hobart were due here about now?"

"Yes sir. General O'Connor will explain."

Churchill took the proferred phone.

"Good evening General. Where the devil are you?"

"The Middlesex Hospital?"

"There's been a what? An accident? Where?"

"Swiss Cottage. Anyone hurt?"

"I see. General Hobart is unconscious. Captain Bush gravely injured. And you, Richard?"

"A bang on the head. Nothing to worry about? Concussion sir can be very serious."

"So you have all the medical expertise needed currently?"

"I see."

"Overnight at least for you? What about Hobart and Bush?"

"They'll need more time. I see. I'll be there in the morning to see you and get an update and Hobo and Bush."

"Indeed. I am glad you found the briefing documents interesting. You can see why I need you both fit and well and working as soon as possible?"

"I hope so. Thank you, General, for calling yourself. I'll send a liaison officer down right away and see you in the morning."

"Goodnight to you too."

"BUGGER," he shouted at no one in particular.

"Sir?" said his ADC.

"Get a good man down to the Middlesex to liaise with the doctors there. Then get me Admiral Keyes. And a brandy!"

**

Whipsnade – Saturday 9th September 1939

"I tell you Cloughie someone's got it in for us," complained Flanagan.

"Now how do you work that out?" said Clough as he paused from hammering a nail into a log.

"Well why couldn't this wait until the rest got here?"

"I think we're building this as a welcoming present."

"Who says?"

"I heard Captain Keeley talking to Major Palfrey. The rest of the 'Commando' is arriving by train and then marching here with all their kit. They get a short break and we give them a show on the jungle gym before doing it themselves."

"What's this new name for? 'Commando' I ask ya? My Da fought them Boers and their 'Kommando's'."

"An' tough buggers they were too according to my Dad," said Clough. "Nasty and very mobile."

"Oi, you two, what do you think you're doing? Get on with it," shouted Sgt. Garrett.

"Yes sarge. Give us a hand lifting this up," said Clough to Flanagan.

When they'd finished their section of logs they joined the other platoon members for a brew and a smoke.

Flanagan looked thoughtful as he considered the partially built assault course, "How far's the station then, Cloughie?"

"Dunstable? A couple of miles, I think."

"Hardly a jog, is it? Even with all their kit."

Sgt Garrett leaned across, "That's where you are wrong Flanagan, because the lads won't be coming from Dunstable Station, they are de-training at St Alban's. That is a distance of 13 miles, with all their kit."

"Poor bastards," said Flanagan.

**

Middlesex Hospital – Saturday 9th September 1939

"How is everyone this morning Richard," asked Churchill?

"I'm fine sir," said O'Connor. "General Hobart is awake now but we've been asked not to disturb him today. It was touch and go with all the blood he lost. The surgeon isn't sure how much use he'll have of his left arm."

"Not amputated though?"

"No sir." He paused, "But poor Captain Bush has lost his right leg below the knee."

"How did the accident occur?"

"It was very dark in the blackout, especially with the rain. Our driver and the lorry's didn't see each other in time and then both vehicles skidded."

"And?"

"All would have been fine but the lorry shed part of its load and a piece came through the car door and sliced into Hobo and Bush."

"What on earth was it," asked Churchill?

"Oddly enough sir something that' supposed to keep people safe. A section of Anderson Shelter."

"Bloody hell!"

"The surgeon thinks Captain Bush will recover, unless infection sets in."

Churchill nodded his head.

"Do they have any of the 'wonder drug' we keep hearing is coming along?"

"Penicillin?"

"No sir. I have heard the scientists are still trying to scale up production. I believe the Americans are working on it too." "Hm," replied Churchill, non committedly. He paused whilst pondering the US conundrum. Franzi had made it plain that he believed that engaging with the United States to some degree was acceptable but only to a certain level. Churchill considered that If Roosevelt could shake his country out of isolationism then Hitler might be made to see some sense and end the war without too much bloodshed. However, getting Hitler to give up Poland might still be impossible without a clear military conclusion.

O'Connor watched the First Lord and waited for him to continue.

"Are you ready to meet with Admiral Keyes and his team?"

"Is Lord Gort happy to dispense with my services?"

"Yours and Hobo's," replied Churchill. "For a while, at least. You can see there's some interesting work to be done with my new Commando."

"The idea of a mixed arm, mobile force ready for rapid deployment does appeal to me. Fuller and Liddell Hart would approve. I have questions though?"

"Yes?"

"Why is the Navy undertaking this and where on earth are you going to get the tanks from?"

"Don't you worry about that. I'll let Admiral Keyes explain everything when you get to HMS Whipsnade later today."

"Yes sir."

"As soon as General Hobart is fit he'll join you."

"Sir."

On the way back to the Admiralty Churchill lit up a cigar.

I wonder, he mused, whether Franzi knows anything about pharmaceuticals?

**

Whipsnade – Saturday 9th September 1939

Franzi ended his mutual grooming session with Daisy after she clouted him particularly hard around the head. For what reason he couldn't imagine other than he was grooming near 'certain bits' of her body and she had already pushed him away three times.

She loped off to her shelter and he could hear her crunching away on her food.

Looking around he noticed that the sun had set. He shrugged his shoulders, picked up his slate and tucked a piece of chalk behind his ear before letting himself out of the compound and stealthily making his way to Lucy's house.

"Franzi," Lucy said cautiously after they'd been 'chatting' for a while trying to use the slate as little as possible.

'Yes?'

"Erm, you really smell you know."

'What? More than usual?"

"I think so," she said sniffing and pulling a face.

"The smell has been getting stronger for a week or so. Mum commented that my room smelt as though a bear had been hibernating in it. I've been very careful to leave the window open when you've gone but it's getting cooler at night now."

'Oh dear. I'm very sorry. I'll try and take a dip before coming over.'

"Jane has noticed it too in the office, but she's been too polite to mention it to you."

'Right. Thank you for telling me. I'll be off now then and hopefully see you in the HQ tomorrow afternoon.'

"I haven't upset you have I?"

'No Lucy. All's well. Can I still get a hug or is Franzi too pongy for that?'

Lucy smiled and they had a hug before he leapt out of the window and headed home.

As he came in sight of the compound, he had an overwhelming urge to vocalise and he let out a series of long, uuuuooooa calls.

Now why on earth did I do that he thought? Then chuckled to himself as he settled down on his nest in his shelter.

**

Whipsnade – Sunday 10th September 1939

Sandy Mackenzie was nervous. He'd had a letter from Shimi Lovat asking him to join him at a new unit the Marines had just established. His request to travel south and join Lovat was immediately approved by Colonel Leslie-Melville.

He packed his things, loaded his motorbike and sidecar and took two days to travel from Inverness to Whipsnade.

When he arrived at HMS Whipsnade, as a newly erected sign at the entrance stated, he reported to the Guard Tent.

Shimi had been sent for and now he and Sandy were discussing sniper training with Admiral Keyes.

"Lieutenant, Captain Lovat tells me that for one so young you show a remarkable aptitude for sniping and training snipers."

"Ah would not presume to boast sir but I am pretty competent in sneaking around and putting a single bullet to best use."

"Good. I am pleased to hear it. I want a number of the Commando to be proficient snipers. How many is it again, Captain?"

"Five sir," said Lovat.

"And they will only be the start of it. The First Lord has determined that there will be at least three Commandos, two Marines, and the third, if he can get General Gort to agree, will be Army."

"And we'll need replacements to be ready too sir," suggested Lovat?

"We certainly will. Well, that will be all gentlemen."

The two Lovat Scouts turned to leave Keyes tent and pushed open the flap just as Jane Wiess was coming in with an armful of papers.

She and Sandy inevitably collided as the Wren tried to get out of the Lieutenant's way and he, being chivalrous, tried to get out of hers.

They both stammered out apologies and Lovat took Sandy's elbow and shoved him outside.

"Franzi has asked if you could look at these sir," she said, still flustered from her encounter with the young Scot.

"Thank you Jane," said Keyes, "Please tell Franzi I will and perhaps discuss the content with him this evening."

"Yes sir," she said.

"That will be all," said Keyes noticing that she was still somewhat dazed and surmising the reason.

"Sir," she said, returning to her normal self then coming to attention, turning about and leaving the tent.

Interesting, thought Keyes.

Chapter 13

The Toyshop - Sunday 10th September 1939

Goodeve was sure he could take the suggestions provided to him by Mr Whyte and turn the Navy's venerable QF 12-12 into an all-purpose weapon. It would fire High Explosive shells, a giant shotgun rounds termed 'canister', and an anti-tank round which Mr Whyte had christened Armour Piercing Discarding Sabot containing a tungsten dart.

The trouble was there was no way that a 10' gun would fit into a turret made for a 6'10" one. Weight wise the odd thing was the 12-12 was lighter at 510kg to the 2lb antitank gun's 814kg. The 12-12 had a slower muzzle velocity but range wise it was fine. The weight of the rounds used was 4.5lb with a 2.4lb projectile compared to 12.5lb but if a wooden former was used around an armour piercing 'dart' then that dropped to 6.5lb. Still, surely some modification or other could be undertaken by a competent engineer, even if the resulting turret wasn't quite what was normally expected on a tank. The size of the 12-12 rounds would limit the number that could be carried, but again provision would have to be made. Thank goodness, he thought, that I'm not a tank designer.

**

Burney liked the look of the drawings he'd been provided with. They echoed his own work on his recoilless weapons but his large calibre bullet had been replaced with a much more potent munition. A 'Dr Whyte' had described a high explosive 'squash head' round of just 5lbs in weight including the plastic explosive and casing. The anticipated range of 1000 yards was impressive and the whole weapon was quite portable. All in all, it would give German armour and fortifications a bit of a headache.

**

"Sorry to interrupt you sir," said Sgt Mowe. "There's a Lt Colonel Blacker at the gatehouse with a letter from the Admiralty asking him to meet with you."

"Pardon," said Jefferis, "It is Sunday for heaven's sake and I've had no notification about Colonel Blacker."

"Sorry Sir, but he's insistent."

"Is he by God?"

"He said the letter is from a Mr Whyte."

"Ah, why didn't you tell me that in the first instance?"

Sgt Mowe was long in the tooth and didn't interrupt the officer as he continued,

"Right get brought up here straight away and have some tea brought in, please."

"Yes sir."

**

HMS Whipsnade – Monday 11th September 1939

Marine sentries were posted outside Keyes Headquarters tent to keep passing personnel at a distance.

Keyes, Jones, and O'Connor sat around a large table drinking tea.

"General," said Keyes, "I hope you're recovered somewhat from your knock after a full nights sleep?"

"Yes Sir. No after-effects as far as I can tell."

"Good, good," said Keyes. "You've had a chance to read the briefing notes that the First Lord provided you with?"

"Yes sir. I re-read them yesterday. The First Lord also provided me with copies of the addendums specifically charged to Hobo, General Hobart."

"Hobo is fine," said RV, "As is Roger, RV, and Churchill, don't you think?" he went on addressing Keyes.

"Quite so, RV," replied the Admiral.

O'Connor nodded and smiled, "Dick."

RV started to smirk. "Ignore him, Dick. He's picking up some bad habits from Franzi," instructed Keyes.

"Who's Franzi?"

"Sorry Dick. Franzi, well you could say he's the reason we're all here. We'll take you to meet him this evening," said RV.

"Getting back to business Gentlemen," broke in Keyes. "What do you think of the plans?"

"It took me some time to accept that the Navy is establishing a mixed arms unit and also seeking to integrate artillery and air support," said O'Connor.

"And Naval support if the geography allows," Keyes said.

"Yes," said O'Connor. "How do you intend to get hold of all the weapons detailed on this TOE, especially the armour? Churchill said you'd provide details."

"The small arms aren't too difficult. Some of the support arms are still in development but I've been assured they'll be available by March next year, at least in a form we can train with. The armour, well, we have several vehicles to be modified to increase their mobility and hitting power. We must acquire sufficient Bren Carries, trucks and cars. Our 'supply' team have shown themselves to be very resourceful in the short time they have been with us. I believe our needs will be met. I will introduce you to their officer later."

"I see that the troops you have here are marines?"

"That is true. Churchill wishes to expand the training to a further two Commandos..,"

"Odd choice of name for a British unit I thought?"

"Yes. That was Franzi. He expressed a great deal of admiration for the Boers and the trouble they caused the Empire. He seems to think our Commandos will cause Hitler as much tribulation, if not more."

"My task, with Hobo, is to make all this work?"

"Yes. Training to be here, Salisbury Plain and Scotland. Drive the men as hard as you like, which I am told you two have been doing in Egypt."

"We have indeed. We've high hopes of the units there."

"Drive these men harder, as necessary. Any, including officers, who do not come up to scratch will be transferred out."

"I see."

"Once you've three commandos, two Marine, one Army, operational then Churchill hopes to get you posted to Montgomery's old division as CO. From there he'd like you, if you are able, to spread the training and operational doctrine. Do not, however, rock the boat too much."

"More tea, Roger, Richard," asked RV?

"Yes please."

**

After dinner that evening Keyes and RV took O'Connor for a stroll around the zoo. It was a pleasant diversion after almost nine hours of concentrated work.

O'Connor had met with the Marine officers currently at Whipsnade and also two Lovat Scouts officers and their 'quartermasters'. He'd had some difficulty with understanding the two NCO's and it had been difficult to tell if they were being insubordinate or not. Lovat and Mackenzie had assured him that they were 'fine fellows' and that he should be confident they could get hold of any equipment he might desire for his Commandos.

As they walked back up the hill to the park entrance the Admiral and RV took a detour. They went to the 'House' where O'Connor was introduced to the 'Captain' and Mrs Beal. After bidding them 'good evening' instead of backtracking to the main gates he was led down a path towards an old army hut which stood on its own.

"Sentries here Roger? And barbed wire? No mines I hope," he joked?

Keyes and RV laughed.

"No Dick, no mines. Well not yet anyway," replied Keyes.

The two Marine sentries on duty at the front of the hut presented arms smartly as the men approached.

RV knocked on the hut door and waited for a response.

"Come in," said a pleasant female voice.

They entered and O'Connor was surprised to see a pretty WREN standing by a desk inside.

"Good evening sirs," she said.

"Good evening Jane," said Keyes. "How is he this evening?"

"Busy as ever Admiral, but he is expecting you."

"General O'Connor this is Jane Weiss. You'll be working with her a lot I expect."

"Sir," she said.

"Hello Jane," said O'Connor.

"This way please," said Jane as she tapped on an inner door.

"Don't make any sudden moves Dick," said RV gravely, "You don't want to startle Franzi."

"RV please?" said Keyes.

O'Connor entered the room behind Keyes and Jane. And then stood stock-still.

"Bloody hell, an orangutan's got loose – where's Franzi?"

Franzi rose from his desk chair. Stood up, bowed, walked to a large blackboard and wrote 'Good evening General. Let me introduce myself. Franzi Whyte, at your service.'

**

Air Ministry – Monday 11th September 1939

"Good morning Dr Jones," said Air Chief Marshall Freeman.

"Yes I have spoken with De Havilland. He told me all about the 'Mosquito'."

"Ah, so you work with Mr Whyte?"

Freeman smiled, "I did indeed have a lock of hair enclosed with a letter."

"I would be very happy to meet with you and De Havilland at the works on Friday."

"Very good, let me know if there is any change in time and date after you've spoken to Geoffrey."

"Goodbye."

Vickers Armstrong – Monday 11th September 1939

"It won't do Sir Charles, it just won't work," said Claude Gibb, the chief engineer of C.A. Parsons Ltd.

"Well that's what this says here," replied Sir Charles, head of Vickers Armstrong.

"I don't think Mr Whyte is being prescriptive. He is making suggestions. He specifically told me that people working on his 'projects' need to make their own decisions. He's just trying to give a steer and avoid dead ends," said RV.

"Well I can see roughly what he wants to do," said Claude. "We can hack the turret about and get your 12 pounder in and make room for ammunition, in as safe a way as possible. But it's no to the engine. There's not enough room. Hacking the back off would compromise the overall structure, not to mention the poor suspension that wouldn't be able to cope with that power or more speed."

"So what do I do with all the engines that Fighter Command is sending me?" asked Sir Charles.

"Don't get rid of them," said Claude, "Your Mr Whyte's brainwave about using them as a tank engine is splendid."

"I'll have a word with Churchill about getting them moved to a secure location until they're needed," said RV. "With respect to the Matilda's can you do what needs doing, Sir Charles?"

"I'm sure if Claude comes up with a design we can deliver. I'll have to take men off other jobs though, at least for the time being. Will Churchill be happy with that?"

"He's said do what needs doing. A slight delay in certain ships is acceptable. He's having a major re-think about what ships the Navy really needs," said RV. "So Claude can you make Frankenstein from Matilda?"

"Mr Whyte's letter surprised me," said Claude, "I hadn't considered working on tanks, but I can see some mileage in it. I can make you your 'Frankenstein' but I'd like to talk to him about the other plans he sent to me."

"That could be a little difficult," said RV thinking rapidly, "He's not very well at the moment."

It's all well and good, Franzi, he mused, asking me to take on these tasks but when the chaps at the sharp end start asking questions in a field I don't know they can tell if I'm giving them a load of bull. I've never overseen the design and build of a tank before, and this beast he'd sketched, well...

"I'll see what I can do," said RV. Franzi, he thought, you and I need to have a little chat about 'surprises' he determined. "Can I see those blueprints again please Claude?"

Claude passed them over and RV unfolded the sheet.

Although he was no expert on tank design the monster shown was impressive, the annotations even more so. Weight approximately 50 tons, Hull Length 25 feet. Width 11 feet. Height approximately 10 feet. And the title 'Centurion'.

**

HMS Whipsnade - Tuesday 12th September 1939

'Two hundred and fifty-six marines, Officers, NCO's and men make quite a racket when marching on a metalled road,' thought Franzi. And this lot were singing too! Nice lyrics, filthy but nice. Oh, there we go. A shouted order reset the song to something less risqué as the column approached Whipsnade.

The original contingent was drawn up on parade to receive the newcomers as they marched into camp.

Salutes were given and exchanged, arms and kit bags arranged neatly as the men fell out and jogged over to trestle tables loaded with bacon sandwiches and tea.

15 minutes later the entire Commando, less the duty officer and guard section, marched out of the camp in full combat order, across the road and into Whipsnade wood then down past the chalk Lion and on to the woods utilised in their daily 'morning stroll'.

The assault course was impressive, given it had been constructed in under 3 days. In length it stretched back and forth through the woods for 5 miles. Ditches, climbs, a Tank trap water Jump, a 5ft wall, a Cargo net crawl, zig zag log walls, monkey bars, a rope climb up to high rope obstacle, a suspended wooden 'bridge', a 12 foot wall with footholds, a log 'tunnel' and then back to the start.

Major Palfrey lined up with the 'originals' at the start waiting for the gun. At the rear of the Marines, the Lovat Scouts waited to display their prowess. Shimi was sharing some joke with the MacFeegles and Sandy Mackenzie was nervously looking around, the 'unproven' new boy aware of his need to deliver and uphold the Scout's honour.

Keyes and O'Connor stood at the start with the Captain, who was taking a keen interest in the 'race'.

To one side of the startline mostly hidden by trees stood John Baker, immaculately turned out for the 'event' in his keepers uniform and Jane Weiss dressed in improvised battledress. Next to them, crouched impassively on the ground sat Franzi, puffing away on a Churchill 'special'.

"Who's your money on, Roger?" asked O'Connor, "The 'Originals' as they insist on calling themselves?"

"I think they'll do well but Major Riley informed me that the 'Newcomers' have been training hard in Plymouth."

"Isn't it interesting that there's always some good-natured competition between units?" said the Captain.

"Nothing changes much Captain," said Keyes.

"I wonder how both teams will take the outcome?" said O'Connor.

"That's going to be priceless," replied Keyes.

RV fired his Webley and they were off. Sandy glanced back into the trees at the sound of someone blowing an enormous raspberry. He was sure he saw a keeper and that lovely WREN looking at him with a smile. And on the ground to her left, its head coming up to her waist at least was a bloody huge orangutan!

Captain Baines and two senior sergeants from the newcomers following the 'originals' to check out the way almost ran into Mackenzie as he came to a near stop to check what he'd seen. Baines swore at the young Lieutenant to 'get a bloody move on' and the sergeants thought it fun to pick him up bodily and propel him after his team-mates. Shaking himself free of the NCOs he sprinted to catch up with the other three Scouts.

The 'Originals' came back into sight and raced for the finish. RV fired twice, once to record the first man back and the second time for the last. O'Connor recorded the times in his notebook.

Mackenzie was pleased, neither first nor last but in the first ten alongside Lovat and the smaller MacFeegle. He looked around as he passed the finish line and spotted the WREN but not the keeper, nor the orangutan. He shook his head and went to take a breather and a drink.

The 'Newcomers' lined up. RV fired his pistol once again and they raced to the first obstacle.

They were back soon enough and crossed the finish to the accompaniment of two more shots.

After the 'Newcomers' were permitted a drink and brief respite both groups were paraded as a body where Keyes and O'Connor could see them all be able to address them.

"Very good, gentlemen," began Keyes. "You've performed well. I hope, with more training, you'll perform better as One Commando, Royal Marines. You might even be able to emulate someone who is going to show you how this course should be done, don't you think General?" he asked O'Connor.

"I very much hope so Admiral. Let us prepare to be amazed, men," O'Connor responded. "John, could you present Franzi to the parade please?"

John Baker stepped forward from behind a tree followed closely by Franzi who still had the cigar butt in his mouth and an ostentatiously draped collar and chain over one arm.

A murmur ran round the men. "Silence there," ordered Colour Sergeant Bourne.

"Now, men," said O'Connor, "This is Franzi. He wishes to apply for the position of One Commandos mascot."

Franzi nodded solemnly at this.

"But he'd like to demonstrate that he does not intend to be a burden to you. RV who were the fastest marines from 'Originals' and 'Newcomers' around the course?"

"Marine Flanagan and Corporal Phillips."

"Hey sir ah wis aheid o Flanagan," shouted Corporal MacFeegle.

"Be queart min," ordered Lovat.

"Sir," said Corporal MacFeegle, the Big Yan as he was known in the Scouts.

"One minute Captain Lovat. Dr Jones is this true?" asked O'Connor.

"It is General."

"Well then we have three men versus one ape."

"Excuse me sir," piped up Flanagan, "but that Franzi fella has a bit of an advantage on us. We've been running about since dawn and then done the course in battle order whilst he's fresh as a daisy and carrying nothing at all."

"He's right, you know," said Keyes.

"Would it suit if you didn't carry weapons?" O'Connor asked the men.

"No sir, we'll take that chance, Sir," said Corporal Phillips.

"Aye sir," agreed MacFeegle.

Flanagan stared at the two corporals in disbelief.

"That is most sporting of you, men," smiled O'Connor. "But let's make things even. What's say Franzi takes some kit on the course."

"Oh yes sir," Flanagan said with obvious relish.

"What would you think fair?" asked the General.

Flanagan smiled a cunning smile. "How about a Bren Gun, sir, and ammunition."

Keyes and the Captain worked hard to hide their smiles.

"So be it," said O'Connor. "Captain Lovat will you do the honours please?"

Lovat collected a Bren and five magazines in a bag and took them warily over to the keeper and orangutan.

John Baker helped Franzi with the webbing and bag much to the amusement of the marines.

Franzi looked around at them then picked up the Bren making as much of a hash of it as he dared without damaging the weapon. He noted, with interest that the magazines, in bag and gun, were all fully loaded, and a mischievous idea came into his head.

The competitors set themselves ready and RV fired yet again to start them off.

The men sprinted away. Franzi put on a show of being 'puzzled' whilst looking around for his mark.

He then hefted the Bren in a most practised manner and loped off at a relaxed pace after the men.

A cheer went up from the assembled marines and Colour Sergeant Bourne instructed a handful of junior NCOs to follow the ape to ensure that the obstacles were completed correctly.

Franzi could see the three men ahead of him. With scarcely any effort he caught up to them, overtook them and passed them on the way back to the start. Once back in front of the assembly he waited for Phillips, Flanagan and MacFeegle to cross the finish. The men were cheering for the result. They felt that Franzi had proved his point. When the following NCO's caught up they confirmed he'd completed every obstacle fair and square.

Franzi had one last point to prove to 'His' Commando. He swung the Bren up from the ground, cocked it and fired off the magazine at his target neatly cutting a sampling in two at 100 yds and causing all the humans except Keyes, O'Connor, John and Jane to dive to the ground.

He carried out the unload procedure and handed the gun back to Lovat as he got up from the mud.

"Parade, atten shun," bellowed Bourne. "Sort yourselves out now. General on parade."

"Thank you Sergeant," said O'Connor.

"Thank you Franzi," said Keyes. "Most edifying."

Franzi turned to the parade, bowed and delivered his best raspberry.

"Your mascot, men? Or no?" asked O'Conner.

Two miles away a gamekeeper working with his two lads wondered about the roar.

**

HMS Whipsnade – Thursday 14th September 1939

The café was crowded with officers and senior NCO's.

The weather was poor, wet and windy, so the closure to the public wasn't an issue.

O'Connor had consulted long with Franzi about the enhancements he'd insisted upon and, after several heated 'debates' over the past two days, had eventually accepted their efficacy.

Franzi hadn't explained where the kit was to come from and dismissed Dick's concerns with the repeated phrase 'It's in hand'.

Their interchanges had been somewhat surreal in that some had been conducted with Jane as the intermediary, which had a moderating effect on both man and apes language; others had been straight orangutan to General where the exchange had been far less 'restrained' as Franzi chalked furiously on his large blackboard and illustrated various points with sketches.

However, now an agreement had been reached O'Connor had One Commandos leadership to present to. He felt sure there would be some protests and wondered if this might help identify those who would be better back with their old unit.

"Gentlemen," he began, "after some considerable research and thought, " he paused, it would be so much easier if he could just say 'Franzi, your mascot, tells me that this will increase your efficiency and effectiveness and save bloody lives', "we will be having some changes in uniform and equipment."

There was some shuffling but no one demurred.

"A new 'smock', suitably camouflaged, is to be worn during combat. New rubber-soled boots will replace the hobnailed variety," he smiled at the men, some were nodding sagely.

"Officers, NCO's and Marines will all carry similar weapons. Some new weapons will be issued over the coming months. The Thompson submachine gun is familiar to most of you and I know some of you have seen the American Colt 45 automatic pistol. However, some support weapons will be coming straight out of design and we will be expected to work with the developers to ensure they can fulfil their promise."

That brought a big groan from many of the audience. They had had experience of new equipment and how it could go totally wrong, in some instances fatally, and that had been in peacetime. You didn't want some new 'toy' doing that when you were knee-deep in SS.

"I know, I know," said O'Connor, "I'm sure we've all had similar experiences but be reassured that the promised equipment is apparently so safe that I'd let Franzi have a bash with it."

That brought a laugh.

"Finally, except for formal parades, there is to be a change in battledress insignia. No badges of rank will be shown openly. Tags have been produced which can be turned to reveal the persons rank when it is safe to do so."

"Excuse me sir," said Captain Lane.

"Yes Captain."

"Surely that will lead to all kinds of muddle, if not insubordination?"

"That may be, Captain. It is something we will have to work with the Marines to eliminate. The Commandos will lead the way in this as in many other aspects of military development. I hope the rest of the services, particularly the Army, will follow."

Captain Lane, shook his head and turned to one of his colleagues, obviously mouthing his displeasure.

"Or is it, Captain, that you'd rather have a sniper pick you off because you're obviously an officer with insignia and officers' weapons?"

"No sir," replied the Captain.

"Any questions? No, well I would like you to now go and brief your men accordingly. Dismissed."

"Major Riley," said O'Connor, "A word please."

"Sir," said Riley as he approached the General.

O'Connor waited until the room was almost clear and then leaned toward the Major,

"Lane and Boyland, his friend."

"Yes sir?"

"Please return them to their unit and send someone sensible to brief their men."

"Sir!"

Chapter 14

De Havilland Works - Friday 15th September 1939

"So there you have it, gentlemen. An absolute wonder in such a short time made possible by the information supplied by Mr Whyte," said De Havilland SNR. as he finished his presentation.

"A 'Wooden Wonder' one might say," said Freeman. "And you say furniture manufacturers should be able to assist in production?"

"I believe so," replied De Havilland.

"The next question is when can we get them into service?" said RV.

"Our problem at the minute isn't engines, which is usually where delays occur, Stanley Hooker has been as good as his word, but the 20mm cannon for a full load test."

"I see," said RV, "I'll make sure support is provided to resolve that. I assume you can rig something to mimic the weight and position of the cannon and ammunition?"

"That's not a problem."

"You have blueprints here for three versions, fighter, fighter bomber and long-range unarmed reconnaissance/bomber," said Freeman.

"We do."

"Do you think Dowding and Hewitt will be receptive?" asked RV.

"I can't see Stuffy being a problem," said Freeman.

"I should hope not, he's been very helpful to us so far."

Freeman and De Havilland stared at RV.

"Your Mr Whyte has been busy, I take it?" asked Freeman.

"He has indeed."

"Just exactly who is 'US'? asked De Havilland.

"That's quite a question. I suppose you could say it's a 'Brains Trust' what wants to ensure we are going to win this war as soon as possible, without wasting time and lives on dead ends."

"And exactly who is going to ensure the purse strings are loosened and vested interests are controlled?"

"For the time being funding has to come from supporters like yourself using their resources in the best places. I take it you've been on the receiving end of vested interest pressure?"

"Yes. Directly and from their MPs. There is trouble brewing and if it goes further than the Air Ministry?"

"It does."

"Then it'll go to the top and they'll demand answers."

De Havilland looked at the two men, "Am I to proceed with the project?"

"Your decision," said RV to Freeman.

"Yes, I'll ensure you get what is needed."

"Good because I've something to show you if you'll come with me to the hanger."

As they walked across the tarmac de Havilland went on, "Well, we were hoping to have a mock-up for you to look at today. But it's been hard work and a rush, even with the relatively simple build process."

As they neared the hanger doors de Havilland waved at a team of men standing by the entrance.

"I think we'll stop here, gentlemen."

The hanger doors were rolled back and two engines burst into life with the unmistakeable Merlin signature.

After a slight delay, an aircraft taxied out and past them. The pilot waved and continued to the runaway.

"Quite the showman, Geoffrey," said Freeman, "A mock-up indeed."

"He isn't going to take off, is he?" asked RV.

"Watch," said de Havilland.

The powder blue Mosquito taxied to the threshold, turned into the wind and then opened the throttles.

The aircraft sped down the runway and lifted off.

"Who's flying?" asked Freeman.

"My boy Geoffrey, of course, he wouldn't let anyone else."

There were no fancy manoeuvres just graceful flypasts, climbs and dives.

"Magnificent," said RV and Freeman in unison.

Obut Pikatan, Sarawak - Friday 15th September 1939

The Iban consider orangutans as allies.

Jugah anak Barieng looked carefully over the letter which had come to him privately that morning.

It was very polite and deferential, but it was plain the author considered himself an equal to Jugah.

The 'maia' reminded him of the long family connection back to time before memories and how his tribe had lived alongside Jugah's people. Iban and maia worked as co-Guardians of the Forest. They still continued in that role after the White Raja and his descendants were given rule of the land by the Queen Empress.

Now Jugah was being asked to help.

His spirit guides had already visited him repeatedly since the Germans had declared war on the Empire. They warned of the Japanese joining them to attack and seize the King's lands and of the bloodshed the invaders would wreak. Last night his dream had told of a maia 'general' who would defeat the Germans and the Japanese.

Maung of the Skrang River, seer and tattooist, had visited him yesterday and told him of similar dreams and of 'seeing' District Officer Whyte's companion now fully grown at the head of a mighty host.

There was no doubt in Jugah's mind, he would help. He would have a letter written and countersigned by District Commissioner Whyte before despatch to the First Lord of the Admiralty.

**

HMS Whipsnade – Saturday 16th September 1939

One Commando paraded for the First Lord's inspection.

Two days of needlework, in some cases painful, had removed rank insignia from shoulders and arms, although the unfaded evidence of stripes and badges on uniform blouses still gave the game away.

Now each man wore his rank, or lack of it, on his chest on a tab which could be hidden away as necessary. Alongside that tab was another emblazoned with the word, 1 Commando.

No rubber-soled boots or camouflage smocks had yet appeared, but requisitions had been submitted and if they didn't deliver promptly there were always the MacFeegle quartermasters.

Churchill was accompanied on the inspection by Major Palfrey whilst O'Connor, RV and Franzi looked on.

"A fine show, Major," said Churchill, "Thankyou men. I believe you're going to demonstrate your prowess of arms after a little 'stroll' through the woods?"

"Colour Sgt Bourne," said Palfrey.

"Sir!"

"Get them moving."

"Sir!"

"Parade, parade atten shun!"

Stamp stamp.

"Parade left turn!"

"Stamp stamp.

"Forward march!"

"If you excuse me sir," said Palfrey, "I will join the column."

"Certainly Major," replied Churchill.

The Major jogged over to the column and nodded to the Colour Sgt.

"At the double!"

Churchill joined Keyes, RV and O'Connor.

"It's good to see the integration of officers and men," he said.

"It is early days yet," said O'Connor.

"The General has already dispensed of the services of two officers," said Keyes.

"Really?" said Churchill.

"The wrong type for this new sort of soldiering in my opinion," said O'Connor. "I'm not sure what Hobo will think about it but as long as he gets to combine all arms I think he'll accept it."

"Bugger," said RV, "Where's Franzi gone?"

**

The Commanders arrived before the commandos at the quarry which had been requisitioned as a temporary firing range.

Churchill travelled in his own car with Keyes and O'Connor. Walter and the driver sat in the front.

RV followed them in a Tilly with Jane.

"By the way Jane, did Winston, I mean the First Lord, inform you that he has got the WRNS to part with two other girls who can sign?"

"No sir, I haven't seen him. That is good news though. Franzi is so busy."

"I'm glad you're pleased. How's young Lucy doing?"

"That's supposed to be secret sir. How did you find out that she knew about Franzi?"

"I had to work out who he got to post letters for him before we came on the scene. I've seen Lucy with him in the compound when John takes her in. It's obvious they are close."

"Well we're trying to not make too much of it. Not sure what her parents would think."

"I understand and have forgotten all about it already."

Jane smiled.

One Commando doubled into the quarry with Franzi at their head.

"RV," Jane asked, "is Franzi supposed to have a Bren Gun today?"

**

Franzi's HQ – Saturday 16th September 1939

"You are sure about these men?" asked Churchill.

"Yes Winston, absolutely sure," said Jane as she read Franzi's signing.

"How long have they been in Stalin's employ?" asked RV.

'Since their time at Cambridge,' said Franzi.

RV let out a low whistle.

"And their positions will give them access to many of our secrets," said Keyes.

"I'm not happy with this. It will need to be handled sensitively," said Churchill.

'I suggest Admiral Godfrey takes charge,' said Franzi.

"Agreed," said Churchill, "Who else should be informed and utilised?"

'It rather depends on what we wish to do.'

"They're traitors," said Keyes, "hang the lot of them!"

'A solution,' said Franzi, 'Rather like what we will do when all the German spies have been rounded up. Yes?"

"I'm sure Special Branch and MI5 have that in hand," said Churchill.

"After questioning," said RV?

Franzi blew a mild raspberry.

"You disagree," said Keyes?

'Better to turn this Cambridge lot and these Germans,' said Franzi handing each man a typed list of names headed GERMAN SPIES, 'And have them feed to our enemies what we want them to know."

All three jaws dropped. How the hell did Franzi know these things?

'Come now,' he signed, 'why would I only give you a list of Soviet spies?'

**

Over brandy and cigars, Franzi continued to bombard his audience with information and suggestions (well orders really). 'Can't give the humans much leeway or they'll mess things up,' he thought.

'Gentlemen,' he chalked, 'You've seen today One Commando at the start of their training. There is only so much we can do here in Bedfordshire.'

"What do you suggest?" asked Churchill.

'That Whipsnade be an initial selection centre, staffed by some of the best men who can also ensure security. Once a coarse filter has been applied here then move the survivors to somewhere remote and wild for real training and toughening up.'

"You've somewhere in mind, haven't you? Just as you had 'The Firs' picked out for the Toyshop," said RV.

'As a matter of fact, yes. I sent a letter off to the head of Clan Cameron, Sir Donald, about using Achnacarry Castle as the main training depot. It's accessible by rail, well it's a pleasant march of 7 miles from Spean Bridge railway station. The chaps won't notice that after all their marches and runs here."

"See here Franzi," started Winston.

'Oh it's all fine,' Franzi cut in, 'He knows Shimi Lovat and the Scouts and has agreed to it for a modest annual rental.'

Keyes and RV laughed out loud and O'Connor smiled at Churchill's obvious discomfort when outmanoeuvred, yet again, by an ape.

"I see," said Churchill, "anything else you've like to spring on me Franzi?"

'No, I don't think so, for now.'

"Good. RV may I trouble you for a refill as a nightcap before I go back to London?"

"Certainly Winston."

'Ah, I forgot,' chalked Franzi banging the blackboard and making them all jump. 'We need to second a number of officers, I have the list here somewhere, and short men.'

"Short men? Whatever for?" asked Churchill.

'Tank crews. Strong short men."

**

The Admiralty – Monday 18th September 1939

There was a hush in the room whilst Admiral Godfrey, Head of Naval Intelligence, and John Masterman, intelligence analyst, senior tutor at Christ Church Oxford, and sometime champion tennis player, pored over the notes that Franzi had prepared for them.

Churchill and Keyes stayed silent until the other two men had finished reading.

"Quite a list," said Godfrey.

"An interesting lot," replied Churchill.

"Dangerous," commented Keyes.

"I'm not sure what you need me for," said Masterman.

"Well I have been advised," said Churchill, "to set up a team, under your chairmanship, to handle this 'problem' and turn it to our advantage."

"I see."

"Do we know this is the complete roster of spies?" asked Godfrey.

"For the time being," said Keyes, "but Hitler and Stalin will, no doubt, try and insert new agents."

"And will MI5 be handling their detection and arrest?"

"Once we are sure our whole Intelligence Service is secure."

"Why haven't you taken this to the Prime Minister and Home Secretary?" asked Masterman.

"We don't want anything to leak out before we've got them all in the bag," said Keyes.

"Our first step is to set up a team. I'd like you to sound out David Petrie and if he's amenable to joining us then you and he can recruit who you need, subject to checking with me," said Churchill.

"When do we round them up?" asked Godfrey.

"The German spies? As soon as possible. I will get 'Bubbles' at Portsmouth to sort out a detention centre."

"Bubbles?" said Masterman raising an eyebrow.

"Ah yes, sorry. 'Bubbles' is Admiral Sir William James," said Churchill smiling.

The other two Admirals were wearing broad grins too.

Masterman still looked puzzled.

"The Pear Soap boy, it's him!" said Keyes.

"Ah, I bet that fact has dogged him somewhat?" said Masterman.

"Only in the nicest, one might almost say, 'clean' way," added Godfrey.

Masterman smiled too.

"What about the 'Russians'?" he asked.

"I was thinking about inviting them to a conference next Saturday and sending some Special Branch officers to ensure they turned up," said Churchill.

"Good," said Godfrey, "I'm sure we can have the new team operational by then, eh John?"

"I believe so. What designation is it being given?"

Churchill referred to his notes, "That would be Section Twenty, Roman numerals XX."

**

Middlesex Hospital – Monday 18th September 1939

Sister MacDonald eyed the three men in front of her with suspicion. Here they were wanting to see General Hobart, which was all well and good, but they also wanted to not be interrupted AND leave one of their number, a very tough looking marine in combat order including pistol, outside to make sure they were undisturbed.

"Well I suppose it will be alright, Admiral," she told Keyes. "But don't tire the General please, he's grumpy enough at the best of times."

"Yes Sister," replied Keyes, "I'm sure we'll be able to take him off your hands by the end of the week and let him recuperate with us."

"In you go then," she said.

The officers went into the private room leaving the marine outside.

"And don't you be annoying any of my nurses."

"No, ma'am."

Hobart was sat up in bed reading.

"At last," he said, "I thought I'd been abandoned."

"You have Winston's man here for company," said Keyes.

"Yes but he's NAVY!, no idea about how to get hold of army information from France."

"You're not going to be happy with the news I'm afraid," said O'Connor.

"Don't keep me waiting then Dick."

"The French have pulled back in the Saar."

"Forced back?"

"No, offensive called off."

"Did they take any ground, did they hurt the Germans?"

"No, as far as my source on Gort's staff has it they just gave up."

"Bloody hellfire."

"Keep it down Hobo, that Sister told us to keep you calm," said O'Connor.

"Calm? Calm? How can I be calm stuck here with a gammy arm when there's so much to do?"

"How's Bush?" interjected Keyes.

Hobart took a deep breath before replying, "Not good. There's an infection and he's fretting about the loss of the leg."

"I think I'll have a word with the First Lord and see what can be done."

O'Connor and Hobart nodded.

"Now then General," said Keyes, "we're not here on a social call."

"I can see that," said Hobart, "there are no grapes."

O'Connor smiled, "We're going to spring you before the end of the week and you can come and help me with Winston's project."

"Ah, I wondered when you'd get around to that. I've read the briefing documents over and over and am intrigued. The Marines and then the Army to set up specialist all arms units, including tanks. Now when did the marines get interested in tanks Roger?"

"It's a short story but best told by the originator. He chose you two and got Churchill to talk to Gort. Surprisingly he didn't raise any objection to your secondment."

"Ha, that's not surprising," said Hobart, "most of the staff think we are disruptive cranks!"

"Well that attitude," said O'Connor, "is going to come back and bite them!"

"I take it you're having a good time then?"

"It is very interesting," he agreed.

"And my role?"

"To take over all of the innovation and training in due course. In the interim to work with the mechanised elements and weld them into an effective force to work alongside the footsloggers," said O'Connor.

"Not so much footsloggers," said Keyes, "you've seen Franzi's plans for transport?"

"I have, these units will be quick on their feet."

"What about communications," said Hobart, "No point in men and tanks going off all over the place unless they can co-ordinate their actions."

"Radio improvements, procedures and new radios are all being taken care of," said Keyes.

"Good. Air support?"

"All in hand."

"Not Battles I hope, the Germans will slaughter them. Do you know they have quite a contingent of AA guns with their panzer regiments? The 88mm was used very effectively in Spain both for anti-air and ground support work."

"We've yet to see the aircraft but RV, that's R V Jones, has seen a prototype and if it works to order the Luftwaffe and Heer are in for a nasty surprise."

"If," said Hobart.

"So what tanks have you managed to lay your hands on? Some cast-off light mediums?"

"We have a modified Matilda II coming to us, before January," said O'Connor.

"Good enough. I bet Ironside and Gort weren't happy to give them up."

Keyes and O'Connor said nothing but broad grins appeared on their faces.

"Well? What's so bloody funny?"

"We'll tell you when you get to Whipsnade," said Keyes.

Hobart harrumphed.

"Why aren't Liddle-Hart and Fuller part of this picture?"

"Because Fuller has those leanings and connections with the Nazis and Liddle-Hart is too close to him. So no, they won't be joining us in this effort of transformation," replied Keyes.

Hobart paused and looked at his friend. "What's the whole plan then Dick?"

"Why the entire bloody army, Hobo, every last bit of it. That'll stuff those hidebound donkey wallopers!"

**

Scapa Flow – Monday 18th September 1939

Sir Charles Forbes, Commander in Chief of the Home Fleet, greeted Captain Makeig-Jones warmly.

"Flags, get the Captain and I one of Hudson's 'special' gin concoctions would you please? So Captain are you all ready for sea?"

"Yes sir. It has been a little tedious here in port but I recognise the wisdom of withdrawing carriers from anti-submarine patrols."

"The First Lord was very insistent that they should be stopped before they started and ships recalled for other duties."

"I had heard rumours," said Makeig-Jones.

"The hanging around is over. Tomorrow you sail with HMS Southampton. You're to link up with Harwood's South Atlantic squadron and see if you can help to track down that pocket battleship."

"I see sir."

"The First Lord is confident he will have some intelligence that will help with the task. Ah, here's our gin fizz. Your very good health Captain and 'Good Hunting'"

**

Walter Young, a seaman servant in the FAA officers mess, was off duty and on deck when the Captain returned.

The Captains side party greeted Makeig-Jones as he climbed aboard his ship. As he stopped and saluted the ensign, Walter had a terrifying vision. The ship was sinking and the Captain was staying with her to the end, saluting the ensign as she went down.

He shuddered, blinked and the vision was gone. HMS Courageous was still there, and she was off to hunt.

**

Franzi's HQ – Tuesday 18th September 1939

Franzi considered his notes and then began to type his list.

Churchill had been taken aback at the number and range of people Franzi wanted to 'recruit' but had finally given in after Franzi had explained each case.

Barnes Wallace would hopefully work with the Toy Shop team and have the special ordinance ready for testing with the Mosquitos by February.

The training depot at Achnacarry would be constructed and go operational in November. He didn't envy the troops who'd be training there. The coming winter was going to be very chilly. He'd already warned the Captain and work was underway on warmer quarters for the animals.

There was one thing for sure if the men coped with the winter training in Scotland they'd be acclimatised for their first major operation in April.

The instructors he'd chosen had all performed well in their original timeline so there was no reason to believe they wouldn't now, albeit they were somewhat younger than before.

He had written up suggestions for making the Commandos into the crack units they should be. No actual camp. Billeting with locals and living off the land. The 'Me and My Pal' system. Encouraging independent thinking and rewarding success. Fitness and durability. Climbing, skiing, small boat work. A high level of expertise in all weapons, including those of the enemy. An offensive mindset tempered with caution so lives would not be thrown away uselessly.

Then the men selected, Charles Haydon, Charles Vaughan, then two famous mountaineers, John Hunt and Frank Smythe who was currently engaged in training the Lovat Scouts. They wouldn't be happy to lose him but it might bring them closer to the Commando. They would certainly be useful during the training. Perhaps they could form a cadre for the first army Commando.

It was getting late. He paused. Enough for now. Tomorrow two more WRENS were due to turn up. He was sure One Commando would comment about his 'hareem'. He couldn't expect total silence from the sentries who guarded him night and day.

Got to see Lucy and tell her about the new arrivals. Shell be pleased. Then go for a smoke with the MacFeegles and their new friends Cloughie and Flanagan? And maybe a drink.

Chapter 15

Whipsnade - Wednesday 19th September 1939

The WRNS had pushed hard to have an officer in charge of the small detachment at Whipsnade. Not only was there Jane but now two other signers had joined her and a half dozen clerks. Keyes had finally accepted a Petty Officer WRN, the daughter of a Chief Petty Officer who'd served with him in 1918, and who he felt would fit into the somewhat unusual establishment of HMS Whipsnade.

Petty Officer Margaret Meake's reaction to being excluded from the guarded hut that housed three of her charges was admirable. "If it is that secret, Admiral," she told Keyes, "then it is. Admirals have no need to apologise for anything."

Keyes smiled, he saw the same steadiness and practicality in her as he had in her father at Zeebrugge.

"In due course things might change," he told her.

For now she had to be content with seeing with Jane, Rosie Dowell and Susan Corbell, the three WRN signer clerks, when they weren't in Hut F1. She wasn't sure how it would work but the Admiral was clearly very happy with Jane Weiss and had already recommended her promotion to Leading WREN.

**

Late in the day Churchill put in a call to Franzi over the scrambled line.

The new girls had yet to be introduced to Franzi. It was felt that should be undertaken at the Captain's home with Keys, RV, O'Connor, and Jane present as well as the Captain and Gladys so it was Jane who took the call in Hut F1.

"Yes First Lord," she said. "Right away sir."

She tapped on Franzi's door and went in.

"The First Lord wants to speak to you Franzi."

'Did he say what about?'

"No just that it was urgent."

She crossed to Franzi's desk and switched on the speakerphone.

'Ook.'

"Good evening Franzi."

'Ook.'

"Look I don't know if you can help but I have a member of my staff who'd very poorly in hospital."

'Oook.'

"He was in the accident with Hobart and O'Connor."

'Ook.'

"He lost his leg and seemed to be making a recovery but infection has set in and the doctors think he might die."

'Ook, Ook!'

"I know. Is there anything that can be done? By you, I mean, you seem to be knowledgeable about many things."

'Ook,' said Franzi and chalked on his portable board.

"One moment sir, he's writing."

"Yes?" said Churchill.

'He says he'll get in touch with a team working at Oxford University and give them information to allow for a rapid distillation of 'penicillin'. I'm sorry I don't know what that is."

"Who is he going to contact?"

"He says he'll get RV to take briefing papers to Howard Florey and his team, Ernst Chain, Norman Heatley, and Edward Abraham."

"Many thanks Franzi. I hope we can save Captain Bush and then make use of his services if he fully recovers."

'Ook, ook.'

"Before I go Franzi, I think this is the first occasion when you've not fired a raspberry at me."

Franzi paused and then laughed whilst chalking on the slate, 'Bugger off Coppernob, I'm busy.'

"Franzi I am not repeating that to the Frist Lord. That is out and out rude," jane scolded.

"What's he put?" asked Churchill.

Franzi wiped the slate and hung his head in mock remorse after being chastised.

"Nothing at all sir," said Jane.

"Well then good night Franzi, goodnight Jane."

**

Whipsnade Thursday 20th September 1939

"Now girls," said Petty Officer Meake, "Jane will brief you about who you're are going to meet in Captain and Mrs Beale's home."

"Yes, Petty Officer," choruses the three Wrens.

"Peggy is fine amongst ourselves when no officers are about. Off you go then, Jane. I'll make myself scarce."

Jane waited until the Petty Officer was out of earshot and led Susan and Rosie to the garden bench to sit down.

"We have been selected," she began, "for a very important role for two reasons. We can sign and we've passed all the tests and been given the highest security clearance possible in England."

The girls made no comment and waited for her to continue.

Good, she thought, no giggly chattering Wrens here.

"I believe you were added about working with animals too?"

"Yes," said Susan.

"Although I didn't find any connection to signing and security clearance, " said Rosie.

"Listen carefully and I'll explain. You are going to meet the most important person in the Empire."

"The King?" exclaimed Rosie.

"The Queen," said Susan, "I've heard she wears the trousers at the Palace."

They laughed.

"Seriously girls," said Jane, "please."

"Sorry, nerves," said Susan.

"Not the King, or Queen," said Jane etei g Susan with mock severity, "or the Prime Minister nor the First Lord. You are meeting Mr Francis Whyte,

Franzie to his friends. He's chief advisor to the Admiralty. And he's a mature male orangutan."

**

Whipsnade – Friday 22th September 1939

Hobart arrived at Whipsnade just before lunch.

He was greeted by O'Connor and Keyes and introduced to the officers off One Commando.

The Commando was paraded for him to inspect despite the light rain that was falling.

"Cloughie," said Flanagan out of the corner of his mouth, "another bloody general. Do you think we're going to get one per company? That'll upset Lt. Tomlinson."

"Will you give over, Flanagan. You and that mouth has already got us assigned to the Franzi."

"Well how was I to know that Bourne and Todd were prowling around the camp. Besides Franzi's a fine fellah and he only wanted a smoke and a drink."

"Poteen though, I ask ya."

"He out drank you, me and the MacFeegles."

"And now we're his babysitters when needed."

"Corporal Clough, is there a problem?" barked a voice.

"No Sergeant Todd."

"Well shut it or it will be Marine Clough."

"Sergeant."

**

Keyes introduced Hobart to RV at lunch.

"Glad to have you join us," said RV.

"It is strange being seconded to the Marines. My father in law, Colonel Field was a marine. Dorothea commented on the fact when she came to see me in hospital."

"So you hadn't been totally 'abandoned' then at the Middlesex?" said O'Connor.

"Well of course my family visited. Be that as it may you gentlemen said you'd satisfy my curiosity as to where you got hold of the Matilda's, and 24 for of them at that."

"Well, Hobo," said O'Connor, "we have some very enterprising chaps in this unit. In this case they're currently attached to us on secondment from the Lovat Scouts."

"Go on."

"They managed, to divert a trainload of Matilda II's to Armstrong's Yard on the Tyne."

"And no one's found out?"

"Not yet," said Keyes. "Questions might be asked when strange vehicles turn up at Otterburn."

"Especially if anyone sees how they preform in gunnery practice," laughed RV.

**

Post lunch O'Connor escorted Hobart to Hut F1. Just like O'Connor had questioned the security of the single hut so did he.

"Is this Mr Whyte so valuable he needs all this to protect him?"

"You can't imagine," said O'Connor. "Now I remember you weren't very keen on camels?"

"Filthy beasts, worse than horses."

"You have dogs though?"

"Yes. What does this have to do with the chap in here?" Hobart said as he returned the sentry's salute.

"Just keep an open mind," replied O'Connor as he led the way inside.

"Good afternoon Generals," said Jane.

"All set?" asked O'Connor.

"Yes, if you'll follow me. Rosie, Susan I'll handle this one."

She tapped on the door and waited for the Generals to enter before following them inside.

Franzi was casually lounging at his desk. Cigar butt in mouth, pencil in hand, scribbling on a piece of paper.

"Dick, there's a bloody ape at the desk."

Franzi stood up on his chair then leapt gracefully down by his blackboard, picked up a chalk and waited.

"Yes Hobo, this is our genius, the one Winston would gratefully sacrifice half or more of the RN to keep safe. May I present Francis Whyte, Franzi to his friends."

Franzi chuffed modestly and wrote on the board 'Hello General Hobart. May I call you Percy like your wife, or better still Hobo?"

For once Hobart was lost for words.

**

After a long and intriguing discussion with Franzi Hobart was hooked. The opportunity to discuss how a combined arms war could, no would work, if Franzi had his way with the British Armed Forces, was invigorating. It tickled his fancy how Keyes and the team, and particularly Churchill, were going to bring this about.

The advanced plans for new tanks and aircraft looked excellent, on paper. The new infantry and artillery tactics tied in well to the thoughts voiced by many post World War 1.

Changes to the Navy and the re-direction of construction to carriers and escort vessels seemed sound.

All in all the establishments of the Navy, Army and RAF were in for a shock and shake up. Battleship Admirals and Captains, Cavalrymen and Bomber enthusiasts would be retiring in droves if Churchill succeeded.

At dinner Keyes sounded him out,

"General, Dick tells me you spent all afternoon with Franzi."

"I did sir."

"Call me Roger please. And what do you think?"

"If it can be pulled off without the military dinosaurs and Whitehall warriors stopping it all... well I guess we've got a chance in putting up a good show."

"You're worried about Churchill's foes blocking him or sacking him if they find out what's going on?"

"That's about it Roger. If Chamberlain, Halifax, Hore-Belisha and the other Service Chiefs discover the plan there will be hell to pay."

"One thing, Hobo, that Franzi didn't tell you is that Churchill will be prime minister sometime in 1940," said O'Connor.

"Yes," said RV, "we've only got to box clever until then."

"I see. Will the German's give us that time?"

The men fell silent. They honestly didn't know and Franzi hadn't offered up any thoughts.

**

Later that evening Franzi sat with RV and Keyes in Hut F1.

Susan interpreted trying to keep up with Franzi's busy hands, her nerves causing her to make a few mistakes until he spotted her and slowed down to a gentler pace.

'Gentlemen, I'd like you to ask Winston to form a new navy research team into 'Special Weapons'. He needs to get Geoffrey-Lloyd to co-operate.'

"The Secretary for Petroleum?" asked RV.

'Ook.'

"Who are you wanting to post there and coach?" said Keyes.

'Donald Banks, Quarter Master General, 50th Division and Barnes Wallace.'

"To do what?" asked RV.

'Petroleum weapons and special ordnance, which I hope Barnes has been working on since I wrote to him.'

"Franzi, it would be kind of you if you could supply a full list of people you've written to and what you've asked them to do," said Keyes.

Franzi let rip with a raspberry, 'What and spoil the surprises?'

**

Switzerland, Muttenz – Friday 22nd September 1939

"Are you going now?" Anita called down to Albert as she tucked their two children into bed.

She looked down at them lovingly and patted her tummy bump.

Albert was going out for his regular Friday evening drink with his friends. Anita knew he enjoyed relaxing and letting off steam after a long week in the laboratory.

"I won't be late tonight," called up Albert.

"You always say that. Hans is a bad influence on you. Anyway, I am tired so shall have an early night. Be quiet when you come in."

Albert walked down to the kneipe where he met his friends for a beer and maybe a game of cards.

When he arrived at the 'Wildschwein' he found Hans, Fritz, and Nick sitting with a stranger at their usual table. Nick and the stranger stood to greet him.

"Albert this is Mr Bond," said Nick.

"Yes, Bond," said the stranger, "James Bond."

"So, Mr Bond," began Albert.

"James please."

After he was seated and a full stein was placed in front of him Albert considered the young Englishman in front of him.

"What brings you to Muttenz, James?" asked Albert.

"Research and business."

"I see, what sort of 'business? There are a lot of fit young English, French and German men in Basel at the moment. Is your 'business' similar to their intelligence gathering work?"

"Oh I'm not in that sort of game," he lied. "My company would like to do business with Sandoz."

"I see. We all work at Sandoz in Basel-Landschaft. What are you interested in?"

"Ergot and it's properties if you want specifics."

"Ah."

"We're concerned about grain storage. The last thing we need is an outbreak of ergot poisoning on top of enemy action, eh?" he laughed.

"I've done some work in that field," said Albert.

"Really? We should exchange notes."

"Come on Albert, James, we're not here to talk science. It's cards and beer and admiring Uschi and Lina," interrupted Hans.

"Albert has to be careful doing that, Hans," said Fritz, "If Anita found out she'd have his dumplings."

The men laughed and looked, non too subtly, at the pretty waitresses.

"When's the next baby due" Nick asked Albert?

"Two months, if the calculations are correct."

"Number 3. What do you want? Another boy?" asked Fritz.

"Anita would like a girl. She says she is outnumbered already."

"More beer and let's get on with the Jass," exclaimed Hans, signalling Lina across.

"James, can we interest you in a game of cards," asked Nick?

"I don't think I've heard of Jass so I wouldn't be much use I'm afraid."

"What games do you play?" asked Albert.

"Poker or a game you may not have heard of, Baccarat."

Albert smiled. "I'll have you know we're not unsophisticated bumpkins in Basel, some of us have even travelled to Monte Carlo."

"Before Anita," Hans added.

"We can play Chratze," suggested Nick.

"Chratze?" said Bond.

"It is akin to your whist but with fewer tricks to play for and it uses our pack of 36 cards."

"Well then when in Rome and all that."

"Don't mention the Italian's please, not in the northern cantons," said Albert.

"What are the stakes?"

"20 cents per person except for the Chratzer who has to double the pot."

Bond sighed his plan had just gone to pot.

**

Three hours later the cards were pushed aside. Bond was up a whole franc. Everyone was much tipsier than when they began and all the best of friends.

Bond tried a new gambit. "So what do you think about the Jews fleeing Germany?"

"Should go somewhere else," said Hans, "not here."

"Not our problem. Let them try France or Britain," said Fritz.

"They've got children," said Nick.

"Have you seen them being turned away at the border," said Albert, "It is distressing to see them. Their hopes of safety dashed and the SS soldiers rounding them up. Where are they taking them?"

"Surely just to camps before they emigrate?"

Bingo, thought Fleming.

The men paid up and said their good nights to the innkeeper and the two girls. Albert disappeared in the direction of the gents.

"I'll wait for Albert," said Bond. "He's a little unsteady on his feet."

"S'alright," slurred Nick as he staggered into a table, "I'll walk him home."

"I think you need to concentrate on getting yourself home safely. I'm fine."

"Ok then, Goodbye."

Bond waited patiently by the door but after a little while, when Albert didn't reappear, he went to look for him.

He had to chuckle when he saw poor Albert trapped in the corridor. He was saying all the right things and putting up a spirited defence but Uschi obviously had a crush on him and was showering him with kisses.

"Ahem," Bond began.

"Yes goodnight, Uschi," stammered Albert.

"Goodnight Bertie, goodnight Herr Bond,"

"Goodnight Uschi. Come on Albert, let's get you home."

**

Fleming instructed Albert in the removal of lipstick from his face and some spit and dirt helped disguise that on his collar, before he took the keys and opened the door.

"Shushhhh," said Albert, "Sleeping."

"Albert, is that you?" said a woman's voice quietly from the staircase.

"It is Anita my love. I've brought a friend."

"Oh Albert, what am I going to do with you. Every week the same," she said descending the stairs.

The table lamp lit the room only dimly but Fleming could see that Albert's wife was very attractive, even though she was clothed in a long dressing gown and seven months gone.

"He is fine Frau Hofmann. Just a few beers. I thought I'd best make sure he got home safely."

"Nick usually does that," she replied.

"Er he was a little 'tired' and unsteady too, so I volunteered."

"That was very kind of you, Herr?"

"Bond, James Bond."

"Thank you."

Albert had sat himself down in an armchair and dozed off.

She sighed, "Perhaps he's safest there for the night."

"It might be best. I'll be off now back to my hotel."

"It's late. The police will want to question you if they see you out at this time. Stay here, if you don't mind sleeping on the settee and being woken early by two boisterous children?"

"Thank you. I'll make myself comfortable. And keep an eye on Albert."

"Good night, Herr Bond."

"James, please."

**

Muttenz – Saturday 23rd September 1939

Fleming's only 'close up' experience of children to date had been his nephew, Nicholas, who arrived in January 1939. He'd reluctantly attended the Christening at the invitation of Peter and Celia and then had his arm twisted into becoming a Godfather. The reception had been agreeable, but he hadn't been sorry to hand back the young Fleming to his lovely mother before driving back to town.

The arrival of the two Hofmann boys at 6 a.m. had been noisy in the extreme. They'd quietened a little at the sight of a stranger but soon overcame their shyness and took to throwing themselves at him in a rough and tumble.

Albert surprised Fleming. He showed no ill effects from the night before as he fed the boys and took their mother breakfast at 7.

"Sorry about the boys James," he said.

"I can see why Anita would like a girl. Three 'tornados' in the house would be trying."

"Would you like anything to eat?"

"Just a coffee please."

The boys decided to take themselves off upstairs as the men settled down for a smoke and coffee.

"Thankyou for seeing me home last night. It was a most enjoyable evening, yes?"

"Not a problem and yes it was."

"Did Anita say anything much?"

"She tut tutted in a loving way. I guess she's used to your Friday evening excursions."

Albert smiled. "Yes, she's very tolerant, and I'm fortunate not to suffer hangovers."

"You'll have to watch that little minx at the kneipe," suggested Fleming.

"I know. Perhaps I'll give Friday evenings a miss for a couple of weeks. Let her find some other man. Hans would be happy if she picked him."

After a pause Fleming decided to play his hand.

"Albert, last night you showed more concern than your friends about the refugees trying to come in from Germany."

"I don't like what's happening there. Anita says it's evil treating people that way. Switzerland should let them in or through at least."

"England isn't much better you know."

"Even with the war on?"

"Perhaps now things might change. People need to be protected from Hitler and his cronies. The Nazis need to be stopped."

"France and Britain should put an end to his adventures. There's little Switzerland can do."

"Switzerland might not want to upset the bully, but you could do something to help the Allies."

Albert looked up sharply. "So you are a spy?"

"Yes and no. I've been asked to speak to you about your work on lysergic acid."

"What on earth for? There's not much of interest there. My notes are all filed away."

"We've a scientist johnny who thinks there could be some use for LSD."

"Really? And that might help the Allies in some way?"

"He seems to think so. Would you be happy to provide me with a copy of your research?"

Albert paused. "It is difficult. Sandoz have the rights and.."

"If you can help those people at the border in some way then don't you dare use that excuse," said Anita as she came down the stairs with the two boys. "It is your Christian duty to help them."

Albert took a deep breath. "It is as you say Anita."

"So?" she asked.

"I have a copy of my work here, James. You may borrow it and return it to me when you have copied it."

"That is very kind of you, Albert, Anita. I will make sure they are safely delivered to our boffins, copied and returned. His Majesties Government will be very grateful."

"What would you have done if I had been sympathetic to the Nazis like Fritz and Hans?"

"Albert!"

**

Fleming bid goodbye to his hosts and went straight to Cyril Bryant, ostensibly the Honorary British Consul in Basel but actually MI6's head of station.

Fleming was kept waiting which didn't sit well with him. Eventually he grew bored with the delay and barged into Bryant's office.

"Well I say sir. Who the devil are you and what makes you think you can barge into my office unannounced?"

"My name is Lt. Fleming. I work for Admiral Godfrey, head of naval intelligence and I need to get these documents copied immediately before a kind Swiss chemist has a change of mind."

Bryant paused for thought. "Important is it?"

"Yes. Once copied can you get someone to drop the original papers back to Herr Hofmann whilst I signal London and set off for home."

Bryant nodded. "Certainly Lt.. Elsa?" he shouted.

**

Whipsnade - Saturday 23rd September 1939

Keyes re-read the signal from Basel and turned to RV.

"Well at least there is good news from Fleming."

"Agreed. But Franzi isn't going to be happy about Bush."

"Do you think we should scratch him from the Bedford operation?"

"See how he is. If he doesn't come then we've got out notes and they are pretty comprehensive."

**

Franzi was working at his desk when RV, Keyes and Jane entered his office.

"Franzi," RV began, "Couple of bits of news for you."

'Ook?'

"We received a signal from Fleming this morning."

'Ook.'

"He's obtained all Hofmann's notes and research papers."

'That is good news,' translated Jane.

"We received a call from London earlier," said Keyes.

'Ook?'

"Unfortunately Captain Bush succumbed to the infection and died at 4 a.m."

Silence.

"Are you alright Franzi?" asked Jane.

Franzi rose from his seat.

'I need to go to the assault course.'

"Of course," said Keyes.

They watched Franzi as he left the hut in a slow and composed manner. Once outside he sped away over the hill in the direction of the woods.

"Should someone go with him?" asked Jane.

Keyes nodded.

Outside F1 Clough and Flanagan were on sentry.

"Corporal, you two go after Franzi. See he's alright but I don't suggest getting in his way."

"Sir!"

The two marines set off at the run until they were out of sight of the Admiral when they slowed down to a controlled jog.

"We'll never catch him," said Flanagan.

"Keep going," said Clough.

"Where to?"

"The Admiral didn't say."

"Wonderful."

**

As they went on keepers pointed the way. It was the usual route for the marines run.

"Hey, lads," shouted John.

"Can't stop, John, orders to stay with Franzi," said Clough.

"As if," panted Flanagan.

"What's the problem," said John trying and failing to catch up with them.

"Don't know," said Clough. "he came out of his hut and took off."

"Loik the Devil his self was after him," added Flanagan.

"I'll follow on then," said John.

As the marines got into the wood proper they could see a number of large saplings had been snapped in two. In the distance they heard more cracks.

"Somethings upset him right enough," said Clough.

"I wouldn't like to get on the wrong side of him and that's a fact," said Flanagan.

**

They found Franzi up a large tree. He was making kiss squeaking noises and hitting the trunk with a fist.

'Stupid idiot Franzi. Arrogant Franzi. Unthinking Franzi. But for you that man would have been alive. If you'd have thought more about peaceful science and medicine, he wouldn't have died. How many people are dying in this country and the Empire and beyond who you could save? Is it more than the war will kill?'

"Franzi," shouted Clough up to their friend.

"Come on down, Franzi," added Flanagan.

Franzi hit the tree harder.

"Franzi, Flanagan here has some poteen for you."

"Who says?"

"Flanagan, I know you, remember?"

Flanagan ignored him. "Hoy Franzi. I've a drop of the good stuff for ye. Come on down will ya?"

Franzi didn't answer and continued to squeak and hit the tree.

John came into the clearing and joined Clough and Flanagan at the bottom of the tree.

"Oh dear," he said. "I've never seen him this upset before."

"Franzi, Franzi," Flanagan called up.

"Leave it to me boys," said John. "Franzi, old lad, it's me, the Gaffer."

Franzi paused.

"That's right lad. Come on down and we'll sort it out."

Franzi made a move.

"Stand clear boys," instructed John.

Franzi launched himself from the tree, landed, jumped up and ran to John before enfolding him in a massive hug.

"What is it, lad?"

Franzi unfolded himself from John and picked up a stick.

In the dirt he wrote 'I've fucked up John.'

"Jesus would you look at that Cloughie, he can write."

"Shush will ya."

"What about Franzi? The Captain says you're doing a wonderful job."

'No I fucked up. Caused a man to die.'

"How?"

'I forgot about medicines.'

"We all do that. Forget things, don't we boys?"

"That we do," said Clough, "If Flanagan didn't he'd be a sergeant by now."

"How about a fag?" asked John.

'Ook.'

"Deoch poteen, Franzi?" said Flanagan.

'Ook.'

**

John and the marines saw Franzi back to his compound.

'Ook,' said Franzi to his three friends as he gave each of them a hug.

Clough and Flanagan waved goodbye and walked off up the hill back to report to Keyes and RV.

When they were out of sight Franzi went to his shelter and returned with his slate and chalk.

'Please tell Roger and RV that I'm not going with them to Bedford today. Let Jane know so she can take the day off.'

"Alright Franzi. I'll be about if you need me."

'Ook.'

"What are you going to do, just so I can reassure them?"

'Write about medicines and treatments.'

"Is there anything you want?"

'Later I'll come and see the Captain. Tell him to make sure he's got lots of brandy.'

"I will," laughed John, and he 'locked' the compound and went to find the officers.

Franzi called over to Daisy, a mournful cry. She ignored him but when he repeated the cry she came and groomed her strange mate.

Some time later Franzi felt calmer. He went into his hut and pulled out a writing pad and pencil. Then a large cigar, courtesy of Churchill, and the flask of poteen he'd 'borrowed' from Flanagan without being noticed.

Chapter 16

Whipsnade - Wednesday 23rd September 1939

Keyes and RV gathered their notes and, with a strong marine escort, drove off to Bedford. They promised John that they'd call on Franzi as soon as they returned. In all likelihood they believed they would find Franzi with the Captain in the evening.

Jane was delighted with the news of her unexpected weekend off. She and Rosie determined to travel up to town and surprise her parents.

Their transport problem to the station was solved when Lt. Sandy Mackenzie caught sight of the Wrens waiting at the bus stop.

Noticing their small suitcases he pulled up beside them. "Off somewhere Miss Weiss?"

"Yes Lieutenant. We're off to London if we can get to Dunstable or Luton station," she replied.

"We've been waiting for the bus for ages," said Rosie, "isn't that so Jane?"

"Well we can't have that can we? I'll run you down to Luton. Unfortunately I haven't the time to take you all the way to London."

"We wouldn't want to trouble you Lieutenant," said Jane.

"No trouble at all, Miss," said Sandy. "Hop in."

Rosie made sure she pushed Jane into the seat beside the Lieutenant, despite her protestations.

"Perhaps, Lieutenant," she said, "you might come into Town with us both some weekend , if you've got a friend?"

"Shush Rosie," said Jane.

"I'd really like that," he said. Summoning his courage he went on, "Perhaps, Miss Wiess you might accompany me on a walk on the Downs sometime before the weather changes?"

Jane sat still and didn't reply immediately, until Rosie thumped her on the shoulder.

"I would like that Lieutenant."

"Sandy, please."

"Sandy."

**

Spitalfields, London - Saturday 23rd September 1939

Isaac and Rebecca Wiess were very pleased and surprised to see their daughter. It was Shabbat and certain rules were adhered too even though they weren't strict followers of the faith.

They welcomed the girls in and plied them with tea and sandwiches swapping news about home and family and the limited information about the Wrens posting.

Rosie excused herself after lunch and told Jane she'd see her back at camp on Sunday evening.

The weather had turned foul and a rain shower was being made worse by a blustery breeze. Rosie set out for the tube and was very pleased when a smartly dressed man offered her shelter under his umbrella. One thing led to another and she accepted his proposal of afternoon dancing and then dinner.

He hailed a taxi and they drove off into the West End.

**

Bedford School, Saturday 23rd September 1939

Keyes and RV arrived promptly at Bedford School at 10 am.

Their marines de-bussed and assembled in the playground despite the rain.

Other marines were prominently placed around the gates to the grounds and the doors of the school building.

A Captain splashed across the yard to Keyes and RV and escorted them inside.

He led them to a door signed 'Headmaster', knocked and showed them inside.

John Masterman and David Petrie stood and welcomed the newcomers.

"How went the roundup John?" asked Keyes.

"Tolerably well. We got all of those in England this morning before dawn except Bob Stewart, Moura Budburg and Edith Tudor-Hart. Special Branch is still searching for them. Maclean was detained in Paris. Here's the list," he said handing over a file to Keyes.

"And those three, did they escape or were they not found?"

"They had lost their 'shadows' and disappeared. We don't believe they knew about the swoop."

"They'd better not. It would cause a problem if they got the information out to their masters."

Masterman and Petrie nodded in agreement.

"Right, we have here Blunt, Burgess, Cairncross, Driberg, Gow, Norwood, Philby, Rees, Springhall, and Wynn."

"Any trouble?" asked RV.

"Not really. A couple had a go at dropping out of windows but were caught straightaway. The sight of armed marines and police seemed to take the wind out of their sails."

"Where are they now?" said Keyes.

"Separated and undergoing initial questioning," said Petrie.

"Is the plan as we discussed?" said Masterman.

"It is. Unfortunately, our special advisor had something come up so he couldn't be with us. I think we've enough material on each of them to convince them we know all about their activities," said Keyes.

"I wonder how many will choose gaol or execution?" said RV.

"It depends," said Masterman, "The true zealots might hold out."

"We do have another 'fear factor' to play if they won't budge," said RV.

"That is?" asked Masterman.

"Oh only a trip to the zoo," said Keyes, smiling.

"I don't understand," said Petrie, "If we can't persuade them gently why on earth would a trip to the zoo serve?"

**

Masterman and Petrie moved around the school interviewing the prisoners. From time to time they returned to the Headmasters study and discussed matters with RV and Keyes.

The spies were kept isolated from each other and cross-questioned but there was no violence or threats. All were well treated, fed and watered.

By mid-afternoon both men were shattered.

The first round of questioning was over.

"Catch your breath gentlemen," said Keyes.

"I'll be mother," said RV as he poured them all a cup of tea.

"Thank you," said Masterman.

Keyes offered cigarettes which were gratefully accepted.

RV lit his pipe and readied his pen and paper.

"How did it go?" asked Keyes.

"They've all been very shocked," said Petrie.

"Clearly they've had some training from their handlers on how to react in such circumstances but they've been floored by how much information we have on them," said Masterman.

"Let's take them one at a time," suggested RV.

"Fine. I can give you the general gist of their position. David here has detailed notes."

"Skip the detail for the moment let's know their reactions," said Keyes, "And whether they'll co-operate with us."

"As you wish. Alphabetically then. Blunt. He is a canny one. He's being very stubborn, he admits nothing until confronted with evidence. At the moment he is not onside."

RV wrote 'Z' by Blunt's name.

"Burgess is playing on the fact that he is MI6 and that some of his work might be misconstrued. He wasn't happy when we told him his Soviet code name or that of his handler."

"So turned or not?" asked RV

"Not so far," said Petrie.

'Z'

"Cairncross," continued Masterman, "admitted he is a member of the BCP but denied any contact with the Russians in respect of intelligence gathering. Yes he knows Maclean is also a member of the party but they aren't 'friends'. They drifted apart after graduation. He feigned total surprise that he should be accused of being a spy and is continuing to be uncooperative."

'Z'

"Driberg caved in almost immediately and is 'happy' to help his country. Gow broke down and he too will help us. He tried to justify what he had done and then stated he'd not spied for anyone. We put the scenarios to him and he's come around to our way of thinking. I'm not sure he'll be much use, other than in identifying new 'talent' for the Russians."

"Good," commented Keyes.

"Norwood was totally unrepentant. She actually smiled when we confronted her with evidence."

"So she won't turn?" asked RV.

"Not a chance as far as I can see," said Masterman.

'Z'

"We had a bit of luck picking up Philby. The Times has him in France following the BEF, fortunately he popped back to London for a break with a boyfriend."

"Hah," laughed Keyes.

"He's a thoroughly nasty piece of work. A champagne communist. No remorse for working for the Russians. He detests the British establishment. He had the gall to point out that he hadn't actually done anything yet to harm us."

"A zoo trip then," said RV, Keyes nodded.

'Z'

"Rees was open about his past with the Soviets but is adamant he distanced himself from any contact after Poland was stabbed in the back," went on Masterman.

"That ties up with our information," said RV.

"Why did we bring him in?" asked Keyes.

"For completeness and to reactivate him as a double agent. He knows some of the others and might be useful in getting things out of them," answered Petrie.

"Springhall," said Masterman, "a real thug that one. He attacked his interrogator straight off and it took four marines to restrain him. His response to anything put to him is 'Fuck Off'."

"Nice," said RV as he wrote another 'Z'.

"And finally Wynn. He seemed proud of himself when we told him the Russian's thought he was likely to be a better asset than Philby. He's seen sense though. We should be able to use him to send the Soviet's up a number of scientific blind alleys," concluded Masterman.

"Not a bad result," said Keyes.

"Mostly as we expected," said RV.

"What now?" asked Masterman.

"Those who decided to help us should be returned to their homes, under supervision and surveillance of course. The others can have a night in Bedford Gaol to consider their plight," said Keyes.

"And a trip to Whipsnade tomorrow afternoon or evening?" suggested RV.

Keyes nodded.

"You weren't joking about the zoo then?" said Petrie.

"Not at all," said Keyes.

"What are you going to do with them?" asked Masterman.

"Well you'll see because we'd like you to be there to pick up the pieces, so to speak."

"I thought we were all agreed on no Nazi torture methods?"

"What on earth are you suggesting John, we wouldn't stoop so low. But a zoo at night is very atmospheric I'll tell you. Makes a man, or woman think," replied Keyes.

**

The Admiralty, Saturday 23rd September 1939

Frederick Lindemann had returned to his office after another 'odd' meeting with Churchill. Something wasn't quite right, he felt, with their friendship and collaboration. It was as though some great secret was being kept from him and he couldn't deduce what it was.

Rumours abounded about scientists and military men disappearing off to secret locations to work on who knew what and the rumours were pretty clear the Admiralty had something to do with it.

Still, Winston had given him control of 'S Branch' and consulted him on a weekly basis about various matters pertaining to the war. That in itself was peculiar, they used to converse almost daily. Perhaps Winston was just very busy with the war, or was he deliberately holding something back?

What had become of R V Jones, he wondered? Where had the annoying little man got to?

He decided to instruct Bensusan-Butt, his private secretary, to make enquiries.

**

Whipsnade - Saturday 23rd September 1939

Franzi reviewed his notes, made amendments and annotations and filed them away in his new HMG briefcase.

He was feeling much better now he had set down all the useful medical knowledge that 1939 science could get to grips with. Medical procedures were likely to be harder to have adopted but some people, like Archibald McIndoe and Harold Gillies, were probably going to champion the new approaches to wound treatment and reconstructive surgery.

John checked him throughout the day and was pleased to report back to the Captain that his mood had improved almost to the point of being normal.

The poteen had little effect on Franzi other than giving him a warm glow. He wondered where Flanagan got hold of the stuff now he was restricted to camp. He chuckled to himself when he considered the likely answer, the MacFeegles. They were very useful men and seemingly had free rein to go anywhere they pleased as long as their travels benefited the Commando.

It had almost fallen dark when he heard Keyes and RV's convoy returning to camp.

Franzi decided to pay Lucy a call, drop off his notes at Hut F1 and then go on to see the Captain.

He was interested to hear what Keyes and RV had to tell about the Soviet spies.

**

Lucy sensed Franzi was upset and went out of her way to cheer him up.

"We've got evacuees coming, Franzi. More children from Regents Park, some of my old friends. Dad says Bert and his family are coming. That'll be nice for you."

'Oook,' said Franzi. 'I'm happy about that.'

"Mum says we might have a full school in the village."

'I hope Miss Mason will be able to cope with all you monkeys!'

Lucy punched him playfully.

"Dad says there's been talk of getting the chimpanzees back, so the island will be occupied again."

Franzi 'jumped' at that information. 'What?'

"Well it'll be all the chimps from London, you must know them?"

'I do. A right bunch of jokers. Noisy too.' Hell, he thought, if they do come back someone might find his secret files. Better move them to the office now he'd got his own combination for the safe.

"Happier now?" asked Lucy.

'A bit. You're fun.'

"Do you know the visitors are coming back more and more now things have calmed down?"

'Ook'

"Well some of them are disappointed that you don't do any of your 'shows' now."

'I did promise not to do the Hitler one after Churchill and the Captain thought I might have upset the Nazis.'

Lucy harumphed, "Who cares about the silly Nazis?"

'I care if they send people or aeroplanes here for me and mistakenly hurt my friends or the animals.'

"Well do something else then."

'Ook'

"Please?"

**

Franzi left Lucy feeling much better. He popped into his HQ and asked Susan to accompany him to the Captain's house.

When they arrived they found Keyes and RV had beaten them to it and were already relaxing with the Captain. They'd been furnished with a drink and had lit up.

"Come in Franzi, Susan too," said the Captain. "I told the Admiral and RV that you were going to put in an appearance."

'Ook,'

"Evening Franzi," said RV.

"Are you feeling more composed Franzi?" asked Keyes.

'Ook. I've spent the day fruitfully. I hope you fellows can persuade people to take notice of my medical suggestions.'

"Your province RV," said Keyes.

"I'm going to need help soon. An office to handle all the different science that Franzi is providing."

"Speak to Winston."

"Franzi, Susan, refreshments before I leave you alone to hear the news from the Admiral and RV?" said the Captain.

"A lemonade please," said Susan.

Franzi signed and motioned for his usual brandy and cigar.

"Capital," said the Captain.

**

Sometime later, after Keyes and RV had told Franzi of the day's events, Franzi leaned back, inhaled deeply from his cigar and signed,

'Our prime targets to try and turn have to be the people the Soviets value and trust the most,' signed Franzi. 'We turn them and then we can feed the Soviets choice disinformation or even things they are interested in, such as German troop movements.'

"Who has provided them with the most intelligence so far?" asked Keyes.

"Your notes on that are somewhat vague, Franzi," added RV.

Franzi raised his hand. He had no intention of sketching out the role of the spies for the next 20 or so years, too many 'butterflies' might come of that.

'Trust me. Philby and Maclean, they'd be very good. Blunt, Burgess and Wynn would be useful. I don't think we'll have much luck with Springhall and Norwood. Cairncross isn't really relevant.'

"How do you suggest we proceed?" asked Keyes.

'We have plenty of time. No need to rush at this,' said Franzi.

"So cancel tomorrow? Allow Masterman and Petrie to continue with their attempts?" asked RV.

'Not for everyone. Perhaps we only see Blunt and Philby here tomorrow evening, when we've set up their 'surprises'?'

"No strong stuff or deaths please," said Keyes. "We had enough trouble with the polar bear killing. The Zoological Society wouldn't thank us for getting the place closed down due to a poor safety record, would they?"

'Ook, ook, ook,' laughed Franzi.

"Franzi! I don't see it as a laughing matter," scolded the Admiral.

'I could just imagine a letter to the papers,' said Franzi

"Dear Sir,

I must write to you and bring your attention to the terrible safety record that Whipsnade Zoo is gathering.

It wasn't enough that merely a month back, a man was savagely mauled by a polar bear, but I see here that another gentleman has been fatally mauled by lions after accidentally finding himself in their enclosure. It would not surprise me if the next thing we hear, is that some poor unfortunate has been found with his arms ripped off by an Orangutan or some such.

Indeed, I have written my MP already requesting, nay demanding, that they take the zoo under direct control, and would encourage your noble readers to do likewise.

Yours Faithfully,

Concerned

Dunstable."

RV chuckled at this and Keyes stern look disappeared into a grin.

"Well then, what do you plan?"

'Tell me what you think of this...' began Franzi.

**

Whipsnade, Sunday 24th September 1939

Despite the short notice Gladys and two of her ladies of the Whipsnade Amateur Dramatic and Opera Society (WADOS) delivered Bill's requested props by tea time on Sunday.

He, in turn, delivered them to John and Franzi. They took them off down into the Park.

Two hours before dusk, two trucks arrived at HMS Whipsnade and from each, a man with two attendant marine guards dismounted and was taken into an awaiting tent. Blunt and Philby started when they saw each other. KGB training hadn't prepared them for the events of the last 2 days. They were stripped of their clothes and given rough battle dress in return.

Masterman and Petrie had arrived earlier and met with Keyes and RV. Now all four of them nursed a drink and turned their attention to the evening's programme of 'entertainment' as RV insisted on calling it.

"You have my word, John," said Keyes, "that, despite appearances, neither Blunt or Philby will be harmed."

"Thank you Admiral," said Masterman.

"If you two gentlemen can take a last crack at them, just in case they've changed their minds."

"Indeed," said Petrie.

"Pass the word for Sergeants Bourne and Todd, if you please Roper," said Keyes to his flag lieutenant.

"Aye aye sir."

Within minutes Roper returned with the sergeants.

"Sgt Bourne, would you escort Dr Masterman and Mr Petrie to the prisoners please? Select a section to assist you in carrying out whatever orders these gentlemen give you."

"Aye aye sir," responded Bourne.

"You might consider including Corporal Clough and Lance Corporal Flanagan in the task," suggested RV.

Bourne glanced at Keyes who nodded his approval.

"Aye aye."

**

Keyes and RV watched the inquisitors and marines depart. Finished their drinks and stood.

"Shall we?" said Keyes.

"Certainly," said RV, "It's a nice evening for theatre."

"Really RV must you?"

"You know I must."

They left Keyes tent and walked into the zoo. They took up position on a bench in front of the café where they could see the whole of the Park stretching away downhill before them. The sun was setting slowly in the west and the evening was most mild for late September.

"Do you think they'll have any joy with either of them?" asked RV.

"It's possible, but I doubt it," said Keyes.

"Ah, look here," said Keyes pointing to a group of seven men walking up the Central Avenue towards Flamingo Island.

"Is that Philby?" asked RV.

"I believe so. He looks somewhat different stripped of his sartorial elegance eh?" said Keyes.

Once by the flamingos the party halted and turned to face downhill.

Two marines appeared near Chimpanzee Island seemingly frogmarching a civilian between them. They forced the 'prisoner' into a boat and rowed him over to the island. He was unceremoniously dumped ashore and left. The body did not move.

From his hiding place, Franzi waited for a reaction but Philby stood stoically and said nothing.

'Oh well,' thought Franzi, here we go. I am not a gorilla so I do not charge in. He slowly walked up to the body. Sniffed and then ripped it's head off. Blood and gore sprayed about as it was clear this prisoner was dead.

Masterman, Petrie and Philby shouted and screamed. Flanagan leant across and cuffed him Philby around the head. "That's what'll happen to you, you queer, if you don't help these gentlemen."

"That's enough, corporal," ordered Todd.

"Sorry sarge, I don't know what came over me."

"Take him away," said Masterman to Sgt Bourne.

The marines dragged Philby away, not back to the camp but further down into the zoo.

"Come with me David," said Masterman, "I want a strong word with the Admiral."

"As do I. I've never seen anything so barbaric," responded Petrie.

They strode quickly up the hill to Keyes and RV. Masterman's face was livid with rage.

"You promised me, gave me your word," he started.

"To do what?" said Keyes.

"Not to harm the prisoners and that damned ape has just ripped off Blunt's head, doubtless at your command."

"One moment, please?"

"One moment? I will not have anything more to do with this terror and I shall be speaking to the Home Secretary and Mr Churchill in the morning!" stormed on Masterman.

"If you will turn your attention to your left you will see Mr Blunt with a military escort walking towards Flamingo Island where you should be to do your duty," said Keyes.

"What the hell?" said Masterman and Petrie in unison. They looked and saw it was true. Blunt was there large as life and unharmed.

"I, I, I, ..." started Masterman.

"No time man," said RV, "the light's going."

"Come on John," said Petrie taking Masterman's arm and leading him away downhill.

They met with Blunt and his escort, two sergeants, Lovat Scout flashes on their shoulders, and two marines.

"So no change of mind then, Tony?" asked Masterman.

"No."

"Please observe this then," said Petrie, "I think you might recognise your 'fellow traveller'."

Blunt's attention was drawn to a commotion down the hill. Two marines were dragging a third figure, a civilian, between them towards a small lake in the middle of which rose a single hilled island. Surely, he thought, that's

Philby. He wasn't putting up much resistance and he didn't move after he was dumped and left ashore.

Blunt watched with fascination as a large male orangutan appeared from the back of the hill. It moved slowly towards his fellow spy. Examined the body then tore its head off showering blood and gore about.

"Oh my God," shouted Blunt.

"No," shouted the men about him except one. The giant sergeant on his right gripped his arm and growled in his ear "You're next poof, if you don't co-operate. If the ape don't do it I will!"

Blunt threw up and whimpered. "I'll do it."

Chapter 17

London, Sunday 24 September 1939

"Rosie, about time," said Jane, "I thought we were going to miss the train."

"Sorry, but I had to make time up with my family after yesterday."

"Pardon? What do you mean?"

"When I left your place a really nice man whisked me away for lunch and a tea dance," said Rosie.

"Rosie!"

"I say nice man but after the dance I gave him the heave ho."

"Was he fresh?"

"No. That was part of it. He was charming to begin with then started asking lots of questions about you. I ask you, can you believe it."

"What did you tell him?"

"That we was stationed together at a military establishment."

"Nothing else?"

"No, but he kept asking. It was very fishy so I went to powder my nose and slipped out of a side door."

"Good for you."

"Did you see anyone near your place today?"

"I wasn't really looking."

"I think we should tell the Admiral or RV," said Rosie.

"Tomorrow morning," agreed Jane.

**

HMS Whipsnade, Monday 25 September 1939

Franzi's office was crowded.

Rosie related her Saturday encounter to Keyes, RV and Franzi whilst Jane signed.

"So sir, it was very odd, first him taking no proper interest in me and then all the questions about Jane and what we did."

"Quite," said Keyes, "Most odd him ignoring a Wren like yourself."

RV stifled a laugh.

"In all seriousness," he said, "this needs looking into."

'Ook'

"I agree," said Keyes. "Thank you, Rosie, for bringing this to our attention. You may return to your duties."

Both she and Jane rose to leave. "Not you Jane please," he said.

She sat down and Rosie closed the door behind her.

"Have your parents noticed anything odd lately?" he asked.

"Well, the internment people have been interviewing people, you know, people from Germany."

"That would be right, Roger," said RV.

"I suppose we've taken steps to see the Jane and her family won't suddenly be whisked off to who knows where?" he asked.

'Ook. The Isle of Mann.'

"Really?" said RV. "To answer your question, Roger, we've done nothing specific as far as I am aware."

"Then we'd better jump to it."

'Ook. And find out who's observing the Weiss family home.'

Jane looked upset. "They will be alright won't they?"

"Certainly, my dear," said Keyes. He turned to Jones, "Pass me the phone RV."

"Operator please get me the Director of Naval intelligence. Yes I'll hold."

"Ah good morning to you John, Roger here."

"What do I want? Nothing as complicated as Berne I assure you."

"Yes, it did go well did it not? Now I have another confidential job for Lt Fleming if you can spare him."

"No, it shouldn't take long. A few days. Right. He's to find out who is watching a house in London. Get him to ring Roper, my flag lieutenant, he'll give him all the details."

"And to you. I owe you another dinner when I'm next up in town. Many thanks. Goodbye."

**

Whipsnade, Hut F1, Tuesday 26 September 1939

Franzi finished listening to Churchill and sighed.

'I told you that Professor Lindemann would likely kick up a fuss.'

"I know," said Churchill, "but I can't just sack him. He does have some uses."

'Let me explain,' said Franzi, 'He's using that department of his to influence you and to manipulate others. They'll provide him with a report, based on his terms of reference, to support whatever he happens to be peddling.'

"Are you saying he's lying?" said Winston huffily.

'I didn't say 'lying'. He's manipulating the facts and using those to manipulate others.'

"Including me?" he snapped.

'Alright, if you want it plain, yes, especially you,' said Franzi showing his right palm and smiling at Churchill.

"It's no laughing matter," said Churchill.

Franzi slammed his fist down on the desk and glared.

"Erm, I think you'll find, sir, that Franzi is somewhat angry," said Jane.

'Oook'

Churchilll was shocked and taken aback. Even when Franzi had 'lectured' him before he'd never got angry. He drew in a deep breath, swallowed his not insubstantial pride and said: "I'm sorry Franzi, please forgive me."

Franzi mastered his anger and nodded.

'Let me set out what your friend, and I know he has been all through your wilderness time, believes in.'

Churchill nodded.

'He believes that a small circle of patricians and scientists should run the world. He believes in eugenics. He's quite happily colluding with others on how to visit genocide on the German people. He cares not a jot for the people of the Empire and Commonwealth. He sees society as those who rule and those who serve. And you have heard him express these views over the years, haven't you?'

Churchill nodded again and hung his head.

'I cannot lend any support to a man like that, or any of his friends.'

"But.."

'No 'buts'. Do you want to be seen as a great statesman and saviour of the free world or as one who could have been, except for the blood on his hands.'

Churchill considered Franzi in silence.

"The former," he said.

'Good. Now let me add some scientific facts to this tale of woe.'

"Go on," said Churchill reaching for his brandy.

'He has no idea about rockets and missiles. He has flawed ideas about radar and air defence. He won't listen to anyone who knows more than himself on virtually any subject you care to mention. He's a bully and a sneak. In short, he is a liability.'

After a pause Churchill responded.

"I see. What do you suggest?"

'Pack him off to America as a scientific liaison. There are people in the US administration that he already has a certain rapport with.'

"He won't like it."

'Oh dear. How sad. Never mind.'

**

Whipsnade, Hut F1, Tuesday 26 September 1939

It was dark outside and stormy. Marine sentries stood guard and cursed the rain as it found ways to get passed their capes. Inside the hut, Franzi and his team began their review.

Each member of the group had been provided with an agenda and several colour coded files. All were stamped "Most Secret".

Keyes stood and began.

"Since Franzi arrived we have been recruiting the best military and scientific brains from Britain, the Commonwealth and Empire and further afield if he was sure of their allegiance. Some were contacted directly by Franzi, others have been brought onboard by friends and colleagues. You can see from the summary that we have projects covering aircraft, engines, armaments and ordinance; similarly with special weapons and science for all three services. We have persuaded service chiefs to take measures to improve their operational capabilities. We have been instrumental in curtailing the German and Soviet intelligence services activities in Britain. We have established One Commando as a model for frontline ground forces."

"Quite an achievement in such a short period of time," commented Churchill.

'Ook'

"This is only the beginning. I would now like to hand over to our director, Lt Colonel Francis Whyte of the Iban Scouts, who will outline what is to come."

'Oook?' said Franzi.

"Let me explain," said Keyes, "by way of reading this letter."

"Dear King George," he began, "in this time of trial, the Iban peoples wish the other peoples of the Empire to know that we will contribute to our fullest in defending freedom and defeating tyranny. Unfortunately, we cannot send our warbands to aid you but I know that one of our Maia brothers is with you already in England. He is of the Iban and Maia and a chief amongst them. I am glad to name him a lieutenant of Singalang Burong, our War God.

Francis Whyte is known to one of your war chiefs, Churchill, and I respectfully ask that he is treated and honoured as the warrior he is.

Yours courteously,

  Jugah anak Barieng."

"Here, here," said RV.

"Quite so," said Churchill, "so the King was happy to have Franzi gazetted as a Lt Colonel with immediate effect. But I have had to put him off from meeting our Maia for the time being!"

'Ook, ook, ook,' laughed Franzi and the others.

"The next stage is ensuring we have the new equipment ready for testing, training and then deployment. To some extent, we will be unable to keep this secret. Aircraft have to be flown, tanks and weapons range tested. In short, people are going to notice and become curious. Especially people in the Prof's circle. I am hoping to head that off by despatching him to

Washington to work with the US Navy and Army Airforce on air defence issues. As you know he's very 'keen' on that."

"Oh yes," said RV. "I wish the Americans well."

"Thank you, RV," said Keyes. "We know your views to the Professor. Can I ask General O'Connor to take us through our personnel requirements as outlined in Franzi's paper?"

"Certainly, Admiral," said O'Connor. "You will see that we have a list of three middle-ranking officers and twenty junior officers, NCOs and other ranks."

Churchill glanced at his paper.

Staff

Major Brian Horrocks, Staff College, Camberley

Gp Captain Arthur Coningham, Bomber Command

Lieutenant Colonel Dudley Clarke, War Office

Others

Jim Almonds, Coldstream Guards

Jack Churchill, Manchester Regiment

Philip Dunne, MP

John Durnford-Slater, RA

John Howard, formerly of King's Shropshire Light Infantry

George Jellicoe, awaiting Sandhurst admission

Dave Kershaw, Grenadier Guards

Geoffrey Keyes, Royal Scots Greys

Robert Laycock, BEF

Jock Lewes, Rifle Brigade

Paddy Mayne, RA

David Stirling, Scots Guards

Charles Vaughan, The Buffs

"This is not going to be easy. The enlisted men and NCO's fine. The officers from the Army, especially those already with the BEF, very difficult," said Churchill. "What do you think gentlemen?"

"Do we need them immediately?" asked Hobart.

'The tankmen,' signed Franzi, 'although Marine or Navy gunners will serve, will be needed before the end of November. The staff officers, Captain Laycock, Colonel Horrocks, Group Captain Coningham, need to have some time to assimilate the tactical doctrines and working practices we're introducing. Better that than being currently underemployed in their current roles. Do you know they have Laycock swanning around France telling people how to react to gas attacks? I ask you. Durnford-Slater is serving as the adjutant of an anti-aircraft unit in the West Country. What a waste!'

"Franzi, please can you slow down a little?" asked Susan, "You're hard to follow when you go that fast."

'Oook. Sorry Susan.'

"And you're certain the Germans won't employ gas? Just as a surprise tactic to launch an assault?" asked O'Connor.

'Totally,' said Franzi. 'By the way, when you get Horrocks and Laycock back from France they'll be able to provide you with first-hand information about the state of the French Army. You won't be happy, gentlemen.'

"We'll do our best, Franzi, to get everyone you want," said Churchill.

'You need Charles Hayden to set up the Achnacarry depot. Men for 2 Commando. And the specialist instructors for the Arctic Warfare School, Frank Smythe and John Hunt.' They'll need a full programme defined to ensure they deliver what we and our troops need."

For that matter what do we expect?" said Churchill. "Where is this winter war going to be?"

'Don't worry, not France,' said Franzi. 'The Germans haven't had it all their own way in Poland, even though it'll be over soon.'

"Poor bastards," said O'Connor, "cavalry versus tanks."

"Only one outcome there," commented Hobart.

"So where then, Franzi? At least tell us that," demanded Churchill gently.

'Norway. In the Spring.'

**

Whipsnade, Wednesday 27th September 1939

"No dummies this evening then?" said Keyes.

"No," confirmed RV. "Petrie and Masterman are just going for a walk in the Park with Burgess and Maclean."

"Together?"

"No, separately."

"And Franzi is going to put the willies up them?"

"Something like that."

**

"Look you are 28 years of age. You've been working for the Soviets since your Cambridge days alongside your fellow Apostles. It is now over. We know everything you've done. We know about your lifestyle, and actually don't give a damn. But let's face it we could lock you up for espionage or have you shot for treason or you could work for us. The choice is up to you," Masterman told Burgess.

Burgess was silent. His handlers had prepared him for interrogation but their advice seemed mute given the information Masterman already knew.

They continued to walk in the still autumn evening. Two Marines followed a short distance behind.

"Why don't you sit down here," said Masterman indicating a bench overlooking an enclosure, "and I'll leave you to think about it."

Burgess did as he was asked and was surprised when Masterman and then the two Marines began walking back up the hill leaving him alone. He was sure they must have someone watching him but couldn't see anyone.

A cry brought his attention to the enclosure to his front. An orangutan seemed to be waving at him.

He ignored it and closed his eyes. His mood was sombre and depressed. All the academic arguments about overthrowing the capitalists and spreading the rule of communism seemed dead and dry as dust.

The orangutan whooped again. When he looked up fear banished his depression. The ape was out of its enclosure and bounding over the grass towards him.

He thought about running but his legs had turned to jelly. Think. Surely this was the same orangutan that had delighted the public with its Hitler parodies?

As it came closer the run became a steady measured, menacing walk until it stopped an arm's length away and smiled at him. The smile and grunts weren't reassuring.

He considered shouting for help. Surely the hidden watchers would act. Seconds turned to minutes and still the orangutan smiled and grunted.

His mouth was dry, he was close to losing control of his bladder and bowels. The ape stopped smiling and grunting and sat down.

In the dirt in front of him it wrote 'Help and Live or Die, Your choice Hicks'. Then it leapt up and screamed in his face.

He lost control of himself, half scrambled half fell off the bench and ran back up the hill shouting for help.

He didn't look back.

Two Marines and Masterman appeared from around a corner.

"Help me, there's an orangutan there trying to kill me. It's out."

"Where," said Masterman, looking back won the hill.

"By the bench."

"No, there's nothing there."

"It has to be. It wrote on the ground."

"Corporal Clough, would you take a look please?"

"A pleasure, sir," said the marine.

Burgess thought he detected a smile on the corporal's face.

"Now if you'd come with me, Mr Burgess, shall we talk some more about your choices."

"No, no need for that, I'll help you."

**

Petrie and Maclean heard the shouts from the other side of the Park as they were walking by Wolf Wood.

The wolves howled and the marine guards had readied their weapons but Petrie motioned them to relax.

"It seems as though something may be amiss," said Petrie to Maclean.

"Really?" replied Maclean with disinterest.

They resumed their walk down Dukes Avenue until they came level with Spicer's Field with its heard of zebras. They were nervous after the disturbance and gave voice to their distress.

Petrie didn't respond.

Maclean stopped and turned to him.

"What are you going to offer me Mr Petrie? I have already told you that I do not fear prison or execution."

"Yes, you have. So you have given up on your 'Crusade'?"

"My Comrades will carry it on."

"Ah. You mean Blunt, Burgess, Cairncross, Driberg, Gow, Norwood, Philby, Rees, Springhall, Wynn, Stewart, Budburg and Tudor-Hart?"

Maclean's jaw dropped.

"Oh yes, we have all of them. Some have already agreed to work with us. I won't insult your intelligence by saying all."

"Who?"

"I'm afraid I can't divulge that information. And couldn't even if you agree to work with us."

"Go to hell."

"Perhaps, but not, I feel, before you do."

"Hah."

"In any event let us not trade insults. You are an intelligent man. If you had more information about the Soviet Union and Comrade Stalin would you be prepared to consider your position?"

"Propaganda? I am aware that the General Secretary has been accused of many things."

"The Nazi-Soviet Pact?"

"Done to secure the western border and allow the sphere of influence to increase peacefully."

"I'm not sure the people of Poland and the Baltic states would accept that description of their annexation."

They continued downhill in silence once more until they reached the polar bear pit and Petrie indicated they should stop.

"I see, for all your polite words you are showing me the pit where that man was killed by the polar bears. Is that to be my fate so I don't embarrass anyone at my trial?"

Petrie smiled. "I don't think you'll get any trial where you can embarrass the government. In any event what do you know? Foreign office matters, the possible plans to intervene in Finland?"

Maclean stared at him coldly.

"I'll tell you what, I'll leave you in peace to consider things. It's much nicer here than the gaol and it's a pleasant evening," said Petrie and with that he and the two guards wandered off back up the hill.

Maclean's mind was racing. What sort of trick was this? He couldn't decide whether to sprint to the boundary fence he could see beyond the polar bears or not. He could see no guards, but a sniper might well have him in his sights.

He walked slowly past the bears. He jumped when one of the lions roared as he continued by them.

Just beyond the lion enclosure was another which had been partitioned in two. Each section contained a small hut or shelter as well as a sort of assault course comprised of logs, ropes and tyres. The light was fast fading but he could see a shape atop one of the obstacles and as he looked it held up an arm. Something white showed up in the twilight.

Maclean smiled and as his tension eased. What to do? Get out, call his handlers, tell them about the others then flee the country.

It was full dark now and there was no moon. He couldn't see any sentries but they must be there.

Perhaps he could find a phone in the Park's buildings? He saw a signpost but couldn't make out the words. He took out a box of matches and then shook his head. Lighting up would give him away to any watchers. Going on instinct he began to walk up the hill. The animals had calmed down but there were still nocturnal noises and calls emanating from all around the Park.

He ignored side turnings and continued uphill. Now the path branched left and right. Shouts to his right and flashlights showed where people were searching for him. He went left. Shouts to his front. He looked for a way off the path. A shelter on his left and an enclosure beyond it looked promising, then he saw the large notice describing the inhabitants, "Black Rhinos". Perhaps not a good choice. To his right was a small stand of trees. He climbed over the fence and quickly discovered another path. He was at the apex of a V, in front of him was a small lake and an island.

Voices and flashlights to the left and right with little time to choose, he hurdled the small fence and splashed into the water. Cursing he tried to move as quietly as possible as he waded across to the island.

Lights flashed but none picked him out. He stalked ashore and looked for somewhere to hide. A path led into a sort of cave. It was pitch black but he was now out of sight of any pursuers.

His trousers, shoes and socks were soaked but his jacket, pullover and shirt were dry. He took out his matches and cigarette case and lit up. The cave was some 12 feet in diameter. Some straw and old clothes lay discarded on the dry earth floor. He extinguished the match and sat down. Things could have been worse. He wondered if there was anything on the island that he could use for a fire if the searchers didn't find him. Perhaps he could evade them and then slip out or find a phone.

Shouts continued to sound outside for some time until they finally died away.

He lit another match and used the light to retrieve the old clothes he'd seen. The battle cress jackets were covered in dried blood but one set of trousers wasn't too bad. He stripped off his wet clothes and pulled them on.

Now only his feet were cold. Notwithstanding the dried gore he used the other clothes as cover and settled down to rest and think in the straw.

He woke and had no idea how long he'd been asleep nor initially could he remember where he was. He glanced around. It was no longer dark in the cave. A small fire burned cheerily near the entrance, its smoke rising and disappearing up and out into the roof. His clothes and shoes had been arranged to dry and sitting opposite him was a large orangutang smoking a cigar.

He wondered if he could stand and then beat the ape to the cave entrance before it caught him and tore him to bits.

His fear must have shown because the orangutan gestured to him to be calm and remain seated.

It pointed to the cave wall near the fire.

On it he read, 'Hello Mr Maclean. It's nice here, isn't it? Well compared to the condemned cell at least.'

He fixed the ape with a wide-eyed stare.

It got up and approached him.

He shrank back, not daring to offer provocation.

'Oook,' it said and handed him a large envelope, a cigar and hip flask.

It motioned for him to have a drink and light up.

Shakily he opened the flask and took a swig. The brandy warmed him through and calmed him enough so he could light the cigar.

The orangutang picked up the flask and sat down, took a good gulp of the spirit and resumed smoking his cigar.

Maclean looked at the envelope, then the orangutang, then the wall.

He was obviously going mad.

'Ook, ook,' said the ape pointing to the large envelope.

He opened it and took out the papers and began to read.

The information was obviously capitalist propaganda. It detailed atrocities perpetrated by Stalin. Betrayals and show trials which had condemned friends of his, all good Communists, to death. Purges of the Red Army. Terror and atrocity after terror and atrocity in stark detail. He threw it down.

"Rubbish. Who expects me to swallow these lies?"

The orangutan shrugged and stared at him.

"It is rubbish, propaganda. Isn't it?

What the hell was he doing talking to an orangutan? Was he going mad?

The ape got to its feet. Crossed to the wall and rubbed out the chalked message.

It shook it's head and then chalked a new sentence on the wall.

'You've always had expectations and morals thrust upon you. You rebelled. That's understandable. Now it's your choice.'

He watched in fascination and read.

It was true, his father, his headmaster and school all forced him along the 'moral path'. His handler's had fed his rebellion against them and then his country. Used him. Well no more, he would choose his own path now.

He nodded and the orangutan rubbed out the words. Raised a hand and then left.

In the morning he left the cave and saw Petrie and one marine waiting for him on the path.

Time to make amends.

Chapter 18

Lutterworth, Friday 29th September 1939

"Good morning, Squadron Leader," said RV as he shook hands with Frank Whittle. "How's the engine doing?"

Whittle looked quizzically at him. The work on his engine was 'Most Secret'.

"Please sit down, Professor Jones."

"RV, please," he replied as he installed on the hard office chair.

"Erm. Well," said Whittle. "To what do I owe the pleasure of your visit?"

"I understand that you were contacted by Air Chief Marshall Freeman?"

"I wouldn't have seen you otherwise," said Whittle.

"Let me put you at your ease," said RV. "I believe you've had some correspondence with a mutual friend of the mine, and of the Air Chief Marshall." So saying he took an envelope from his pocket, showed Whittle the address and then plucked out a clump of Franzi's hair.

Whittle's jaw dropped and he held out his hand to touch the hair. A smile played across his lips and he nodded at RV?

"At last. I wondered when or if there was a real person behind this. Thank you, RV, for helping me hang on to my sanity."

"Not a problem, Frank, if I may?"

"Of course. When will I see Mr Whyte? He's an absolute genius. He helped me sort out the surges and he's now sent me these incredible designs for this 'Ghost' engine."

"Yes, he did tell me," said RV. "It might be some time before you see him though. He seems to have thoughts about so many developments. It was only yesterday I was talking to BSA and Martin-Baker about aircraft guns and escape methods."

"I see. A polymath then?"

"Very much."

"He does believe in driving a man hard though. I'm going from an engine with an output of 850 lbf to this new 5,300 lbf. Will I get the backing?"

"Oh yes. But it comes at a cost"

Whittle's face fell and he looked very suspicious. "Go on."

"You have to work with De Havilland and Hawker to get a plane operational by the end of next year, at the latest."

"Bloody hell."

**

Shoeburyness Ranges, Saturday 7 October 1939

It was a cold morning but the sun was bright. Little or no wind disturbed slack water and the seabirds went about their business of finding food unconcerned about the hustle and bustle inland.

Churchill, Keyes, RV and Generals Hobart and O'Connor stood outside a large tent drinking tea with their guest, Air Chief Marshall Freeman, Barnes Wallis and the Toy Shop scientists.

Marines stood guard at the range gates and boundary; the regular staff had been given the day off.

Several areas had been sectioned off.

In two, 20-foot towers had been erected. Atop each tower was 250 lb GP bomb. Each tower stood within a circular enclosure of sandbags at 2000 feet. Dummies and several old vehicles stood inside and outside the compounds.

In three areas an old tank had been set up as a target.

In another stood an old 18lb artillery piece complete with dummy crew

"What are we going to see first RV?" asked Churchill.

"I thought we'd start small and work up to a big finish," said RV, smiling.

"Get on with it then, we haven't got all day, don't you know there's a war on?"

"Right. If I could draw your attention to the tank closest to us gentlemen," he said waving at a small party of marines who had taken a prone position 50 yards from the target.

An NCO waved, turned and slapped a marine on the back. The marine settled himself and fired. The crack wasn't as loud as a rifle, more like a 10 bore 'pop'. The effect on the tank was spectacular. The bang and explosion were greeted with a cheer by the Toyshop team.

"Impressive," said Churchill.

"Better than a BOYS," said Hobart.

"Nice to have that handy," said O'Connor. "What is it?"

"Colonel Blacker, would you care to explain?" said RV.

A monocled, middle-aged Lt Colonel came forward and saluted.

"That, gentlemen, is an adaptation of a bombard design I've been working. Major Jefferis had some hand in it too as well as a chap called Whyte. Made things much easier. We call it a PIAT. It's able to destroy any current German tank but it's short-range, 30 yards to 50 yards really. It has a kick like a mule and cocking it for first use really means standing up. Stealthy though, no flash or smoke indicating where it's been fired from."

"A last-ditch weapon then," said O'Connor?

"Or ambush," said Hobart?

"Better than no weapon at all and quite lethal," commented RV.

"You've two more tanks out there. What are your plans for them," asked Churchill?

RV nodded. "Colonel would you like to get your other two demonstrations primed whilst we show off Commander Burney's anti-tank weapons?"

"A pleasure," said Blacker. He saluted and sauntered off down towards the marsh feeling very pleased with the way things had gone. Thank goodness for Mr Whyte's suggestions, it could have taken some time to perfect the weapon otherwise.

"Gentlemen, please observe tank number two," said RV.

Some 250 yards from the tank two marines had taken up position. Both knelt. One held a piece of what looked like a drain pipe. The observers could see the rear end was flared and that the 'pipe' had a pistol grip and a sight mounted at the nine o'clock position near the foregrip. The second marine was positioned to the right of the operator. As they watched he twisted the rear of the pipe, swivelled the breach open, inserted a large round and snapped the breech shut. He tapped the 'gunner' on the head. This time there was a considerably louder bang and a flash from the back of the tube. The results were as good as the PIAT. A direct hit on the target and explosion. The crew reloaded and fired off another round, then another in short order which both hit the target.

"Excellent," said Churchill.

"By Jove, that's got some range," said Freeman.

Hobart just let out a long whistle.

"That's going to ruin the donkey wallopers fun of riding roughshod over infantry," said O'Connor.

"Observe tank number three please," said RV in measured tones.

Looking at the third tank the audience could discern no immediate threat.

As they watched a Bren carrier crested a dune in the distance. Through their binoculars, they could see it mounted a larger 'pipe' with four vents at the back.

The carrier went hull down, stopped, and opened fire on the third tank. The discharge was as noisy as a mountain gun but the effect on the tank was much more devasting then a normal artillery round.

The gun fired again, this time there was a large explosion at the tank and the high explosive round turned it over.

Two more rounds were put into the target before the carrier ceased fire.

The whole process taking less than a minute.

"My God," exclaimed Hobart, "consider the mess a squadron of those would make of a Panzer advance!"

"Wonderful, RV, simply wonderful," said Churchill. "Whose brainchild were those weapons then?"

"Here he is Winston, I believe you know him," he said.

"Deniston," said Churchill, holding out his hand.

"Hello Winston," said Burney as he exchanged a handshake. "You like my little inventions?"

"I do, and I think I can say so does everyone else here."

"Yes indeed," confirmed O'Connor.

"Well, I say my inventions, my ideas plus suggestions from a Mr Whyte and help from the team at the Firs."

"So what do you call them then?" asked Hobart.

"Recoilless rifles. Haven't thought of in-service names for them yet."

"I'm sure the troops will call them something interesting once they've used them," said RV. "We have but two more demonstrations to go, gentlemen. If you'd be so kind as to look at the artillery piece."

He waved at a marine standing off to one side on a dune who turned and signalled to a hidden position.

After 10 seconds a rapid rattle of explosions erupted and a rain of 30 bombs flew over and into the artillery position and exploded. The target was obliterated.

The observers were stunned and delighted.

"Colonel Blacker, Commander Goodeve perhaps you would like to tell us about your weapon?" said RV.

"After you, Colonel," said Blacker.

"Right oh. We call this device 'Hedgehog', which refers to the spigots or 'spines' that are left after the bombs have been fired. Those bombs were a 20lb charge but the Commander here has a suggested a 30lb charge to use against submarines."

"Yes," said Goodeve, "Hedgehog, if it can be fitted, will be far superior to normal depth charges. Mr Whyte was very specific about that."

"The land version is a little limited in range but Mr Whyte suggested it would be very effective against fortifications if it were upscaled say to a single 40lb device," said Blacker.

"Thank you, gentlemen," said Churchill. "An excellent weapon with varied operational capabilities."

The officers saluted Keyes and Churchill and moved back to re-join their colleagues.

"Now for the finale. Which should be of particular interest to you Air Chief Marshall," said RV.

"I was beginning to wonder whether standing out here in the cold was worth it, notwithstanding the spectacular demonstration so far," he replied.

"it is a bit chill, isn't it?" said Churchill.

"Certainty after the desert," said O'Connor.

"Dr Wallace, can you join us please for your part of today's demonstration. Gentlemen, I'm sure you've heard of Dr Wallace if indeed you haven't met him?"

A readily recognised bespectacled and duffle coated figure joined the senior commanders and exchanged 'Hellos' with them all.

"So gentlemen," he began, "I've been working on a few ideas that Mr Whyte suggested to me and, with some more input from him and my fellows at the Toyshop, I've managed to perfect an interesting bomb. You see on those two towers two 250lb GP bombs, except one isn't. Let me demonstrate the difference."

He turned to a Marine Lieutenant off to one side of the group.

"If you please, Lt Mackenzie."

"Sir," said Mackenzie and raised a whilst to his lips and blew twice.

There was a slight pause and then the left hand bomb exploded.

The vehicles and dummies set around the bomb were comprehensively destroyed.

"As you can see we've enhanced the blast radius by detonating it off the ground. We've successfully developed proximity fuses with the help of Mr Whyte and we'll be able to deploy them in artillery shells, as well as bombs, in due course."

Heads nodded and Freeman smiled. Anything to enhance effective bombing, he thought.

"Now gentlemen. Prepare yourselves, please. As you can see the other bomb is much further away than the first. If you please, Lieutenant."

MacKenzie blew his whistle three times.

The explosion this time was by way of a double-tap, the first part a simple bang, the second, after the emergence of a cloud from the casing, was ear-splitting. The flash and roar were spectacular and the watchers were rocked by the pressure wave.

When the dust cleared revealed devastation inside and outside the marked compound.

"Good God man – what was in that?" asked Freeman.

"Nothing too special," said Wallace. "Powdered metal and coal dust."

From the top of a truck parked a quarter of a mile away, Franzi slammed his hand on the cab roof in delight. "Oook, ook, ook!"

∗∗

Otterburn Range, Monday 9th October 1939

It was cold and misty on the hills but it wasn't raining. A skein of geese honked their way south through the lightning sky.

"Fine morning, Captain," said RV.

Captain Moulton, RM Artillery, nodded. "Visibility should be good enough by 0800," he said.

The early start from Vickers Armstong had gone well. The tank had been loaded and covered and out of Newcastle before dawn.

Corporal Alfie Nicholls, 9th Lancers and Sgt Laurie Hall, East Riding of Yorkshire Yeomanry, had been 'seconded' to 1 Commando, 'Motorised Recconaisance' whilst going about their normal army lives. It hadn't been a hard choice. They'd been promised a key role in testing a new tank and training and, some pucka combat. Now they stood around an improvised fire with the Scammel driver and three Royal Marines who'd never been near a tank in their lives but who knew how to load, aim and fire a 12x12 gun.

Laurie had the pleasure of being the tank commander, Alfie the driver.

They'd had some time to familiarise themselves with what was essentially a Matilda 2, A12 or Matilda Senior (depending on who you talked to.)

Claude Gibb and his team had, with some input from Dr Jones and his advisor Mr Whyte had worked a minor miracle on the tank. The hull was same as before, but now there were panniers on the side for the crew's kit. The turret that wasn't a proper turret looked 'odd', given it's increased dimensions and limited traverse of 120 degrees. The engine compartment had been enlarged upwards to the rear of the turret and the two diesel engines had been given supercharger to coax a little more power out of them. Speed was increased but not so much as to break the suspension. The gearbox had also been tweaked to cope with the extra power.

Trials had been run indoors in a great shed at the dockyard but now was the moment of truth before the other nineteen Matilda's were modified.

"Right sir, let's get on with it," said Moulton to RV. "Serjeant mount up, please? I believe that' the proper order?"

"Aye sir," said Hall. "You heard the Captain lads. Get moving."

Once aboard Alfie started her up. The twin engines sounding odd to RV. Franzi hadn't been pleased when he had told him of Gibb's objections to fitting Dowding's gifted Merlins. He'd let it go, he said, for the time being, just to keep Gibb's happy and get the project underway. RV was sure that Franzi had a plan and wouldn't be prevented from implementing it for long.

The tank moved off into the prepared firing position. Two rounds were fired at an old A10 tank target 500 yds away. The first missed but the second, one of the new armour piecing type slammed into the front plate and blew the turret off. Two more rounds, this time high explosive, hit the target and bowled it over.

"Good shooting Fox," shouted Hall, "Next position Corporal."

Alfie complied.pushing the tank ahead at three-quarters speed. They bounced along the track and into place before two targets at a range of half a mile. Another tank was despatched with two AP rounds and an infantry position blown up with HE.

"Full speed to the next position."

Alfie gunned the tank and drove it hard for the third and most interesting test.

An angled target of four-inch armour had been set up at 500 yds distance.

Franzi had told RV that this was even thicker than the armour on the Russian Kliment Voroshilov heavy tank and twice that of the Panzer III that the Germans were producing.

Alfie slid the tank round into position and stopped. Fox took careful aim and fired.

Bullseye. Complete penetration.

Job done.

"I think that tank will do nicely for out armour support," said RV to Moulton.

"I agree sir. Jerry is in for a nasty surprise when he meets a few of these."

The crew were cocker hoop, with back-slapping all around.

"Proper monster we have now lads," said Laurie.

"She's not so pretty though," said Alfie.

"Bit of a Frankenstein eh?"

"Bride of Frankenstein, please. She's a lady!"

"Elsa then, not Matilda."

"Elsa?"

"Elsa Lanchester, Bride of Frankenstein."

**

Whipsnade, Hut F, Monday 9 October 1939

Winston sat with Franzi and began to review the initiatives he had taken since being re-appointed First Lord of the Admiralty.

No aircraft carriers had been sent out on anti-submarine patrols despite protestations from Sir Charles Forbes, CnC Home Fleet. He was adamant numerous exercises had proved that the carriers were in little danger from submarine attack themselves. Franzi had begged to differ and Churchill had deferred to his wishes.

Ships had been despatched to where German raiders were thought to be operating, with input from Franzi, but so far none had been intercepted.

It was a comfortable briefing arrangement, both stateman and ape were well supplied with brandy and cigars, whilst Jane had tea and some of Mrs Beal's non-alcoholic elderberry cordial for refreshment.

'So,' signed Franzi, 'How are the defences at Scapa Flow shaping up?'

"I'm told they are as secure as they may be until the construction work on the concrete barrages can commence. Block ships are all in place at every entrance and the port captain is confident nothing can get into the anchorage without being spotted and blown to high heaven."

Franzi blew an enormous raspberry.

'Twaddle'

"Pardon," said Winston?

'On a rising Spring tide, I would feel that there is a possibility, for a suitably audacious submarine commander, to slip between blockships. I bet the port captain hasn't taken that into consideration.'

Churchill paused with cigar partway to his lips, "You're serious, aren't you?"

'Winston I may be known as a prankster and comedian but I don't make comments about the fleet anchorage lightly. I know the disruption that would be caused by relocating until it is made truly safe.'

"I see. I have been wanting a meeting with Sir Charles since we had our discussion about aircraft carriers and anti-submarine patrols, I was thinking of summoning him down to the Admiralty."

'Then why don't we go up to Orkney this week. Before Friday,' said Franzi.

"I can arrange a flight," said Winston, and then pulled up short. "WE? What is this we? You're supposed to be a secret."

'Ah but I have a good reason and I have a plan,' said Franzi, 'so no one will think it strange that an orangutan appears at the Flow.'

"Go on then, Mr Whyte, I'm listening."

'I'll go and be a ships new mascot,' Franzi replied taking a swig of brandy.

"And I suppose you've already chosen which ship?" queried Churchill.

"Oh yes, Royal Oak could do with a boost, as could all of the R class to be honest, at least until they can be replaced."

"You're plotting something."

"No just thinking of all those Booties who we could use."

"Booties?"

'For the First Lord of the Admiralty, you're sadly ignorant of the Service.'

"Those Marines are needed to serve the guns on those ships," Winston growled. "Are you telling me we don't need those ships or that we have to replace the Marines with Navy ratings?"

'Both.'

**

Achnacarry Castle, Tuesday 10th October 1939

Shimi and the MacFeegles were back where they loved to be, in the Scottish mountains.

O'Connor had sent them, Major Palfrey and two troops of Marines up to Achnacarry Castle to begin work on the new depot.

The Major and Shimi, along with Major Haydon, and Lieutenant Vaughan eyed the grounds from the castle gate.

Nissen huts for accommodation, dining halls and ablutions were a must, although the men would spend a deal of time making the best of it under whatever they could build themselves.

"And we'll be needing a parade ground, Sir," said Vaughan, "can't have any fall off in standards."

"Quite," said Haydon.

"We'll have to stop the locals from coming to see what we're about," said Vaughan, "establish a no go line at the canal, maybe, Sir?"

"That would work well. No one can say they weren't aware they'd strayed."

"Where are we going to have the training and live-fire areas?" asked Palfrey.

"I think we'll have to consult Sir Donald about that and let Captain Lovat here have a shufty. He can make recommendations and we'll get the lads on to it," said Haydon. "Do we have a firm date for 1 Commando coming up?"

"The last week in November, but you'll get a couple more troops up before then to help with the construction work."

"They'll be busy enough," said Vaughan, "we have to put a couple of assault courses together and improvise training equipment."

"They're used to that. They've been working hard down at Whipsnade," replied Palfrey.

"Good."

"General O'Connor said we have to get 1 Commando ready for combat by March."

"What does he know that we don't?"

"He didn't say, just that it was from the best possible intelligence source."

"Military intelligence, Sir," said Vaughan?

Palfrey and Haydon smiled.

"Ah here, I believe are our other 'staff members recruits," said Palfrey as two cars drew up in front of the castle. "Shall we go down to meet them?"

**

It was comfortably warm inside the castle's dining room and refreshments had been provided by Sir Donald's staff.

"Gentlemen," said Palfrey, "if you'll take a seat, please. You'll find a folder for each of you and a pad and pencil for taking notes. Firstly let me make the introductions, "Squadron Leader Smythe, Major Hunt, Major Mayfield and Captain Stirling. I believe most of you know Captain Lovat?"

Heads nodded and affirmation confirmed Shimi was known to all.

"I've got you to thank you, cousin, have I," said Bill, "for getting Bryan and I into this?"

"Actually no," said Shimi, "that'll be a recommendation by a Lt Colonel Whyte."

"Never heard of him."

"Well, he seems to know about you two and young David as well."

"Which regiment is he from," asked Mayfield?

"The Iban Scouts," replied Palfrey.

"You are joking, surely?"

"Not at all. He came over and was promoted sometime in July. He seems to have an encyclopaedic knowledge of all things military, especially who we need to recruit to train the Commandos and their like. If you open your folders you'll find a list of Colonel Whyte's suggested instructors for this Commando Depot, the Special Training Centre at Inverailort Castle, and Breamore. Have a look and feel free to suggest other people. Bear in mind you'll probably have to share these chaps and co-ordinate what you do."

Unarmed combat - Captains Fairbairn, Captain Sykes, ex Shanghai Police

Demolitions – Lieutenant Gavin, Lieutenant Calvert, Royal Engineers

Arctic and Winter Warfare - Serjeant Scott, Serjeant Chapman, Serjeant Lindsay, Serjeant Croft, Seaforth Highlanders

Weapons instructors – Serjeant Mackworth-Pread, Serjeant Walbridge, Somerset Light Infantry

RSM Royle, Highland Light Infantry

Surgeon Commander Levick

Skiing Instructor - Captain Waldron, Scots Guards,

Boats and Small Craft – Corporal Courtney, Kings Royal Rifle Corps, Major Hasler, Corporal Sparks, Royal Marines.

Chapter 19

The Highlands, Wednesday 11th October 1939

"Right, Rob," said Shimi, "Le'ts go and call on the Scouts."

"Aye Shimi ah'll putten ma foot doon. Beauly fur denner an recruiting then on tae Thurso later."

In a rare bit of insight and eloquence the Big Yan posed a question, "Fit mony lads div we wint tae join us, Shimi? Ah can un'erstn the sniping an camouflage bit fit else are they tae teach?"

"How many lads do we want to join us, Shimi? I can understand the sniping and camouflage but what else are they to teach?"

"I was thinking stalking day and night. How to kill, skin, gut and cook deer, sheep and rabbits, said Shimi.

"An don't forget catching mackerel an sea trout. Aire's some fine fash in Loch Ailort," added Rob.

"And don't forget catching mackerel and sea trout. there's some fine fish in Loch Ailort."

"Make sure you tell the lads all about it whilst I'm lunching with the Colonel. The generals only want volunteers mind."

"Don't worry Shimi we'll get the best tae volunteer," said Rob.

"Aat's if they don't aa step up. It wis a pretty dull war afore we gid tae the Zoo," added the Yan.

**

Scapa Flow, Friday 13th October 1939

The Captain of the Coastal Command Sunderland delivered the news to Churchill in person.

"I'm sorry to say, sir, that the Fleet has dispersed."

"What do you mean, Squadron Leader," asked Churchill.

The Squadron Leader was tempted to say 'They've left, gone, buggered off,' but instead answered "The Control Tower advised that Admiral Forbes ordered the dispersal yesterday. Something about a U-Boat threat."

"Wonderful," commented Churchill. "Any ships left at all?"

"We'll make a pass over the anchorage before landing, sir. Then you can see for yourself."

"Fine. Mackenzie, you stay here. I'll go and see the others.

Winston made his way carefully down the ladder to the wardroom.

The two Marines, Franzi's permanent military handlers, Clough and Flanagan, sprang to attention, as did Jane. Franzi, on the other hand, turned from the window he'd been staring out of, and said 'Ook?'.

"Sit down, sit down," said Churchill, "we're just about over Scapa and the captain is going to make a circuit to see what's left of the fleet."

"What's happened to it sir," asked Jane?

"Admiral Forbes ordered it dispursed yesterday, then didn't tell me."

Cloughie and Flanagan looked at each other.

"Yes, you're probably right, he did it on purpose. Doesn't like me taking a detailed interest in the Fleet's activities."

'Ook.'

"You two make yourselves scarce please, I wish to discuss something with Wren Weiss."

The marines started to get up again when Franzi waved them to sit.

"Franzi says it's fine, sir," said Jane, "Sgt Clough and Corporal Flanagan are close friends."

"For heaven's sake, is this true?" Winston asked the marines.

"Yes Sir," said Clough.

"It is, Sir," said Flanagan. "He's a wonderful fine fellow is the Colonel."

Churchill slapped his hand to his head.

"Fine secret this is, Franzi."

"Don't go blaming him, Sir," said Flanagan, "It sort of came out when he got all upset about that officer dying."

'Ook.'

"Does Lieutenant Mackenzie know?"

"No sir," said Jane.

'I wonder for how long that will be?' thought Churchill. He'd seen the sparks flying between the Wren and Marine.

"Look there," said Clough, "Barely a ship at all, sir," he said pointing out of the window.

Churchill stared at the most empty berths. The serjeant was right.

'Ook,' said Franzi pointing to the east side of the anchorage.

"Yes?" said Churchill.

'Royal Oak. Not a wasted journey at all.'

**

HMS Royal Oak, 13th October 1939

"I must thank you, Admiral and you Captain, for an excellent luncheon. Apologies once again for turning up on you unannounced," said Churchill.

"Not at all, sir," said Admiral Blagrove, "It would be a fine thing if the First Lord isn't permitted to visit the Fleet whenever he wants."

"Indeed sir. I hope our plain fayre wasn't too dull. We seem to be overly well supplied with mutton at the moment," said Captain Benn.

"It was superb. I deduce that your chef has served for some time in the Far East, he makes an excellent curry."

"He did indeed sir," said Benn.

"I don't plan to inspect the ship today, gentlemen, that would be too much of a surprise but I would like to in the morning if that is convenient?"

"Yes sir," said Benn.

"I'd also like to present the ship with a new mascot."

"Sir?"

"Yes. Somewhat of a favourite of mine."

"If I might ask, sir, what is it?"

"You'll see in the morning. I'll come aboard at 1100 hrs."

"Yes, sir."

**

Shimi and the MacFeegles found their way after direction, to the billets occupied by Clough, Flanagan and Franzi. Jane had been housed by the Wren section officer and was relaxing until she was needed. Franzi had his slate and chalk, which he kept hidden from Shimi, if he needed to converse with his 'mates'. They'd quickly swept away the cards when Shimi came into the hut. 'And a good job too,' thought Flanagan since Franzi was beating the pants of Cloughie and himself.

"Hello men," said Shimi, "and you Franzi."

"Sir."

'Ook.'

"Serjeant Mac Feegle you may carry on this afternoon visiting the Lovat's who are on Orkney. I'm off to see Mr Churchill and Lieutenant Mackenzie. I'll see you at 1800 hrs."

"Sir."

**

The RN tender Daisy 2 was the pride and joy of John Gatt. Sub-Lieutenant Gatt felt privileged to be in command of a fleet tender of the Home Fleet. Not quite the destroyer that he yearned one day to skipper but it would do for now. At least he was getting noticed by senior officers on a regular basis as he carried out the multiplicity of tasks allocated to his boat.

He was not due on duty until 2000 hrs so he'd dropped into the 'unofficial' bar at the Highland Park Distillery for a dram or two.

He was surprised to see some strangers in uniform were already there, then he recognised the giant of a man known as the 'Big Yan' and immediately looked around for Rob MacFeegle whilst checking his wallet was still in place.

Rob appeared from around his brother and waived John over.

"Guid e'en tae ye young captain. Cum ben an hiv a dram o fuskie," he said.

'Oh no,' John thought, 'I can't get into a session with these boys.'

"I can't stay long," he said, "Just for a couple of drams only. I'm on duty at 8."

"Aat's nae a problem ah ken ye hiv yer jape tae div. In fact ah wis wondering if ye can div me a favour an take me an the lads on a boat trip afore ye hiv tae ging back tae yer battleship?"

"That's not a problem. I know you have your job to do. In fact, I was wondering if you can do me a favour and take me and the lads on a boat trip before you have to go back to your battleship?"

John looked at the 'lads' nervously. There seemed to be a dozen of them, mostly Lovat Scouts but including two Marines in what looked to be like non-standard uniforms, lounging around. What the hell was that?

He stared open-mouthed and pointed at a red-haired ape dressed in a ghillie suit, sat in an armchair with a large cigar and glass of malt. And this was before he'd taken a drop!

**

Special Operation P, Friday 13, Saturday 14 October 1939

The tension and excitement amongst the crew manning the conning tower of U47 was almost palpable. Prien had tried to follow the plan but got it wrong.

The photographs had been taken by a mad Luftwaffe pilot, Siegfried Knemeyer. He'd decided, on a whim, to finish a Narvik reconnaissance with a pass over Orkney. The RAF scrambled two Spitfires that intercepted him over the base. After fancy flying in and out of clouds, he'd evaded the fighters and made it back to Germany. His photographs eventually came to the notice of Donetz. After consideration, the Admiral and his staff had come up with an audacious plan. Kapitänleutnant Günther Prien and the U47 were handpicked to execute it.

U47 was supposed to pass north of Lamb Holm, a small, low-lying island between Burray and Mainland. But Prien mistook the more southerly Skerry Sound for the chosen route. His sudden realisation that U-47 was heading for the shallow blocked passage forced him to order a rapid turn to the northeast.

On the surface, illuminated by a bright display of the aurora borealis the submarine edged towards the gap between sunken blockships towards the open waters of Scapa Flow ahead. Suddenly they were caught in the headlights of a car travelling along the coastal track. They froze. Seconds ticked by and the car didn't turn or sound its horn. A collective sigh and nervous laughter came from the crew members, Prien uttered a low 'Achtung' and silence once more descended on the boat.

Within a minute the submarine ground to a halt caught on something between two of the blockships.

"Scheisse," exclaimed Prien in a low murmur. "Slow astern. Muller take Klopp and Grubber to the bow and tell me what we're caught on."

"Sir."

The petty officer and two seamen scrambled down the conning tower ladder onto the deck and made their way for'ard.

"All stop," instructed Prien as the boat pulled free from whatever was preventing their forward progress.

A minute later Klopp raced back to the base of the conning tower and called up "A cable, Kapitan, between the blockships."

"The tide is rising, can we push over it," asked Prien?

"Muller says he thinks we can, but slowly," came the reply.

"Tell him to use whatever he can to help us over."

"Sir," and Klopp turned and ran toward the bow.

"All ahead slow," ordered Prien.

The submarine edged forward once again.

"Mein Gott," came a loud shout from the bow.

Prien could see the three figures of his crewmen had a fourth shorter, bulky figure, with them. Before he could ask what was wrong or make an order, searchlights from the blockships flanking the U47 lit up and dazzled everyone on the conning tower. His two manned machine guns swung towards the light but bursts of automatic fire cut the sailors down.

Splashes came from the direction of the bow and foredeck.

"Full astern," shouted Prien, as he tried to get a grip on what was happening. "Get us out of here."

The crew from below appeared and tried to bring weapons to bear on their tormentors aboard the blockships.

"Head 180 degrees as soon as we're clear. Dive when we can. Ready codes and machine for throwing overboard."

What an absolute disaster, thought Prien as more of his crew were caught in machine gunfire. His men managed to take out first the left and then the right searchlight. As his and their eyes tried to adjust to the darkness they were assailed on the bridge by a Rübezahl from the German folktales of the of the Krkonoše Mountains. Bodies flew left and right off the conning tower. Shots rang out, muzzle flashes illuminated the melee and then stopped. A parachute flare lit the scene of mayhem. Prien had enough time to glimpse of the red-haired woodwose in front of him before it thumped the top of his head and darkness descended again.

**

HMS Royal Oak, Scapa Flow, Saturday 14th October 1939

The guard boats and other small craft had turned out en masse after the action.

Prisoners were ferried ashore and the submarine searched but of the signal and codebooks and the 'Enigma' machine, no trace could be found.

Prien woke in the Naval Hospital with a very sore head. He looked around and saw some other wounded members of his crew, and then the armed guards.

It had all been going so well, now he was likely to be a prisoner until Germany won the war.

**

Churchill was livid when he heard what had occurred. Britain's greatest asset had risked his life to capture a submarine.

"What the hell were you thinking of, Franzi? Sorry for my language my dear," he said to Jane.

"I told him off too, sir," she said.

Franzi eased back in his chair and had a long draw on his post-breakfast cigar.

"Well, sir? What have you to say for yourself?"

Franzi held up his hand and then rang a small bell which had sat, incongruously, on the breakfast table.

There was a knock on the door and then the MacFeegles and Franzi's marine minders brought in two large kit bags.

From the first, they produced code books and papers. From the second a complex looking typewriter machine.

Franzo indicated they should be put on the table.

'Now, Winston, we have the German navy at our mercy, for a time at least.'

**

Churchill and his party, including Franzi, were piped aboard the Royal Oak.

"Welcome aboard once again sir," said Admiral Blagrove, staring past the Royal Marine officer and pretty Wren at the orangutan standing between them.

"Good morning, sir," said Captain Benn, trying hard to keep surprise and amazement from his tone.

"Good morning, gentlemen," responded Churchill.

"The ship is ready for your inspection, sir if you'd like to follow me," said Benn.

"Thank you. Lieutenant Mackenzie, Wren Weiss and Franzi will accompany us."

"As you wish, sir."

**

Once the inspection was over the ship's company assembled on deck and Chruchill mounted a platform to address them. The ship's tannoy system had been rigged, as much as possible, to allow the crew to hear him but, inevitably, there were going to be some of the men who would have to get his words passed onto them by their shipmates.

"Officers and men of the Royal Oak," he began, "you have a great ship, old she may be but potent she still is. I am very pleased with what I have seen today and what I have heard about your efforts to ensure that the 'Mighty Oak' can carry out all her duties in the days and months to come. We are not sure how long it will take us to win this war but win it we will and the Royal Navy, and the Royal Oak, will do their bit. Last night, as many of you may now be aware, there might have been a major catastrophe. A German submarine nearly penetrated the defences and who knows what destruction she might have wrought if she had done so."

A great shiver went around the entire crew at that. Some of the one hundred plus ships boys felt tears welling in their eyes and Admiral Blagrove felt a tightening in his chest.

"Thanks to the work of the harbour patrol and some marines this attempt was foiled and the submarine sunk." He didn't bother to add that it had been sailed off to a secure port so the Germans wouldn't have a clear picture of her fate.

"Today I have with me a new mascot for your ship, his name is Franzi and he's come a long way to be with you. He, by the way, insisted that he should be appointed your mascot. I hope you approve."

Franzi cam forward, goose-stepped for a couple of paces, gave the Nazi salute and then blew a tremendous raspberry.

It broke the strange ennui that has taken the crew and they cheered as one.

"Three cheers for the First Lord, three cheers for Franzi," shouted Captain Benn.

**

HMS Whipsnade, Wednesday 18th October 1939

"How did you get on, Shimi, with the Scouts," asked Major Palfrey.

"Quite well sir. We have enough people who will be on detachment for training in Scotland."

"Good."

"And sixty who've got fed up of riding their ponies and want to join the Commandos or whatever we might become."

"I'd like you to go up to Achnacarry when the lads move there. Keep an eye on the training and liaise with us back here. I'm sure the General's would like a briefing in person today. I'll suggest 1500 hrs to them."

"Thank you, sir."

"By the way where are Lieutenant Mackenzie and the Band of Four?"

"Band of Four, sir?"

"You know to whom I refer Captain."

"Yes sir. They've gone on a little mission to Bletchley Park, at the First Lords order, sir."

"Anything to do with that fracas in Orkney that rumours are running rife over?"

"I couldn't really say, sir. Mr Churchill asked us to forget all about it."

**

Bletchley Park, Wednesday 18th October 1939

"This isn't really the correct protocol you know," said Mackenzie. "We should be handing these over to Naval Intelligence and letting them bring them here."

"The First Lord's orders," said Jane, "The machine and papers to be given to the named person."

"We can't just go in and ask for him. Questions will be asked."

"Weel ah might, Sir," suggested Serjeant MacFeegle.

'OOK!'

"And why is Franzi with us, Serjeant Clough?"

"That would be Mr Churchill's order as well."

"I'm getting more and more confused about who is running this mission," said Mackenzie in exasperation.

"It'll be alright, Lieutenant, really it will," said Jane.

'Ook, ook, ook' said Franzi pointing out of the truck window.

They followed his direction and observed an odd sight. Coming towards them was a figure on a bicycle wearing a storm cape and gas mask.

'Ook ook.'

"That's him," said Jane. "Out you get, serjeant."

It wasn't the most concise order ever given and consequently, all three serjeants jumped out to stop the cyclist, closely followed by Franzi. A collision was inevitable and all the men ended up on the floor. Franzi, of course, deftly leapt out of the way.

He was the first to cross over to the fallen cyclist and offer a hand up.

The man removed his gas mask and said "My word a Pongo Pygmaeus."

'Ook.'

Jane got out of the truck and handed him an envelope.

"For me?" he said.

"Yes, read it later in private. The Marines here have a machine and papers for you too courtesy of the First Lord. Provided you are who we think you are?"

"Alan Turing. Pleased to meet you, miss?"

"Leading Wren Jane Weiss."
'Oook!'

The story of Franzi will continue in Part II planned for publication in 2021. And for those who can't wait turn the page for a short extract...

Friday 4th January 1946

"Thank you, Sir Winston, for taking time out from your writing to see me," said Wynford Vaughan-Thomas.

"Not at all Wynford," said Winston. "Brandy?"

Wynford glanced over at the clock in Churchill's study. It showed just a few minutes to noon.

"Thank you," he replied, "I don't mind if I do."

"So, what tales would you like to hear?"

"I've been reading and researching about your work and life just prior to war breaking out."

"Yes, a very frustrating time," said Churchill.

"And dangerous for you too?"

"Oh you mean the assassination attempt?"

"Yes, a near run thing I believe? And one where you had a lucky escape?"

"Indeed I did," agreed Winston.

"Can you recall anything about the police enquiries at the time, once the IRA assassins were under lock and key?"

"They were somewhat puzzled, I remember, about events of that evening. The local inspector came to see me you know......"

**

"Thank you Mr Churchill," said the detective inspector "for agreeing to see me at such short notice,".

"Not at all inspector, very happy to help," Churchill replied.

"The thing is sir, well to be honest the accounts given by the suspects are more than a little puzzling."

"Indeed?"

"Yes sir. If you recall when I and my constables responded to your wife's call we found all three of the would be assassins disabled, unconscious."

"Yes I do recall," said Churchill. "It was rather 'exciting' wasn't it? I'd not been targeted for a while."

"You could say that sir. It's something we'd rather not happen on our patch though."

Churchill laughed, "Surely inspector this sort of thing keeps you and your men on their toes? I know my fellows in the trenches loved a bit of excitement with a trench raid or whatever."

"Different times sir," said the inspector smiling weakly.

"Perhaps to return Inspector, in a very short time," Churchill responded.

"Yes sir. Be that as it may I have to try and clear up the crimes, ordinary and not so ordinary as they are today, and the attack here certainly falls into the 'not so ordinary' category."

"And why is that?" asked Churchill.

"Well it's the stories the three fellows tell. Actually to be honest two of them. Now I know they're Irish and given to flights of fancy sometimes, but the two chaps who weren't shot say they were set upon by someone. And, of course, they say they weren't here to do you harm."

"Poppycock!"

"Well yes sir, I agree with you but I do recall you saying that you'd had some 'assistance' in the incident. I also remember your surprise that whoever it was that had helped you had left as we arrived," said the Inspector respectfully.

"Ah, yes."

"So could you tell me who that was sir, please? The two fellows say they were attacked by someone in a very furry coat, someone who was quite short but inordinately strong."

"Does they now?" said Churchill.

"I realise it's all nonsense sir, but I really need to get to the bottom of it. Can you shed any light on their tale?"

Churchill took a deep draw on his cigar, began to respond then paused.

"I'd hoped to keep this quiet Inspector. You see my neighbours don't hold with my helping some of the travelling community who pass through this area every year. My rescuer was the son of one of my old soldiers who has taken to the road. I help him out when I can. He was here that night purely by chance when he spotted my attackers and was able to intervene."

"I see," said the Inspector.

"He suffered some birth trauma and doesn't like to mix with the general population because they laugh at him and call him names. Fortunately for me he is immensely strong, like his father, and that enabled him to come to my aid," explained Churchill.

"And what about the red coat and odd smell?" asked the Inspector.

"That's easy to explain. I have sometimes provided him with clothes and things. Last year I gave him a coat."

"Yes sir?"

"Yes, very much like that of Mr Flannagan, and definitely red and furry, if I recall correctly."

If anyone wishes to pursue the roots of this story, the author recommends the following sources of reference:

The Story of the Lovat Scouts 1900–1980 (with contributions to 2000), Michael Leslie Melville (www.librario.com)
British Commando 1940-45, Angus Konstam (www.ospreypublishing.com)
Most Secret War, R.V. Jones (Penguin Military History)
Churchill's Ministry of Ungentlemanly Warfare, Giles Milton (John Murrray Publishing)
Churchill's Secret Weapons, Patrick Delaforce (Pen and Sword Military)
It Had To Be Tough, James Dunning (Pen and Sword)
Wilfred Freeman, Anthony Furze (Spellmount)
Whipsnade 'Wild Animal Park - My Africa', Lucy Pendar (The Book Castle)

Acknowledgments

The Zoological Society of London

All Franzi's friends at alternatehistory.com a big thank you for all their encouragement and support

Lt Col. (ret) Grenville Johnston, Lovat Scouts Association for information about Lord Lovat and the Scouts.

Kirsty Tilbury at Colchester Zoo for the information about orangutans: "After speaking with our curator here at the zoo he has mentioned that it is quite hard to describe a smell of any animal. However, male orangutans can have a bit of a musty smell whereas females not too much."

Bill Houston for his wonderful cartoons (www.billhoustoncreative.com)

The Staff and Contributors at http://www.commandoveterans.org/

And Andrew Sparke, lifelong friend, for helping me all along the way.

Printed in Poland
by Amazon Fulfillment
Poland Sp. z o.o., Wrocław